My Favorite Boss

MELANIE MORELAND

WATERHOUSE PRESS

For my Matthew — my favorite everything.
Always yours,
M xx

CHAPTER ONE

Bane

The knock I had been waiting for happened. I recognized it since I knew it well.

Rap, rap. Pause. Rap, rap.

I delayed responding for a moment, just to annoy the person on the other side of the door. Before they could knock again, I called out, "Come in."

The door opened, and Laura walked in, a stack of files in her arms. She sat across from me, not waiting for an invitation. When she spoke, her voice was purposely restrained, hiding the fact that she, no doubt, would like to ream me a new one but, as head of HR, knew she could not. Still, there was an undertone to her voice—one of barely concealed impatience.

I had to let her have it.

"Alexander," she began.

"Laura," I replied, not looking up from the rows of numbers on the page in front of me.

"We need to have a discussion." She paused. "Now."

When I didn't respond, she reached across the desk, closing the file folder in front of me. "And I need your complete attention."

With a sigh, I sat back, pulling off my glasses and rubbing my eyes. "I already know why you're here, Laura. Save your voice, and we can move on."

"That was your sixth assistant in two months, Alexander. Sixth."

"She was horrible. She couldn't assist me getting out of a wet paper bag."

Laura rolled her eyes.

"You need to send me someone better."

"I've sent you the best candidates we've had. You've found fault with every single person." She opened a file folder. "Constantly late, bad attitude, can't handle direction... Smiles too much." She looked up. "Shall I go on? The faults you find are so minuscule, it's ridiculous. You barely give people a chance to settle in, and you fire them. Do you see a pattern here?" She removed her glasses, glaring at me.

"Yes. You send me the wrong people. HR is obviously falling down on the job. I gave you my list of requirements."

She regarded me, her voice becoming pointedly annoyed. "No. *You* are the pattern. *Your list* is ridiculous. No one is going to work the hours you want, be at your beck and call, run around after you, and never talk back. Nor will they have the education level you desire, be able to travel at a moment's notice, and—" she referred to the list "—make a mean sandwich." She shook her head with a sigh. "You're hiring an assistant, Alex. Not a gofer."

"Sally did all those things and more."

"Sally knew you and could handle you. Plus, she was fifty-six and knew how to put you in your place. You frighten all these young women and men we send to help you. You never give them a chance." She narrowed her eyes at me. "And it is not HR's fault. The common denominator for failure here is you."

"Ha," I snorted. "I could do better."

"I thought you'd say that." She handed me the stack of files she'd been carrying.

"What are these?"

"Four of the top applicants for the job. You interview them."

I accepted the folders, pursing my lips. "If you think this is a challenge, you're wrong. I'll find the right candidate." I leaned back. "What do I get if I'm right?"

"You interview, you hire, and they last more than six weeks? I'll admit the fault was ours."

I scoffed. "Prepare to apologize." I grinned, winking at her. "I expect quite the show."

Laura laughed, standing. "When this doesn't work, then I get the apology. I think an office memo stating that your arrogance and ego were the problem all along will suffice. That, plus you buy lunch for the entire HR department. Our choice."

I chuckled. I liked Laura, and I enjoyed our little sparring matches.

"To make it fair, I need to see a list of other candidates."

"Fine. There were only six others who qualified for the position. I'll send them over."

"Great. Now, out of my office. I have an assistant to hire."

She left, and I went back to the spreadsheet I'd been working on. The budget was tight on this project, and I wanted to make sure nothing was overlooked. I would get to the assistant thing later.

How hard could it be?

A short while later, another woman from HR dropped off more files. She paused as she was leaving. "Oh, Mr. Bane," she said, sounding nervous.

"Yes?"

"Laura told me to mention that the interviews were already scheduled—she had me contact the other candidates as well. I got hold of all of them but one. You'll have to make that phone call."

"Fine."

"For late Friday afternoon, between two and six."

I gaped at her. "*What?*"

That was tomorrow. And I had planned on taking the afternoon off. I was certain I had mentioned that to Laura last week. She was doing this to knock me off my game. I waved my hand, dismissing her.

"No problem."

She grinned, obviously in on the little wager. "Have a good afternoon."

The door closed behind her, and I groaned. I was going to have to put in some work if I wanted to be prepared for tomorrow. I was going to ace this interview process and have the best assistant in the company.

I was looking forward to the groveling after.

I reached for the files and began my work.

Given the number of candidates, I divided the folders into two piles—the strongest contenders and the runners-up. Reading through résumés, I made notes, checked references, nodding over some of the comments. When I finished, I had the three top choices, and the rest were graded as to how compatible they seemed. A lot was expected from my assistant—I knew that. I worked hard and anticipated them to do the same. My office needed someone smart, able to think on their feet. I didn't expect them to know how to use CAD—a computer-aided design software—but a general understanding was a bonus. At present, I already had assistants to work with me on the landscape designs when needed. The person I hired was required to run my office and calendar and keep me on track. I needed them to understand the basics of what we did. To go over numbers and budgets. Schedule meetings, bring clients up-to-date, handle small problems, keep up with emails and calls.

And yes, make me a sandwich and coffee when I requested it. The occasional personal errand.

And I expected them to be polite, quiet, and stay out of my way.

And I always got what I wanted.

Friday afternoon, I stared at the dwindling list on my desk.

Who the hell knew how hard it was to find an assistant? At times, I felt as if I were the one being interviewed—and found lacking.

One woman laughed when I went through the list of duties I expected. She took my list, read it, picked up a pen, and stroked off over half the items on it. Then informed me her expected salary was twice what was on offer.

And she had been my fourth choice.

My first and third had been such terrible interviews,

I knew there was no point in trying to offer them a job. My second choice never showed. Number six was married with three kids and spent most of the interview explaining she didn't do overtime, no travel, and needed a lot of time off for kid appointments and personal days if they were sick.

"Which is often," she said with a shrug. "But I can work from home."

I managed to get her out of my office without insulting her.

I had two names left on the list. I glanced at the clock, grimacing. I had a feeling number nine was a no-show as well. It was well past his appointed time, and he hadn't shown up or called. That left a Magnolia Myers. I picked up her résumé, refreshing my memory. She'd been a personal assistant for an account manager who retired four months ago. She'd been working part time ever since with an agency. She had the qualifications I was looking for, but it was the personal letter of reference that gave me pause. Although glowing, the words spunky, eager to help and learn, and always smiling gave me pause. I didn't want spunky and smiling. I wanted quiet and industrious.

But I was almost out of options.

When five forty-five came and went, I sighed. Obviously, Ms. Myers had changed her mind as well. I laughed dryly as I picked up my coat. I was going to have to admit defeat to Laura on Monday and eat crow.

I pushed the button for the elevator, switching off the overhead lights and waiting in the hallway. Realizing I'd forgotten my phone, I hurried back, swiping it off my desk and rushing back as the elevator dinged in the hall. I caught my foot on the edge of a display case as I hurried toward the door, anxious to put this day behind me.

But someone was dashing across the outside reception room at the same time I lurched sideways. We crashed together, my arms automatically grabbing at the person who hit me. We went down to the hard floor, a mass of sprawled arms and legs. I managed to be the one who hit first, a small, warm body landing on top of me. A loud exhale of air escaped me in the form of a grunt, and the person on top of me gasped, a soft, surprised sound, letting me know the stranger was female. The lights around me had gone out for some reason, and for a moment, I was frozen.

It felt like an eternity in which nothing happened, even though I knew it was only a few seconds. Thirty, tops. I was in shock, holding a sweet-smelling woman who seemed content to stay where she was. I lifted my head, realizing the reason that the dim light had disappeared was the heavy fall of hair that covered my head. I reached up to swipe it aside, forcing away the impulse to bury my face into the thick tresses and sniff them. That silly impulse made me angry.

"What the fuck?" I growled.

The woman lifted her head, her hair falling back. I stared into the darkest eyes I'd ever seen. They were round with shock, yet I saw amusement lurking in their depths. A smile played on her full lips.

"Hi."

Her voice did something to me. It was breathy and soft. Sweet, yet sultry. I liked it.

"Hello."

"I'm here for the five forty-five interview." She looked sheepish. "I planned on bowling you over, but not like this."

My lips twitched. "You're late."

"I missed my bus, and then I broke my heel running to get here," she babbled, still lying on my chest. "The guy downstairs refused to let me come up, saying the office closed at six. But I waited until he answered the phone and was distracted, and I ran up the steps," she said, sounding breathless.

And much too sexy to be this close.

"Ten floors," she added.

"You're still late."

"You *have* to let me interview. Please. Ask your boss nicely."

I glared at her. "I *am* the boss."

"Oh," she whispered, her eyes even rounder. "Well, *shit.*"

CHAPTER TWO

Magnolia

It had been a day from hell. Nothing had gone right. Earlier, I'd overslept, missed my bus, and the temporary agency I had been working for let me go. I spent some time dropping off résumés, and while waiting on the corner for a light to change, I had been splashed by a car. I had to go home to change before heading to my late afternoon appointment. I realized I had lost my keys and had to wait for my friend to get home and open my door. By the time he did, I was cold, miserable, and feeling down.

Determined to finish off the day on a better note, I dressed in my best outfit, put on heels, and headed to the interview I hoped would go well. I had been pleased to receive a call the night before, the low voice on the other end asking me if I could come in for five forty-five, giving me the shivers as he spoke. I was quick to agree, jotting down the address as he dictated it, then hung up.

But again, the damn bus took off as I was running to catch it. I started walking, half jogging, and caught a different bus, managing to somehow slip getting off it, and snapping a heel. Then, walking like a drunk on a Saturday night, I made it to the building, fifteen minutes late. The security guard refused to let me up, but I was determined and dodged into the stairwell. I pulled off my shoes and raced up the steps, glad I kept up my cardio.

I hadn't expected to run into someone and get tackled to the floor.

I hadn't planned on the sensation of how good it felt with the stranger's arms around me, holding me as if to keep me safe.

And when I lifted my head and met those intense, icy blue eyes, I hadn't expected his words.

"I *am* the boss."

After muttering a curse, I carefully rolled away, wincing a little as I pushed up off my knees and ran a hand down my skirt. I followed his lithe rise to his feet, staring at him in the semidarkness.

"Mr. Bane, I presume?" I asked, pleased to hear my voice sound almost normal. A little shaky, but okay.

"Yes."

He reached past me, flicking on the light, and I caught my breath. He was tall, broad-shouldered, and wide-chested. His suit was pulled tight across his arms. He had light-brown hair, thick and wavy, brushed off his forehead. His full lips were drawn into a frown, and heavy eyebrows set off his incredible eyes. Clear, brilliant blue. Glittering and frosty, looking at me as if I was a bug he wanted to squash under his fingers. He was handsome, intimidating, and confident. I knew he was thirty-four, eight years older than I was. Somehow, his self-assurance made me feel younger.

He studied me, no doubt finding me lacking. I was far shorter than he was, and I knew I looked anything but professional. I glanced down, trying to hide the fact that I was shoeless, my coat damp, my hair had fallen out of the careful ponytail I had wrestled it into, and I was breathing hard.

Maybe I had to work on my cardio a little more.

"I assume you are Ms. Myers?"

"Yes, Magnolia. Maggie to my friends."

I shut up as I watched one eyebrow lift, effectively silencing me. It was a pretty cool trick, and I wondered how long it had taken him to perfect it.

"I was leaving. You're late, and I'm done for the day. You missed your chance."

I grabbed his sleeve before he could move. "Please. I ran almost all the way here and then...*ten* flights of stairs! You have to give me credit for that. Please. Give me a chance."

He looked down where I gripped his suit jacket. He said nothing. "I can do this job well," I pleaded. "Interview me." I dropped my hand. "Please."

He scowled, turning and heading into what I assumed was his office. "You have ten minutes," he said over his shoulder.

I blinked.

"The clock is ticking, Ms. Myers."

I shook my head to clear it, and I followed him.

Bane

I watched her struggle out of her coat, pulling down the cuffs of her ivory-colored blouse. It was an old-fashioned affair with lace and ruffles on the long sleeves.

It was oddly sexy on her.

Her skirt was black with a slit on the side. It drew attention to her shapely legs and the fact that she wasn't wearing shoes. Her stockings had holes on the feet. I tried not to laugh at the mental image of her darting around Pete downstairs and rushing up the steps. I was surprised he hadn't called up to warn me of a security breach and imminent attack.

Then again, he was old, had trouble seeing from his left eye, and probably didn't notice her sneaking past him. None of us had the heart to fire him. He was retiring in a year, and the "assistant" we'd hired to help out did most of the work. He must have been absent from the desk when Ms. Myers showed up.

She sat down with a small huff, smoothing down her skirt. "Ready."

I knew without looking that her feet didn't touch the floor. Again, a wave of amusement hit me, but I refused to show it.

"Why should I hire you? You're late, unorganized, and, frankly, a hot mess."

"You think I'm hot?"

I blinked, once again fighting a smile. "I didn't say you were hot. I said you were a hot mess. Broken shoes, wet coat, ripped stockings. You look like an orphan."

"I am," she said in a small, broken voice. "I have no one in this world. I'm all alone."

I was at a loss as to what to say next. Then she laughed. "Gotcha. Oh, the look on your face. Priceless." She giggle-snorted.

The sound made my lips twitch again, but I schooled my expression, scowling at her. "You're wasting your ten minutes."

She straightened her shoulders. "I am normally very organized. I don't know much about plants, but I can revise your calendar, make your days seamless, your files perfection, and deliver an awesome cup of coffee and lunch every day without fail. I can work late if needed, be available to accompany you on site visits or out-of-town business trips. I'm very good with numbers and spreadsheets. I'm an Excel genius, and no one will get past me if that is what you tell me to do." She drew in what I assumed was a much-needed breath. "And I am very cordial and friendly on the phone."

I resisted laughing at that. I had a feeling this woman was way too friendly all the time.

She cast her eyes around the room. "I know how to use a 3-D printer, and I am familiar with CAD."

I liked those attributes. No other candidate had them. I didn't need for her to know about plants. As a landscape architect, that was my job. I needed her to run my office.

"Who says I need my calendar revised or that there is anything wrong with my files?"

"Why would you be looking for an assistant again so soon?"

"So soon?" I repeated.

"I have applied for this job four times. This is the first interview I've gotten. I assume none of the other hires have met your exacting demands." She lifted her chin, the light catching on her lovely hair. "You've been waiting for me."

I liked her spunk, although I preferred my assistant less exuberant. I pulled a sheet of paper from a file, handing it to her. "You have a minute to tell me what is wrong with this budget."

I studied her as she looked over the paper. Her lips moved as she read it, her eyes darting from line to line quickly. She bit one corner of her mouth, drawing attention to the shape of her lips. Pouty. Full. Sensual. She ran a finger along the columns, narrowing her gaze, then tapping her cheek. Her skin was creamy and looked soft—much like the petals of the tree she was named for.

Magnolia.

It was pretty.

So was she.

She was different. She wore little makeup, allowing her natural beauty to shine through. Her long, straight hair was chestnut colored. Reddish in the light. Dark in the shadows. Her eyes were a deep brown—so dark it was hard to see where the iris ended and the pupil began.

Her skin was smooth, kissed with a pinkish undertone. My gaze dropped to her mouth again. Her lips were full and soft-looking.

Inviting, if I was interested.

Which I wasn't.

But it was the band of freckles across her nose that caught my attention. Gold in color, they were a perfect symmetry that swept over the bridge and diluted to a fan of dots along each cheek in flawless alignment. I could easily see that when she blushed, the band would be brighter than anywhere on her face.

Some would call it enchanting.

Not me.

I didn't do enchanting. Or sassy-mouthed women who wanted to work for me. No matter how pretty they were. I'd drawn that line in the sand a long time ago, and I never stepped over it.

I didn't date at all, to be honest.

Especially this woman.

Never.

This wasn't a good idea. I would let her finish the interview and get Laura to start a new search next week. She could gloat, and I would keep my end of the bargain.

Ms. Myers's throat clearing made me realize I had been staring. She slid the paper in front of me, tapping the third column. "I don't know much about pricing, but this plant price is listed incorrectly. I doubt it's that much cheaper than the other ones. That would throw the budget off completely."

I had to say, I was impressed. No one else had spotted that. I had tried to make it simple, but she was the only one who'd noticed the price discrepancy.

I handed her a spreadsheet. She said she rocked Excel.

"Error," was all I said. I studied her as she looked over the columns.

It took her thirty seconds. "Incorrect sum in the fifth column."

I sat back, nodding.

She had been late, seemed like a bit of a disaster, but she was the best of all the candidates.

Dammit.

"The salary isn't negotiable."

"I didn't expect it to be."

"A month trial period."

"I won't need it. You'll be lost without me after the first week."

I lifted an eyebrow in surprise. She was confident.

"I don't do Sundays."

"Off to church, are you?" I asked.

"I spend Sundays with my dad at the home. I would rather not throw his schedule out of whack. If it is important, I can adjust, but I would prefer not to."

"Noted." I paused. "There may be some travel. Most certainly overtime."

"That's fine."

Silence fell as I made my decision.

The entirely wrong one.

"You start Monday. Be here at eight. You work until five. You get an hour for lunch and breaks—at least, that is what your employment contract will say. You'll get what I give you and say thank you." I met her gaze, her lovely eyes dancing with happiness. "I work hard. I expect you to—"

"Work harder." She finished my sentence. "I know the drill."

"You answer to me and no one else. You work for me. I don't do the friend thing. I'm your boss. I tell you to jump, you do it."

"I'm kind of short. I hope you don't expect much height. And my butt is kinda round, so that doesn't work in my favor."

I had felt that butt as she'd lain on top of me. My hands had slid over the round cheeks. I could argue with her that it did work in her favor—if this weren't a job interview.

I stared at her, not smiling.

"No jokes. Okay, then," she muttered.

"When you get here on Monday, you'll be sent to HR. You'll fill out the paperwork, get your pass, and report to me immediately after. Do you understand?"

"Yes."

"Do you have any questions?"

"I probably will on Monday."

"Fine. If so, we'll deal with them on Monday."

I stood, holding out my hand. "Welcome to Balanced Designs."

She slid off her chair, confirming to me that her feet hadn't touched the floor. She shook my hand, and I frowned at the feeling of her small hand clasped within mine. It felt oddly right there. I had to look down at her, and I realized I was well over a foot taller than she was. Which reminded me she had no shoes.

"I'll call you a cab to get home."

"No, I'm fine."

I glanced at the window. "It's raining again, and you have no shoes."

"No, really. I'll just break off the other heel and walk to the bus. I'm fine." She shook my hand again, her grip tight. "Thank you for the opportunity, Mr. Bane."

Then before I could speak, she turned and hurried away. I glanced at the chair she'd vacated, rolling my eyes. She'd left her scarf. I rounded the desk, picking it up, and went after her, but I missed her.

Deciding not to chase after her, I returned to my office and inexplicably held the scarf to my nose. Her fragrance, the one I had smelled in her hair, clung to the diaphanous material. Light, floral, and citrusy, her perfume was fresh and feminine. Sexy in an innocent way.

For some reason, I wondered if it would be more potent inhaled from behind her ear or at the base of her throat. Or between her—

I shook my head to stop that thought.

She was my new assistant, and I didn't do relationships with employees. I barked out a laugh as I picked up my coat. I didn't do relationships with anyone.

I headed to the elevator, hoping I hadn't just made a mistake, yet somehow knowing I had. Ms. Myers was far too pretty and quirky to work for me. I needed an old, matronly woman with zero distractions.

Ms. Myers, with her dark eyes and sweet-smelling

chestnut hair, was definitely a distraction. And I had a feeling she was going to be a problem. She was a lot of problems rolled into a small little ball of prettiness.

And I had hired her.

I was an idiot.

Then I shook my head. I handled problems all the time. Made fast decisions and stopped smaller problems from becoming bigger ones with one determined course of action. I could handle Ms. Myers. From now on, she was simply an employee. The fact that I was attracted to her was a problem I could contain.

I could do this.

I only hoped, come Monday, she didn't look as appealing as she had today.

In fact, I was certain I had overstated her attractiveness. She had knocked me off my game when she had...knocked me off-balance. I grimaced, recalling how she'd felt on top of me. I shook my head to clear it.

She was just an employee.

And I only had to remember that for six weeks to win my bet. By that time, I was sure she would have faded into the background.

Then I realized I was still holding her scarf. Fingering the silk like it was her skin.

With a curse, I dropped the scarf on the desk she would be sitting at and walked out of the office.

I only sniffed my hand once on the way to my car.

Handling it.

Yep.

CHAPTER THREE

Bane

She was already there when I arrived on Monday, her coat draped over the chair behind her desk, but the office empty. I glanced at my watch, surprised. It was barely seven-thirty. I looked around, wondering where she was, when she cleared her throat from behind me. I turned to say good morning, the words freezing in my throat.

She wore another old-fashioned blouse. Lace at her throat and wrists. It was a soft mossy green, and the skirt she wore was perfectly modest yet, on her, was sexy as hell. It fit her perfectly, molded to her hips and thighs as if it was made for her.

Her hair was up, swept away from her face. I had a vision of pulling it down and burying my fingers in it as I kissed her. I had to take a step back and shake my head, the lure of her was so strong.

I dropped my gaze to her feet, then met her confused gaze. "Managed to keep your shoes on this time," I observed, my voice clipped.

She smiled, and I instantly regretted my words. I didn't want to have any sort of relationship or inside jokes with her. She was simply someone to make my life easier at the office.

That was all.

"No missing the bus this morning. I'll get your coffee, then head to HR. I was told to come back at eight."

"What time did you get here?"

"Oh, about seven. Pete let me up. We made friends Friday when I left. Lovely man."

She turned and walked away, and I almost groaned at the slit up the back of her skirt and the way the material hugged her ass.

I headed into my office and hung up my coat, then sat at my desk. Ms. Myers walked in, carrying a steaming cup of coffee and setting it down, then took a seat in the same chair she'd been in on Friday. She opened a notebook, her pen poised.

"What shall I call you?" she asked.

"My name," I said drolly.

"First or business?"

"Business."

"All right, Mr. Bane. I have my morning mapped out, but is there something you need?"

I pushed the coffee toward her. "Very pretty coffee, Myers, but I like it black. No milk, no sugar, no foamy designs needed."

She frowned, looking disappointed. "I thought so, but I wanted you to see how great I can make a cup look. I'll drink it and bring you a plain black one." She paused, then grinned. "If you want to impress a client with my coffee skills, just let me know."

"I'll be sure to do that," I replied dryly, trying not to notice how lovely she was when she smiled. "Normally, the only things needed to impress them are my skills, but I'll keep that in mind."

I stared at her, waiting. She met my gaze. Her dark eyes were warm, framed by long lashes. Very little makeup again, which somehow suited her more than a heavy hand with the eyeliner.

I sighed. "I still have no coffee."

"Oh, right." She sprang from her chair, rushing away.

I shook my head and, curious, took a sip of the foamy coffee. I had to admit, it was tasty. There was a slightly creamy edge to it, as well as a flavor I couldn't place. Both countered the normally bitter brew that wasn't unpleasant. My phone buzzed, and I looked down, scrolling through the messages. One was from my mother, demanding to see me. I went past that one, not wanting to deal with her and her orders at the moment. The rest, I could handle later.

Myers walked back in, carrying a steaming cup and setting it down in front of me. Her eyes widened. "You drank the first one!"

I glanced down, surprised to see I had indeed drunk it all.

"I was desperate," I said dismissively.

"Did you like it?" she asked eagerly.

"It was passable."

I picked up the fresh mug and took a sip, pausing before speaking. "Much better, Myers. Now, sit. I need to go over my expectations."

She sat down, clearly unhappy, but picked up her notebook.

"Ready."

Magnolia

The office hummed around me, a constant background noise. People were in and out of Mr. Bane's office all morning. I met the partners, other assistants, and some staff members. Most seemed pleasant. A woman came from the IT department, looking hesitant as she walked into the office.

"Hi," I said brightly. "I'm Magnolia."

"Rylee Jenkins. I have a new computer for you that Mr. Bane ordered."

"Great. This one is awful."

She grimaced, setting down the laptop and speaking quietly. "The last temp kept destroying the equipment. Like, daily. I refused to give her new purchases. But Mr. Bane says you're good." She met my eyes with a droll wink. "Coming from him, that is high praise."

I decided right then that Rylee Jenkins and I were going to be friends.

She departed after giving me a quick run-through of the new machine. I sighed in happiness, trailing my fingers over the keyboard. I would be so much more efficient with this one.

Then I turned my attention to the task at hand. Alexander Bane's calendar was a mess. Obviously, someone had tried to fix it, only to leave it worse off than before. I went from window to window, checking emails, dates, times. Looking over previous schedules. The newer, faster machine made it easier.

The morning flew by. I had a list of things to do—reorganize the files, color code them, change the tabs, rearrange the file cabinet items. I had familiarized myself with the names and projects being worked on. When Mr. Bane shouted out for a file, I would know where to get it from.

He did that a lot. Shouted. Grunted. Made an odd noise of displeasure in the back of his throat. Please was not a word he knew or, if he did, chose not to use often. At least, not so far.

I did a final look-through of his new calendar. It was perfection. I needed to sync his phone with the revised information, and then he would get an updated version constantly. He had disconnected it when the last PA had screwed everything up. It had been my priority once I'd looked at the mess.

I knocked on the partially open door, waiting for the enter grunt. It was different from his displeased grunt or his exasperated sigh. This was one of anticipation, as if he was waiting for my mistake so he could express his displeasure.

I heard a muffled noise, which I assumed was him, and I walked in, finding him on the phone, his eyes shut, his voice pitched low.

"No, Mother, not today."

He listened.

"Tomorrow doesn't suit either. I'm very busy with revisions. In fact, I leave in the morning for a week."

I frowned, glancing at my notebook. I had no notes about him leaving.

"I have a meeting. I'll be in touch."

He hung up, shaking his head.

"You're going away on a business trip?"

"No. Unless my mother calls. Then I'm away."

"You want me to lie?"

He looked at me, his eyes a chilly blue—like a frozen wave on the ocean. Unwelcoming and cold.

"You will do what I tell you." His phone rang again, and he ignored it. "Dammit, that woman is pissing me off. I need her to lose my extension."

He scrubbed his face. "What is it you want, Myers?"

He had started calling me Myers almost immediately. I had wanted to protest, but then I realized he called a lot of people by their last name. Saved him the wasted breath of adding Mr., Ms., or God forbid, the long word Mrs.

His partners called him Bane. Everyone else that I had met so far called him Mr. Bane. I chose to follow the masses. I wasn't sure what he would do if I called him Bane.

But he was rapidly becoming the bane of my existence.

"I need your cell phone to sync your calendar."

His desk phone rang again, and I thought he was going to throw it through the window.

He handed me his cell, and I turned, holding it in my palm.

"What?" he snapped.

"I need your thumbprint to open it."

The phone rang again, and he cursed, answering it. "Mother, I said I'm busy."

I sighed, crossing behind the desk. His hand was on top of the wood, and I grabbed it, shocked when he curled his fingers around mine, holding tightly. I had the strangest need to rub his knuckles. Smooth back his hair and comfort him.

Except he would no doubt throw me through the window, along with the phone he was gripping.

I set down his cell, uncurling his fingers. He seemed to realize he'd been clasping my hand, yanking it away. Calmly, I took it, pressing his thumb to the screen, ignoring his frosty glare and the angry words he was shooting at the woman on the other end of the line.

His phone screen brightened, indicating I now had access. I placed his now-relaxed hand on the desk and, without thinking, patted the top of it. I walked out, pulling the door behind me, daring to glance over my shoulder. I met his gaze, the piercing blue not as angry. Instead, he almost looked grateful.

Then he began to argue with his mother again, and the

fury was back.

I shut the door behind me and went to work.

I knocked, waiting for the master to bid me to enter. I walked in and was met with a steely glare. "Where have you been? I called you twice."

"I was getting things done."

He looked at the tray in my hand. "What is that?"

I set it on the desk. "Your lunch."

He watched as I slid the tray containing a turkey sandwich with a side of pickles and a fresh, steaming cup of coffee onto the side of the desk. "How did you know?"

"I told you I'm good."

He indicated the coffee. "You figured out my lunch, yet again, you brought me the foamy coffee."

"Which you drank this morning and enjoyed. You can have black next time." I reached into the bag I was carrying and brought out a small device, looking around for a plug.

"Ah, there's one," I said, dropping to my knees and crawling under the front of the desk.

He pushed his chair back, crouching by my side. "What the hell are you doing down there on your knees?" he hissed.

I tried not to laugh. "Plugging this in. If you'd turn on your flashlight, it would make it faster."

He mumbled something under his breath but pulled his phone from his pocket and did as I requested. I fumbled, not happy when I realized the plug was partially covered, but I saw another one farther in. "Aim it that way," I instructed, tugging on his arm. He leaned closer, pushing me into the wood, and I had to wiggle to get my arm over to the right spot. It was a tight fit, but I got the plug in and was about to back out when a voice spoke.

"Alexander, I was..."

There was a pause.

"Am I interrupting something?"

Mr. Bane jumped, hitting his head and cursing. He stood, sputtering. "No. Myers was messing around. I mean—"

I pulled myself out from under the desk and stood. "We were trying to find the right hole. It was tight."

The woman in the doorway didn't know where to look. I recognized her from HR this morning, but I didn't remember her name.

"For the plug," I added, holding up my purchase. "For the coffee warmer I bought." I headed her way, my hand out. "I'm Magnolia Myers."

"Jessica Aldridge." She bit her lip, trying not to grin. "I was bringing Alexander some papers."

I looked over my shoulder. Mr. Bane was standing, not speaking. I had a feeling he was in shock. "I can take them. He needs to sign them?"

"Yes. Review and sign."

"I'll drop them off as soon as he's had his lunch."

"Good." She looked between Mr. Bane and me, then started to chuckle. "Good luck."

"Oh, I'm fine."

"I wasn't talking to you."

I could hear her laughing all the way down the hall.

I turned back to Mr. Bane. "You should eat."

He blinked at me. "I can't believe HR...you...me...under the desk."

"It's all good," I assured him. "Now, I noticed your coffee got cold twice this morning. I got you this," I explained as I connected the small device, turned it on, and set his coffee mug on it. "You put your cup on it like that, and it will keep it warm."

He sat down, glancing at it. "Fine."

I picked up my notebook. "Your calendar is synced. Check it out, see if there is anything you want changed."

He took a bite of his sandwich, chewing. He looked at his phone, scrolling through the screens. He nodded, then swallowed. "Fine."

"I'm going to work on the files now. They're a disaster."

I got another nod.

"And you don't have to worry about your mother getting through to you anymore."

That made him pause. "Why?"

"I had your direct line transferred to my desk. All calls will come to me, except your partners and HR. Rylee helped me when she was here, so I knew who to ask. You have an internal extension now that I will transfer everyone else to. When your mother calls, I'll tell her you are unavailable and send her directly to voice mail."

He stared at me. Looked down. Blinked. "Fine."

I stood. "Now I'm going to eat my sandwich."

"Fine."

I scribbled a note.

"What are you writing?"

"To remind myself to get you a thesaurus. Or I could make you a list. Fine is sufficient, but there are other words— for instance, thank you or great job. They sound so much nicer than fine."

He scowled at me. "Do your job."

I smiled. "Fine."

At the door, I paused. "See how boring a word it is? I could have said, 'Right away, sir,' or 'Aye-aye, Captain,' but I substituted 'Fine.' It doesn't have the same ring, does it?"

I glanced over my shoulder, certain Mr. Bane was fighting a grin. I wasn't one hundred percent sure, but I was almost positive I saw his lips quirk.

I sat down at my desk, looking over my list of things to do.

I took a bite of my sandwich, looking at the scribbled notes I had found stuffed into desk drawers. One piece of paper noted my new boss's lunch preferences, which had helped me this morning. Turkey, ham, roast beef. All made the same way, on seeded bread with mayo and mustard. Pickles on the side. The name of the deli where the sandwiches were ordered that had his credit card on file. The underlined note on the bottom made me grin.

No later than 12 or else he gets grumpy.

I tried not to laugh. He was always grumpy. I could only imagine his foul temper if he became hangry.

His list of likes reminded me of my father. He ate a sandwich every day, and those were his top three. Along with egg or tuna salad. I always brought him sandwiches when I went to visit on Wednesdays and Sundays. I left enough for him to have one every day as he said I made the best sandwiches ever.

An idea formed, and I made myself another list. I was going to be so valuable to Mr. Bane, he would never let me go. I'd make sure of it.

CHAPTER FOUR

Magnolia

I was tired the next morning but arrived at the same time as Mr. Bane. The elevator door was closing, and I rushed toward it. "Hold, please!"

The doors opened, and I was met with Mr. Bane's scowling countenance. I hurried, not wanting to keep him waiting. My foot caught on the mat on the floor, and I tripped, closing my eyes in anticipation of hitting the floor. But a pair of solid arms caught me, holding me upright. Seconds passed as neither of us moved. He felt so warm, strong, and oddly safe. I tried not to notice how delicious he smelled. Crisp, clean, woodsy. Reminding me of a fall day in the sunshine. I wondered what it would be like, walking in the forest with him, his large hand wrapped around mine, keeping me safe and laughing with me. Complimenting me on—

"Jesus, Myers, you need to watch where you're going," he snarled and pushed me away, albeit gently. "Try to stay upright."

The doors opened, and he strode away, leaving me still mid-fantasy, his voice in my head not so frosty. I sighed as I went to my desk.

Great start to the day.

♡♡♡

I delivered his coffee, then stowed the bag I'd brought in the fridge in the break room. I made myself a coffee and returned to my desk, determined to do something with the files.

Around eleven, Mr. Bane came out of his office, frowning at the mess. "What—"

I cut him off. "It will all be back in place today. I'm organizing."

"Fine."

I resisted rolling my eyes.

"Staff meeting," he informed me.

"I'm aware. I see your schedule."

"I'll want lunch when it's done."

"Fine."

He did that eyebrow thing, slowly raising it as if he was challenging me. I met his glare with a steady gaze. He waited, then rolled his eyes, apparently not trying to resist the way I had. "Are you coming, Myers?"

"Oh. I wasn't sure I was supposed to. You never said anything."

"Staff meeting indicates staff. Of which you are one. For now," he added after a beat.

I grabbed my notebook and hurried after him, tripping on the cable that ran past my desk. I muttered a curse, rubbing my thigh where I hit it on the edge of the desk. He stopped, shaking his head. "What now?"

I glared. "There's a cable here, and I keep tripping on it. It's dangerous."

"I think you might be the danger, Myers. You seem to invite bad luck. Try to be more careful."

Then he turned and walked out. I rushed behind him, following him onto the elevator, making a face behind his back, then sticking out my tongue like an angry toddler. What a jerk.

"We're using the larger boardroom today," he said, looking straight ahead. "The one on my floor is mainly for the partners and clients."

I nodded, unsure of what else to say.

We stopped on the right floor, and he held out his arm, indicating I should go first. As I went by, he leaned down, his voice a low hum in my ear. "Always look around enclosed spaces."

I glanced up and froze. The panel around the door was glass.

He had seen me. The face I had made. The fact that I had stuck out my tongue at him.

I kept my head down, following him to the staff meeting.

The words *for now* echoed in my head.

They now felt as if my future was set. And not in a good way.

Bane

We entered the room, Myers trailing behind me. I scanned the table, taking note of who was here. I spotted a couple of the vipers at one end of the table and made a fast decision.

"With me," I instructed her. I sat down, indicating the seat beside me. Myers perched on the chair, turning in my direction. "Shouldn't I be at that end?"

"If I wanted you at that end, I'd tell you. Be quiet and listen."

She did that thing with her eyes. Partially shutting them

as if I couldn't see the eye roll behind the lids. I knew a lot of people wouldn't notice it, but I did.

I noticed everything about her. Dammit.

Which was why I was being such a jackass. I needed to keep her away from me. I found her much too attractive and likable.

Not to mention sexy as hell. Even her quirks amused me.

For the thousandth time since I'd hired her, I reminded myself I was an idiot.

My partners came in, the room filling with people. Lawson and Anderson greeted me and smiled at Myers. Their assistants sat beside them as well, and if they were surprised to see Myers to my right, they kept it to themselves. Even Sally had preferred to sit away from me at meetings. She informed me I grumped and made rude comments too much and I was distracting. Little did she know I did it for her amusement. The temporary staff who followed her after she retired kept as far away from me as possible at meetings. Yet with Myers, I felt a strange need to keep her away from some of the other, less friendly people. I felt almost protective of her. Why, I had no idea.

I glanced her way, seeing her head bent over the notebook she seemed to carry everywhere. I had to admit, she had impressed me so far. Even if I made her think otherwise.

Less than two days in, my calendar was perfect, the filing was getting organized, and what she had done about my phone line still amazed me. The thought of not having to listen to my mother and her nasty diatribes all the time earned Myers a lot of leeway with me. Sally had refused to step in where my mother was concerned and had never suggested a different phone line. It was a simple, brilliant idea.

I liked how Myers had noticed how often my coffee went cold and fixed it. I was used to it, always getting involved with my designs and plans, but like my mother getting through on my private line, she decided to change that for me.

Recalling what had occurred with her trying to plug in the little device, I felt the tug of amusement on my lips, and I had to school my features. Once she'd left the office, I had actually begun to laugh after holding it in most of the day. Between the desk incident and her quick comebacks, my jaw ached from locking it down and not reacting to her cheek. She was droll and funny, and it took all I had not to respond. I had a feeling if I did, that would be a slippery slope I would slide all the way down.

I stole another glance, noting how she touched her tongue to her bottom lip as she kept writing, her brow furrowed in concentration. The memory of her pressed close to me, the scent of her filling my senses, the feel of her curves molded to my chest, made my hand twitch with the desire to touch her again.

And I couldn't allow that to happen.

Lawson cleared his throat and began the staff meeting. I lifted my head, giving him my full attention and ignoring the woman beside me.

At least, as much as I could ignore her.

He got at least seventy-five percent of my mind.

The rest—well, I was doing the best I could.

Magnolia

The staff meeting was well-run and efficient. There was no waxing on about things. Instead, information was given, items discussed, and new business delivered. Mr. Lawson said something nice to welcome me since Mr. Bane couldn't be bothered to. I wasn't surprised.

Mr. Anderson stood up close to the end of the meeting, announcing that Balanced Designs was up for five awards at the yearly architectural event being held soon. "We have three tables of ten," he said. "Sadly, not everyone can attend, but there will be a draw if you want to put your name in to attend the dinner. Be advised it is formal."

Lawson stood as well. "One piece of news is that our own Alexander Bane is up for best landscape design for the Beaumont Buildings and grounds. His ideas were ingenious, and we're thrilled for him. Very prestigious."

Everyone clapped, myself included. Mr. Bane waved it off, but I was pleased for him. I had looked at his designs in the files. He was incredibly talented. I had no idea the scope of the things he was involved in. The planning, the intricate designs, the committees he sat on. Sustainable systems, mapping out entire communities, working with varied levels of governments to ensure his designs met and exceeded all required environmental responsibilities. I had seen the awards on his shelves.

No wonder the man was so serious.

The meeting ended, and I stood, heading back to the break room and grabbing my bag with lunch. I set up his plate and mine, carrying them to his office. He was at his desk as I slid the plate beside him. He looked at it with a confused frown. "That looks different."

"Try it."

I waited as he took a bite, chewing thoughtfully. He grunted, but it wasn't in displeasure. "It's..." He paused, and I waited for the usual "Fine." But he surprised me. "Good. I like it. They changed the bread and the turkey?"

"Different deli. All fresh. Better."

"Okay."

"You'll have to sign off on the credit card bill."

He waved his hand. "Of course."

"I might not always be able to get sandwiches there, but I'll try."

"Try hard."

I hugged myself. I was giving my side extra points for this.

"I'm going to find out where to put my name in for the dinner."

"Don't."

Disappointment filled me. "Is this because I stuck out my tongue at you?"

I was shocked when he chuckled. "No. Our assistants are always included. You don't have to enter your name. You'll all sit at one of the tables."

"Oh. Are you sure?"

The eyebrow lifted, and I had to grin at him. It was a great silencer.

Again, he surprised me and returned my smile with one of his own. It changed his face entirely. What was stern and handsome became warm and intoxicating. A dimple appeared high on one cheek. His eyes turned a liquid blue. They resembled the sky on a hot summer day, clear, bright, and warm. He was devastatingly sexy.

"Okay, then," I mumbled. "I'm going to eat my lunch."

He hummed around a mouthful and turned to his laptop. I walked out of his office on a high.

It didn't last long.

I headed to the break room to eat my lunch. It was empty, except for a table with some women I knew were from the assistant pool. Any one of the executives, visiting clients, or even partners had access to the pool if they required a temporary assistant. The four of them had been sitting at the other end of the boardroom. I had planned on going over and introducing myself when Mr. Bane had tugged on my elbow and told me to sit next to him. Watching them during the meeting, I got the feeling they were people I wouldn't want to be around much. They seemed catty. Constantly whispering among themselves and making comments only the four of them could hear. It felt disrespectful to me.

Now, as I sat by myself, they ignored me, talking among themselves again, covering their mouths to hide their words, yet I knew they were discussing me. I was grateful when Rylee walked in, and I smiled and waved. They immediately began with their chatter again. I didn't like that.

She came over after filling her coffee cup. "Hi."

"Time for a quick break?" I asked.

She looked startled, then grinned. "Sure."

She sat with me, her back to the group of women who were watching us, their eyes as sharp as their tongues no doubt were.

"Mean girls?" I asked with a smile on my face, my lips barely moving.

She took a sip of coffee with a nod. "The worst. It's like high school all over again. I ignore them. Luckily, I rarely deal with that department. I give their tickets to others who come through." She smiled sadly. "Still, they always have comments."

"I know the type all too well. Some never move beyond graduation."

There was a round of laughter behind us. Rylee shut her eyes. "They're nice in front of the bigwigs. Other staff. They wait until you're alone to get their digs in. So fake." She took another sip. "They make fun of me whenever they can. My looks, my butt, my nerdiness."

I frowned. Rylee was a pretty woman with soft blond hair and bright-green eyes, plus she was curvy like me and short. She wore glasses that gave her an owlish look, and her outfit was as unique as mine. Whereas I went for lace and silk, she liked leggings and long tunics. Simple, easy.

"I don't care what they think," she added. "I left those needs behind me. I like me. My friends like me."

"I like you too, Rylee. I think we're gonna be great friends."

She smiled, the action lighting up her whole face. "I think so too."

"We should trade numbers and hang out after work sometime."

"I'd love that." Her phone buzzed, and she glanced at the screen with a groan. "Well, that was a short break. I'm needed."

"Have a good afternoon."

She left, and I watched her go, observing the little clique in the corner. The one who looked like the leader made a remark, and they all laughed. I shook my head at their childish behavior, surprised they were allowed to act that way in a business environment. Then I remembered what Rylee said. Nice to her face, mean behind her back. And she wasn't one to complain, especially since it would be her word against theirs. But I liked her, and we could be friends. Maybe somehow we could stop their wagging tongues.

I stood and headed to the door, then stopped and went to their table, deciding to catch them off guard.

"Hi," I said with a bright, fake smile. "I'm Magnolia. I started here this week."

I met the flat blue eyes of the one I suspected was the ringleader. "I'm Verity. This is Rhonda, Maxie, and Susan."

"Nice to meet you."

"You're Bane's girl of the week?" Verity asked with a sneer.

"I'm his new assistant, yes," I replied, ignoring the jibe.

"Don't get too comfortable. They never stay. I doubt you'll be much different." She sat back, eyeing me up and down, no doubt making notes for her scathing opinion of me. "One of these days, he'll realize the best assistant for him is already in the company."

Ah, her dislike of me made sense. She wanted to work for Mr. Bane. Probably more than work.

She wanted to bang Bane.

Bang, *bang* Bane.

For some reason, that silly thought made me smile. I had to bite back a laugh.

She narrowed her eyes at me. "What are you smiling about?"

"Nothing. I'm enjoying it so far. Mr. Bane and I get along fine."

"You should join us for lunch. We can make sure you mingle with the right crowd."

I smiled even wider. "You mean, keep your friends close but your enemies closer? Thanks, but I know the right crowd, and it's not this one. Have a good day, um, *ladies*."

I walked out, hearing their furious whispers and knowing I had just made some enemies.

CHAPTER FIVE

Magnolia

I opened the door to the office, going to my desk. Mr. Bane's door was partially open again, and I heard voices, indicating someone was with him. I was about to sit down when the voices became louder.

"I am not discussing this with you again, Mother. I don't have time, and frankly, I have no interest."

"You need to listen to reason."

"You need to listen when I say no!" Bane roared.

"You said you were going out of town. You lied to your own mother to avoid seeing me. That is horrible behavior, even for you, Alexander." I could hear the censure in her cold voice.

"I didn't lie..." His voice faltered, something in it causing me to spring to my feet, grab my notebook, and hurry to the outer door, opening it, then shutting it loudly. I rushed back to Mr. Bane's door, flinging it open.

"Mr. Bane, the car is waiting for you!" I pretended to hesitate. "Oh, I apologize. I didn't realize you had company, but if you're going to make that flight, you need to go now."

He stared at me, then leaned over, slamming his laptop shut. "Right. I was on my way, and I got distracted."

"Your bag is in the car. I've checked you in, and if you go now, you'll make it. I can't call the client and tell them you've been delayed again. They were already upset enough. You'll be taking them to dinner later to apologize."

"Of course." He grabbed his coat. "Mother, Ms. Myers will show you out. Call next time. I'm very busy." He looked at me. "I'll text you from the plane."

He rushed past me without another word, but he winked as he went by, the relief on his face evident. I tried not to laugh at that or the fact that he'd added a Ms. in front of my name— no doubt to sound professional in front of his mother.

He shut the outside door loudly, his footsteps fading.

"Where is he going?"

"Vancouver."

"For what purpose?"

I crossed my arms over my chest, holding my notebook. "Your son is in demand all over the world, Mrs. Bane—"

She cut me off with a flick of her fingers.

"Mrs. Johnstone. I remarried."

I flicked her right back. "Regardless, he is very sought-after."

She narrowed her eyes. "And you are who, exactly?"

"I am Mr. Bane's assistant. I run his office for him."

"So, you're the one who answers his phone now?"

"Yes, I am."

"Why did that change?"

"New system," I said with a smile. "Why, I'm not privy to. Above my pay grade."

"You put me straight through when I call, do you understand me?"

"I work for Mr. Bane, not you. I will follow the protocols he sets out for me. If he is available, I will, of course, put you through. If not..." I trailed off with a shrug.

A dark flush saturated her cheeks. "Who do you think you are?"

"As I said, your son's assistant. Your very busy son. I suggest you call before you drop by next time. Even better, you should check in with security."

"I'll do no such thing. I am not some common visitor off the street. I am his mother, and as such—"

I held up my hand. "As such, you should understand how busy he is and that he can't just drop everything for you. Now, if you will excuse me, I have to get back to work. He'll call me from the airport, and I need to be ready." I held the door open. "Good day, Mrs. Johnstone."

She stomped by me with a glare. She had the same color eyes as Mr. Bane, but if I thought his were cold, hers were the frozen tundra that hadn't seen light for a decade. Everything about her was rigid. Her posture. Her way of speaking. Even walking. There was nothing motherly about her. It explained Bane to me a little bit—helped me understand why he was the way he was.

She slammed the outer door on her way out, and I sighed. I shut off the coffee warmer and pushed in his chair, making sure his desk was tidy. He'd left in a hurry, but I did notice his plate was empty, so he'd had lunch.

I wondered where he'd gone. Home? A bar? He was smart enough to know there was no car waiting for him, so perhaps he was simply using another office.

I sat down, feeling tired. It had been a day. Between tripping, the meeting, the mean girls, and now Bane's mother, I was weary.

And I had a feeling Bane would be in touch. I wondered what he would say.

I shook my head and went back to filing. I'd know soon enough.

$\heartsuit\heartsuit\heartsuit$

My phone buzzed with a text a short while later.

Is the coast clear?

I chuckled. He was being funny. I could be too.

Yes, the ice storm has passed. Where are you?

At my club. I didn't dare go home in case she checked. She's called four times, and I haven't answered. I'm waiting for her to get tired.

I pursed my lips. He had a club? I didn't know there were such things anymore. Unless...

My fingers flew before I could change my mind.

Like a sex club?

I could almost hear his teeth gnashing and see his eyes rolling.

Completely inappropriate, Myers. And no, there is a private dining club downtown I belong to. I'm sitting in the lounge, working.

                                                    Fine.

I'll work from home tomorrow. I'll see you
on Monday.

                                                    Fine.

I realize you think you're being coy, but I
know what you're doing.

                            No idea what you are referring to. See you
                                                    Monday.

I waited, disappointed he didn't return my text. And feeling oddly sad I wouldn't see him again this week. I returned to my task, working quickly and sorting the files. The afternoon flew by as I did. I put on some quiet music while I went through papers, separating into current, past, and future files. Putting older ones in storage boxes I found in the supply closet down the hall. It was small but well stocked, although the door stuck a little. For a moment, I panicked since I didn't like enclosed spaces, but I got it open. I made a mental note to take something to stop the door from fully closing behind me next time.

I kept busy all day Friday. I rearranged my little outer office to better suit me. I shoved the desk over a foot to cover the cord that kept tripping me. Angled it a little to make it look more welcoming. Adjusted the two visitor chairs. Called building maintenance and had them hang some framed photos I'd found in the walk-in storage area behind my desk on the empty walls. I had no doubt the pictures were of Bane's work. They needed to be shown off, not hidden. When I sat at my desk, it gave me something nice to look at rather than the modern art print that used to hang on the wall opposite me. Once I cleaned out the desk drawers and added a desk lamp I found in the storage area, it looked nice. Part of me wanted to add a few other personal things, but I had a feeling my boss wouldn't like that. He preferred a more minimal style. I thought the small space looked much improved.

I had a few texts from Bane. Additions to his calendar, adjusting some meetings. A request to book his upcoming travel, going, ironically, to Vancouver. Every message was straight and to the point. Nothing personal. There were no thank-yous or pleases in the messages, but I wasn't surprised. As I was finding out, praise from him was rare, and I doubted he even thought to do so. I wondered how much of his nature came from his mother. She had called, demanding to know why her son hadn't replied to her phone calls.

"Mrs. Johnstone," I said with barely concealed patience. *"Your son is away on a business trip. I haven't spoken to him either. Unless it is a dire emergency, I suggest you stop calling him. The more he is interrupted, the longer he will be away."*

That stopped her, and she hung up.

By six, I was done. I looked around the outer office, pleased. I had made it through the first week, mostly unscathed and still employed. I called it a win.

And now, I had the entire weekend Bane free.

Yay.

Bane

Saturday, the sun was bright and the air warm. I decided to go for a run. I needed the release that the long, steady rhythm would give me. After dressing and stretching, I headed out, aiming for the large park not far from my condo. It covered a huge piece of land, dividing two neighborhoods. The one I lived in was filled with skyscrapers and modern buildings. Expensive shops and attractions. On the other side of the park were older houses, more family-oriented. Low-rise apartments and lots of little locally owned shops and vendors. I liked both areas. Although, the more modern area appealed to me more. But the gardens and wider streets of the older area called to my senses. At times, I wandered the streets, checking out the landscaping and lawns. The greenery. All rare in Toronto, yet so vital to the city. All greenspaces were.

My feet pounded on the pavement, the sound and cadence helping to clear my mind. Running always did that for me. I sorted my week into compartments, putting aside those things that didn't matter and concentrating on what did. My mother's visit was actually a godsend. Taking me out of the office and putting some distance between Myers and me had been a good thing. I was able to concentrate and work on a design that had been plaguing me because the client was constantly changing their mind. I didn't have the distraction of her answering the phone. Wondering if her footsteps meant she would be coming into my office to tempt me with her sweet voice and soft fragrance. Tease me over something she found amusing, forcing me to be even terser with her than I should be.

She was a temptation I was finding harder to resist each

day.

When she burst through my door, informing me I had to leave for my business trip and interrupting my mother's diatribe, I could have kissed her for her ingenuity. I had lingered briefly outside the office door, listening to the way she handled my mother, shocked at her ability to do so. Then I headed downstairs, waiting in the alley for my car and driver to show up, and headed to the club. It was the safest place. My mother had no idea I belonged to the club, so she wouldn't show up. And the best part was, even if she did, she couldn't get past the security downstairs. It had been productive.

I went around a group of women out for a run. Or a gab session, more likely, since they were walking—not even very quickly—and they were all chatting. I heard a few low whistles as I went by, but I ignored them. I kept going, finally wiping at my brow, pausing by a small bridge to stop and take a drink of water. I glanced around, surprised not to see many people enjoying the park, then laughed when I reminded myself it was barely past nine. Another couple of hours and the place would be teeming with people. By then, I would be back in my condo, hard at work.

I began running again, slowing my pace. Around a corner, I spied a woman ahead of me, power walking. Or trying to. She wore a tank and leggings but had a heavy, patterned shirt of some kind tied around her waist. It kept getting tangled in her legs, and she would pause and adjust, then start again. I chuckled to myself. For added warmth, she'd be better with a light jacket that wasn't so big, like the one I was wearing. She tripped again, readjusting herself, and I chuckled as she pulled off the flannel, shaking it out.

I stopped for another drink, watching her. There was

something familiar about her, but I couldn't see her face. My gaze dropped to her ass. It was rounded and perky. Quite spectacular in her tight leggings. Then she wound the flannel around her waist again and began to move. She broke into a slow jog, her ponytail swinging with the movement. Again, I felt the sensation of familiarity, but why, I was unsure. I began to run, planning to pass her and then double back and head home. I would see her profile then and perhaps know where I recognized her from.

Except, her foot caught on something, and I watched as she stumbled, falling to the grass with a hard exhale of air. I sped up, dropping to my knee next to her. I automatically reached for the ankle she was holding. "Are you all right?"

I heard a small gasp that was more than familiar.

I looked up, my gaze drifting past the full breasts, pouty lips, and perfectly fanned-out freckles to the dark eyes so well-known to me already.

"Myers?"

Magnolia

I had to get out this morning. I was restless and edgy. I hadn't gone for one of my walks in days. I was too tired when I got home at night. I looked out at the bright sunshine, deciding to go on a power walk now. I got dressed, adding the flannel jacket that used to be my dad's. It was long and warm, far too big most of the time, but I had removed the lining and it was great when I got chilly. With the heavy tree line in places in the park, I might need it.

But as I walked, I got too warm, and I tied it around my waist. It kept slipping, making me stop, readjust, and then keep going. I had been to the other side of the park, had a coffee while sitting in the sun, and was heading home now. I wasn't going as fast since my legs were tired. I hit a rockier part of the path, slipping on some loose gravel and going down hard on the grass.

I was shocked when a man dropped beside me, holding my foot in his hand and asking me if I was all right.

Two things hit me at once. I knew that voice. And that heady, woodsy scent. I gasped, meeting the sparkling blue eyes of my boss.

"Myers?" he asked.

Then he did something out of character for him. He grinned. Really grinned, making him more handsome and sexier than ever.

"I should have known," he said, shaking his head. "What the hell are you doing?"

"Power walking."

He held up a sleeve of the shirt tied around my waist. "Trying to kill yourself tripping over this is more like it."

He leaned closer. "What on earth are you wearing? Is this...*flannel*?"

"Hey, it's Saturday. I can dress however I want."

He studied me, his brilliant eyes glittering in the light. "So, Magnolia Myers, have I uncovered one of your secret weekend fetishes?"

"What?" I asked crossly.

"Rolling lumberjacks for their clothing."

I pushed on his shoulder. "Go away."

With another chuckle, he grasped my waist, hauling me to my feet. "Can you walk?"

"Of course I can walk. What are you doing in my park

48

anyway?"

That one single eyebrow rose, meant to quiet me. But it didn't work outside the office.

"Let me go."

"You own the park, Myers?"

"You know what I mean. Why are you here?"

"I was running. Like I do every weekend."

I frowned. "I power walk every weekend."

"Cruising for lumberjacks to attack?"

I sniffed at his attempted humor. "Please go away now. Continue your run. In fact, run as fast as you can away from me. It isn't Monday, so I shouldn't have to see you today."

"It's a public park."

I huffed out an exasperated noise. Why wasn't he leaving?

I widened my eyes, looking over his shoulder. "Is that your mother?"

"What?"

He turned fast, letting go of my arm. I attempted to move away, crying out when my ankle protested.

He gripped my arm again. "Funny."

"The look on your face was."

"Your ankle is hurt."

"I twisted it. It'll be fine. Let me go, and I'll head home."

"Where is home?"

I indicated the houses near the edge of the park. "Over there, three streets back." I shook off his hold. "See you on Monday."

He shook his head. "Not until I see you walk."

I rolled my eyes, not holding back. It was Saturday after all, and I was on my own time.

I pushed him away, took in a deep breath, and walked. I

held in the groan of pain I felt as I put weight on the ankle, then turned to him. "See? Fine. Now, off you go." I waved at him in dismissal. "Bye-bye."

Taking another deep breath, I began the long, slow process of heading home. Maybe I could find a stick to help. I bit my lip to stifle the little whimper just as I was lifted into a set of strong, firm arms.

"What are you doing?"

"Taking you home," he snapped. "You can barely walk."

I pushed on his chest. It was akin to pushing on cement. "Put me down."

"Shut up, Myers."

"You can't tell me to shut up."

"I think I just did."

"I'm too heavy for you to carry."

He leaned his head back, laughing. "Whatever. Stop squirming and tell me where to go."

"I'll happily tell you where to go," I responded.

Again, he chuckled. "Be nice, or I'll drop you in the pond," he threatened, holding me over the rail as we crossed a small footbridge.

"No!" I grasped his neck in panic.

"Then point me toward your house and be quiet. Your lumberjack-hunting is over for the day."

CHAPTER SIX

Bane

It was hard to stay annoyed at Myers as I held her. She gave me directions, her voice subdued. Otherwise, she didn't talk. She felt soft and warm in my arms. Surprisingly right, as if made to curl against me.

Internally, I shook my head at those odd thoughts.

We arrived at an old Victorian place, and she indicated the steps down located behind a row of bushes at the side of the house.

"You live in the basement?"

"Yes."

With a frown, I carried her down the steps and helped her stand upright. She dug a key out of her pocket and held it up. "Thanks for the lift."

I nodded, waiting.

With an annoyed huff, she unlocked the door and hobbled inside. I stopped her from shutting the door with my foot. Inside, I looked around, pleasantly surprised. It was light and airy. A small kitchen and living area with a short hall leading to what I assumed was a bedroom and bath. The living room was decorated with eclectic pieces. A love seat and a Victorian chaise longue. A huge ottoman. An old wingback in the corner. Bookshelves and tables. Tons of books and knickknacks scattered everywhere. A knitting basket. A small table and chairs tucked in the corner. Old-fashioned pictures and embroidered pieces hung on the walls. Some newer watercolors. The place suited her. It was unique—like she was.

She headed to the love seat and sat down. "There. I'm home safe. You can go."

"Where is your first aid kit?"

"I'm fine."

I waited, lifting my eyebrow at her. Her low huff of annoyance amused me.

"In the bathroom on the shelf."

"Do you have any compression bandages in it?"

Her shoulders dropped. "No. I have one in my bedside table." She shrugged at my confusion. "I used it last week and never put it back."

"Stay there."

"Woof."

I frowned at her. "What?"

"You gave me a command like a dog. I was responding in kind."

"You are a strange girl, Myers."

"Pot calling the kettle black."

I ignored her and headed down the hall. The first aid kit was easy to find in the small space. In her bedroom, I had to stop for a moment. As soon as I walked in, her scent was all around me. Saturated into the linens on her bed. The clothing hanging in the closet. The room was girly. Feminine. Lace abounded. Jewel-colored pillows were on the bed, piled high. A chair in the corner with more pillows. A table laden with books. Bottles and jars on top of the dresser, with hair ties and all sorts of items I wasn't familiar with and didn't want to figure out. Luckily, there was only one night table, and I found the bandage, neatly rolled and ready.

Everything was tidy in her space. Overwhelming, but neat.

Again, just like her.

I noticed a set of glass doors on one wall, and, curious, I opened them, stepping into a small, enclosed sunroom located at the back of the property. An easel was set up in the corner, various canvases piled against the walls. I studied one in particular. It was pretty, feminine. I recognized the subject matter from a few of the paintings I had seen on the walls. I picked up one of the canvases, seeing her initials in the corner. MM. Myers had hidden talents. I studied the brushstrokes, impressed at the way she captured the light. The subtle shading and delicate use of shadows. She was gifted.

I returned to her, lifting her foot onto my lap, tugging off the sneaker and sock, then checking it out. "It's not broken," I muttered. "I'm not even sure it's sprained as much as a nasty twist. Stay off it and ice it the rest of the weekend," I advised as I wrapped it. I tried not to notice how delicate the bones felt under my fingers. How soft her skin was. Pale, the veins in her foot standing out against the creaminess of her flesh. I failed, and my hands tightened on her leg.

I finished and dared to look up. She was watching me, her dark eyes wide. So many emotions were swimming in her deep gaze. This close, I could see the starbursts of green and gold around her pupils. It was lovely. Mesmerizing.

I shook my head. Jesus, it was *Myers*.

I stood, breaking our gaze. "You have ice?"

"Yes."

Her freezer held a large assortment of meat, which

surprised me. Turkey breasts, roasts, and ham. She must cook a lot of big meals.

I grabbed the ice bag and returned to her, making sure her foot was propped up. I handed her the water I had gotten from the fridge and shook a couple of pain pills from the bottle I had found on the bathroom counter.

"You paint."

"Nosy, much?" she asked, her voice all at once teasing and nervous.

"I was curious." I adjusted the ice bag on her foot. "You're talented, Myers. Why are you working as an assistant?"

"Starving artists need to pay rent. Painting is my dream. Working as an assistant so I can eat and help pay for my father's care is my reality. I just dabble."

I recalled her résumé. "You studied art."

"Lots of people study art, but few get to make a living off it."

I had a feeling there was a story there, but it wasn't my place to ask. I was surprised I was even curious to know. I usually didn't bother with people or their stories. I rose to my feet.

"Stay off the foot as much as you can."

"I will." She swallowed. "Thank you, Bane. I mean, Mr. Bane."

"Bane is fine," I heard myself saying. "A lot of people call me that."

"Okay."

"Do you need anything?"

"Isn't that my line?"

For some reason, I reached out and trailed a finger down her soft cheek. "Not today, Magnolia Myers."

She smiled. "Okay. Not today. But no, I am good."

"All right. If you do—well, you have my number."

She nodded. "All right."

I headed to the door, pausing when she called my name.

"Bane."

I turned to see her smiling. "Good job," she said.

I chuckled and shrugged. "It was fine."

Then I left.

I arrived early Monday, anxious to get to work. I had a busy schedule ahead of me, plus the awards dinner coming up soon. I was surprised to find the outer door already open, and I strode in, stopping in shock.

Myers had been busy. Furniture was moved, pictures hung up. Pictures of my work. I had to admit, they looked good. In fact, the entire outer office looked good. Neat and orderly, the same as her little apartment. Inviting as well. She had done an excellent job.

She appeared behind me, carrying a cup of coffee that she handed me.

"How did you know?" I asked, taking the cup and trying to ignore the sensation that hit me as our fingers brushed.

"I sensed a disturbance in the force."

Biting back my chuckle, I shook my head, taking a sip of coffee. "You've been busy. I don't recall you asking permission to change the office or hang those pictures."

"Wait until you see the improvements in yours."

I glared at her, heading to my office, breathing a sigh of relief when I saw nothing different. I turned to scowl at her, seeing the smile of delight on her face.

"I see your fall hasn't changed your odd sense of humor."

"Nope. Stopped a lecture, though."

I sighed and hung up my coat, setting my coffee on the warmer. Myers came in, carrying her notebook. I noticed her walk was still a little off, and before I could stop myself, I asked, "How's the foot?"

"Much better. Flats today, though," she replied, lifting her foot. I tried not to stare as the fluffy skirt she wore fell back, exposing her calf. She smoothed down the layers with a smile. "I went girly today."

A chuckle escaped my throat. "Myers, you're girly every day."

With her skirt, she wore another pretty blouse. Deep blue, with short sleeves edged in lace. The skirt was patterned with flowers in white and black. She looked... I sighed inwardly as I admitted it to myself. *Adorable.* She looked adorable—and alluring. Girly, pretty, yet fine for the office. I was supposed to hate adorable, yet I was finding it hard to do so when it came to Myers.

She laughed. "I suppose I am." Then she got busy, discussing my calendar, upcoming meetings. I handed her a stack of papers I needed her to finish, file, and send to clients. "I need as few interruptions the next while as possible."

She scanned her tablet. "You have two meetings I could shift to next week. That only leaves two, and one is admin, the other the staff meeting."

"I'll sit out the staff one. Lawson and Anderson can handle it. I rarely say much."

"Why is that?"

I was startled by her question. "They are much better

handling, ah, people. I prefer to let them lead. I'm here to work, not be an active admin. I'm part of the decision-making behind the scenes, but I step back otherwise."

"Hmm."

I sat back, picking up my coffee. "What does hmm mean?"

"I think you'd be a good leader. You're confident, smart, and fast-thinking."

I tilted my head, studying her. Her hair was up today, a few wisps around her face, showing off her full cheeks. I could see the freckle band easily, and I was glad she didn't try to cover them up.

"I don't like most people, Myers. I can't stand bullshit and playing games. Trust me, after a couple of HR issues, I was happy to let my partners be the front men."

Her lips twitched. "I see."

I scowled at her. "Back to business." I pushed my coffee cup toward her. "Another cup."

"Boring or foamy?" she teased.

I lifted a brow, and she left. That always seemed to shut her up.

At least in the office. It hadn't on Saturday.

I had to admit, I was glad to see she was okay, aside from the slight limp. It had surprised me how much she was on my mind after I left her. I worried she wouldn't be able to make herself something to eat. If her ankle was swelling more. If she needed anything. The urge to pick up the phone to check had been strong, but I resisted. I even thought of excuses to call her—to ask where a file was on the server, or if she remembered to order the 3-D printer supplies I would need this week—but I resisted. They were flimsy even to me, and I knew Myers was clever enough to see through them. I couldn't let her think I cared.

She returned, carrying a coffee and setting it down.

"Foamy?" I asked with a frown.

"Oops."

I rolled my eyes. "Leave it. I don't want you to walk on your sore ankle unless needed."

"How kind of you," she murmured.

"Get back to work."

She paused at the door. "Open or shut?"

"Leave it open. But make sure I'm not disturbed."

"No problem."

I opened my laptop, skimming my emails. I glanced over the screen, then moved it to one side, sliding my chair the opposite way. With the subtle move and the way Myers had shifted her desk, I now had a good view of her while she worked. Her face was a study of contrasts. Expressive. She pursed her lips, frowned, grinned, bit her lip. Tugged on her ear. Pulled on a stray curl. Tapped her pen on the desk while thinking.

And she talked to herself. Not loud enough that I could hear what she was saying, but her lips moved, and at times, she would nod as if agreeing with herself.

She was quite fascinating to watch.

Then I shook my head, reminding myself that wasn't what I was supposed to be doing.

She was Myers—my assistant. She was there to help me work, not entertain me.

Yet once again, my gaze drifted her way, and I wondered if I would need to shut my door again.

Except, I didn't want to.

This was unexpected.

And that made me angry.

I gave up before lunch and shut the door. I was being an idiot, and I needed to get over this strange fascination with my assistant. She brought me lunch, knocking before coming in. The sandwich was fresh and tasty, and I had to admit, I liked the new deli she had found.

"What are you working on?" I asked.

"Your expenses. Did you know they haven't been done for months?"

"I hadn't noticed," I admitted.

"I need access to your credit card information so I can print off the statements."

"I'll send it to you."

She left, shutting the door behind her. I glared at the wood as if it had done me a grievous disservice.

I stood and opened the door quickly, startling Myers, who was sitting at her desk, eating a sandwich.

"Yes, Bane?"

I startled, then recalled I had told her she could call me that.

Idiot.

"Did you get the email?"

"I haven't checked. I was eating."

"Fine. Let me know when you do. And I want more coffee when you're done."

She stared at me, lifting her eyebrows in question. Then she mouthed a word at me.

I tightened my hand on the doorframe.

"Please," I said through clenched teeth.

"Of course, sir. Anything you need."

I glared at her then swung around and headed back to my desk.

I left the door open.

CHAPTER SEVEN

Magnolia

Later Monday afternoon, I was busy trying to sort Bane's expenses when a deliveryman walked in. He handed me a small vase filled with pretty flowers. I was confused, but they were addressed to me. I opened the card, frowning when I read the simple signature.

Ty

Who the hell was Ty, and why was he sending me flowers?

Bane walked in from a meeting as I was hanging up the phone. He frowned at the addition to my desk. "What the hell are those?" he snapped.

"Flowers."

"Whatever. Take them home. I don't like decorations."

"Again, they are *flowers*. But don't worry. I'll be sending them back since I got them in error. There was obviously a mistake in the flower world, and they were delivered incorrectly."

"Why would you say that?"

I thrust the card his way. "Ty. I don't know a Ty, so the flowers aren't for me."

"Did you call the florist?"

"Yes. They said those were the instructions they got, and they were intended for me." I shook my head. "I don't understand."

"Secret admirer, then. Great," he huffed. "Keep your personal life personal. All right, Myers?"

Then he slammed his door.

I stroked the petals on a flower, smiling. I had never received flowers before, so even if it was a mix-up, I had to admit I loved them. They added a bright touch to my desk. I only hoped whoever Ty was, he wasn't in trouble with his girl when she didn't get the flowers.

I glanced at Bane's door with a scowl. I was keeping them on my desk, and I would take them home on Friday. He could pound sand for all I cared.

Then I got back to work.

The next two weeks were crazy. Bane was hot and cold. Blunt and irritated, then suddenly pleasant. His door was open, then closed. He barked orders, then asked me something in a polite tone. He worked constantly and I stayed late to help him, came in early, and, at times, worked from home. I didn't complain, and he never commented, other than the occasional grunt I took as a thank-you.

Another set of flowers arrived the following Monday afternoon, which earned me a scowl from Bane, although he didn't demand I remove them. The florist insisted they had the right address but refused to give me any other information.

I racked my brain, checked the company directory for a Ty or Tyler, but the only one listed was married, never so much as said hello to me, and worked on another floor. I highly doubted he was sending me flowers. I didn't know a man with that name, so it was a complete mystery. But I was too busy to worry about it.

I didn't know which way was up or down, trying to keep up with Bane. I wondered if he was nervous about the awards dinner coming up, then decided not to ask him. I liked my head where it was—on my shoulders.

I tried my best to stay ahead of him. I made sure he had his lunch every day. That the files he needed for his meetings were at his fingertips. I kept people away from him so he could work. His coffee cup was always full. I added a container of ice water. He looked at me, one eyebrow arched in question when I set it on his desk.

"To keep hydrated," I explained. "You need more than coffee."

He grunted. I took that as a thank-you.

I worked until he left, which was usually past six at night— some nights later. I had been introduced to his driver, and I had his number so I could call him whenever Bane needed him.

When he had explained it to me, I had blown out a breath. "Wow."

"What?"

"I didn't know you had a driver."

"I do. His name is Darryl."

"Landscape architecture must pay well," I quipped.

He frowned. "Old money, Myers."

"Oh." That explained a lot. His suits, his address, his lack of worry about his expense account.

I received one of his rare smiles. "And I do well at my job."

Then he became the Bane I knew the best.

Abrupt and curt.

"Get me a coffee."

"Of course, sir."

During the various errands he sent me on, I got to know the people in the building. Pete, the old security guy. Jenny, one of the cleaning ladies who worked on the floor every day. Mac, the man who kept the front lobby spotless. The other partners' assistants were friendly, although I didn't really know them that well yet. They invited me to lunch, but I had been so busy I hadn't made it yet. I liked them all—hardworking, nice people. I looked forward to getting to know them all even more. As long as I survived my boss.

"Myers!" the bane of my existence called to get my attention.

Again.

Good God, the man liked to bellow.

I rolled my shoulders and went to his door, entering without knocking. There was no point, although he scowled every time I did it. He was shouting for me, so he must know I was about to walk in. Why should I knock?

"You need something?"

"These papers need to go to HR. Now."

I swallowed down my retort. Telling him I was just about to drink my coffee and eat my sandwich would do me no good. I rarely got the chance to enjoy my coffee. Or eat a sandwich in its entirety. In fact, half the time, I didn't recall drinking my coffee. But it disappeared, so I assumed I had. "Of course."

He looked past me with a glare. "I see flowers arrived again. I thought we discussed this."

I sighed. "I have no idea who is sending them, so I can't

tell them to stop."

He waved me off. "Whatever. Take the papers down."

I took a sip and then headed downstairs to the HR office. I gave the papers to Jessica, who asked me how things were going.

"Great," I said with a false smile. "Busy."

She nodded. "Alexander is always busy."

"So I've discovered."

"You're able to keep up?"

"Perfectly," I lied. I came in early, worked late, and did a lot of stuff at home. The man never stopped, it seemed. "I have to get back." I waved and took the stairs up, walking into the office.

I sat down, reaching for my coffee, and frowned. It was empty. I had only had a few sips, hadn't I? I rubbed my forehead. This kept happening to me. I opened my sandwich, taking a bite, then picked up my coffee cup and hurried to the kitchen to make another cup. Luckily, no one was in the break room, so I didn't have to deal with those catty women today. I walked back into the office, surprised to see Mr. Bane standing by my desk. He looked guilty when he saw me, stepping back.

"You got the papers there?"

"Yes."

"Took you a while."

"I was already back. I needed coffee."

"Ah. Well, finish your lunch and get mine."

He headed back into his office, partially shutting the door again. I sat down, picking up my sandwich, now completely confused. I thought I had just taken one bite, but only a bite or two remained of the first half of the sandwich. I rubbed my head, wondering if I was losing my mind. How was my coffee disappearing and my sandwich being eaten? Was I that tired and forgetful?

I lifted my sandwich, stopping as I looked at it. The bite mark was much larger than the nibbles I took. I glanced at the door, recalling the guilty look on Mr. Bane's face.

Had he taken a bite of my sandwich?

Why?

I thought of my disappearing coffees, and once again, I looked at his door. He claimed not to like them, yet they kept vanishing.

He wouldn't.

Would he?

Only one way to find out.

"I'll be back in fifteen," Mr. Bane barked as he walked past my desk.

"Okay."

I waited for ten, then headed to the break room and made my coffee. Back in the office, I set it on the desk and slipped behind his door, peeking through the crack. If I was wrong, I was going to have to explain myself, but it was worth the risk. He strode in, pausing by my desk. I felt my eyes widen as he stopped, lifted my cup, and took a sip. Then another.

I sprang from behind the door, pointing dramatically and yelling. *"Gotcha, coffee thief!"*

In retrospect, I should have thought my actions through.

He spun around, and mid-swallow, he choked. Sputtered. Sprayed me with hot, foamy coffee. I gasped as it hit my chest, dripping down my skin and soaking the material. For a moment, neither of us moved, and then he sprang forward, discarding the cup on the desk.

"Are you burned?"

"No."

He grabbed his pocket scarf, frantically trying to mop up the coffee.

That was soaked into my blouse.

On my chest.

He pressed and stroked, mumbling and cursing. Feeling me up without even realizing. I laid my hands over his, stilling his movements.

"Bane," I murmured. "You have to stop."

"Alexander, you missed a signature—"

Jessica from HR walked in, freezing in shock, the words drying on her lips. I knew what she saw. Bane, looming over me, his hands on my boobs, and me holding them there.

He knew it too.

"Jesus Christ," he swore. "No. No. No."

Jessica shook her head. "I'll come back."

"Coffee!" I squealed. "He was stealing my coffee, and it got on my boobs. He wasn't feeling me up—really."

She looked more confused. "Stealing your coffee?"

I laughed shrilly. "It was a joke."

Bane nodded. "A joke. Yes. A joke."

She grimaced. "Alexander, I think we need to talk. My office. Five minutes."

And she walked out.

His gaze, wild and furious, met mine. "Again," he snarled. "Again, you've caused me trouble that I have to try to explain."

"While you're thinking, maybe you could take your hands off my boobs?"

He tore them away as if they were on fire. But not before we both noticed how hard my nipples were. Or that his fingers had been caressing them the whole time.

"Why were you eating my sandwich?" I demanded.

"I was starving! You never finish it anyway."

"And my coffee?"

"I needed a drink."

"Why don't you just admit you like my foamy coffees, as you call them, and I'll make you your own?"

He glared at me and ran a hand through his hair. Which was still damp from the coffee. He growled in agitation, then turned and went into his office, no doubt to wash his hands before heading to HR.

The way the door slammed, I knew I'd have to knock next time.

By Thursday, I was tired and looking forward to the week being over. Bane had barely spoken to me since the coffee incident. I made a point of making him a foamy coffee at least once a day simply to prove a point. When he returned from seeing Jessica, he told me to forward him any dry-cleaning bills for "splashing" me. I sweetly told him I could get the stains out myself. He had grunted, whether in displeasure or acknowledgment, I wasn't sure. His door-slamming overrode the sound of his grunt. What he and HR discussed, he never revealed.

I walked into the empty lounge and headed into the kitchen. Bane had the only office on this floor. He liked his privacy and being secluded, and apparently, what Bane wanted, Bane got.

The rest of the floor held a private boardroom, this kitchen, and the staff lounge. The other two partners had their offices on the floor below, along with accounting and the main boardroom. The rest of the staff was two floors down. Balanced Designs owned the rest of the building, which was sublet to various businesses.

I rinsed the mugs, muttering as I splashed some diluted coffee on my favorite blouse. I walked down to the bathroom, rinsing my hands and the spot on my cuff, then blotted it dry with a paper towel. I heard people in the lounge, but I wasn't in the mood to be chipper and friendly today, so I decided to make the coffee for Bane and leave.

I measured out the coffee and began to pour the milk when I heard it. Some other women were now in the staff room. They were in the lounge area, so they couldn't see me.

"Did you see the outfit she was wearing today? I swear she buys her clothes from my grandmother's attic. Does she really think she looks good?"

I stiffened, recognizing Verity's voice. I disliked her and her fake pleasantness. I had heard her rip other assistants apart, then smile when she saw them, pretending to be nice— exactly as I thought she would do. I avoided her and her little clique as much as possible.

"Seriously, she has no style. She struts around here like she owns the place just because she's Bane's assistant of the month," she complained. "How she got that job is a mystery."

"Probably on her knees," her sidekick Rhonda said snidely. The other woman with them snickered.

I shut my eyes, shaking my head and continuing to make Bane's coffee. I tried to ignore the fact that my hand was shaking a little.

"She's on borrowed time. He never keeps anyone. I heard he's already complaining about her," one of them said with a snicker.

My head snapped up.

He was? I gripped the counter. Was this about the coffee thing? Was he that upset with me?

"Between her flippant attitude, her embarrassing wardrobe, and her looks, she won't be around long," Verity assured her. "Does she think covering herself in layers and lace hides how fat she is? Can you imagine what sort of getup she'll wear to the awards banquet tomorrow? She'll embarrass the entire company. He'll fire her on Monday. If she lasts that long."

I blinked at the sudden moisture in my eyes, then reminded myself to ignore them.

"I can't stand her. She's a joke," Rhonda said. "Acting like she's a big shot. Friends with all the little people—like that makes her better. Who cares about Pete or the cleaning woman?"

"She's friends with them because she's one of them. The nothings," Verity spat. "I applied for that job. I should have gotten it. I have experience in the company, and I could be so useful to him."

"Behind the desk or under it?" Rhonda asked.

"Both. I'd suck him so good, he'd forget everything and everyone else."

There was another round of laughter. I couldn't listen to them anymore. I headed out the back hallway door, coffee forgotten. I was horrified at what they were saying. Not only about me, but Mr. Bane. The disrespect. The horrible image of Verity doing that to him. Being close to him at all.

And she had hit the proverbial nail on the head when it came to me. Poking at my clothes, my weight, my attitude, and my work ethic. The fact that I was embarrassing.

I slipped into the bathroom, closing the stall door behind me. I leaned on the cold metal, taking in some deep breaths.

They were jealous. Spiteful. Nothing they said mattered.

I kept repeating those words to myself.

I heard the door open and a quiet voice say my name. "Magnolia? Are you okay?"

I recognized Rylee's voice. Unlike the other women, she was sweet and kind. Friendly. We hadn't gotten the chance to hang out together yet, but I liked her.

"I'm fine."

"I heard those cows," she said. "I told them off."

I opened the door. "You did what?"

She was short like me. Curvy, too. Sweet and soft-spoken. Usually quiet. Everyone liked her. Her stature and disposition hid an incredible talent for all things computer. I had heard she was the smartest of them all and could write code no one else could. I knew the partners, including Bane, thought the world of her.

But imagining her going against Verity made my head spin.

"Why would you do that?"

Her normally warm green eyes flashed. Right now, they looked like hard pieces of jade. "They're horrible, and they were all lying to make themselves feel better. Jealous bitches."

"They aren't wrong. I'm not like the other assistants."

"That's why I like you. You're real and nice. You're polite and friendly. Honest." She smiled, dimples appearing on her cheeks. "And I like the way you dress. You always look so pretty."

"Thank you."

She stepped forward, laying a hand on my arm. "Ignore them. Don't let them get into your head. Be you."

I smiled, patting her hand. "Thanks, Rylee. Are you going to the awards banquet tomorrow?"

She nodded with a frown. "I was told I had to."

"We could sit together."

"Oh, I'd love that!"

"Okay. It's a date."

She chuckled. "Awesome."

She left, and I stared in the mirror, wiping my eyes and blowing my nose. I straightened my shoulders and headed back to my desk.

I sat down, frowning at my computer. A moment later, Bane yelled my name, and I went to his door, which was ajar.

"Yes, sir?"

He looked displeased. "Did you get lost?"

"Lost?" I repeated.

"On the way to get my coffee." He made a show of glancing at his wrist. "It's been twenty minutes."

"Oh. Um... We're out of milk."

"Then give me a black coffee." He frowned. "What's the matter?"

"Nothing. I, ah, my tummy was a little upset. I forgot. I'll go get it now."

I turned and hurried off, praying the witches had gone back to their caves and I wouldn't have to deal with their snide remarks and looks.

Bane

She returned with my coffee, one of her foamy ones, setting it down with a fast smile.

"Someone got the milk." She paused. "Anything else?"

I studied her, noting how pale she looked. Her eyes looked odd. Almost as if she'd been crying. For some reason, the thought of her being upset bothered me. Recalling what she'd said earlier, I cleared my throat.

"Are you feeling all right, Myers? Do you need to go home?"

She shook her head, her gaze bouncing everywhere. "No, I'm fine. I'll get back to work."

She hesitated at the door. "Um, sir?"

"Yes?"

"Is everything, ah, satisfactory?"

I frowned. "Everything is fine. I would tell you if it were otherwise."

"All right. I was just checking. I can take direction if required."

I was confused. "I am aware of that, and I have no complaints with your work." Wanting to bring a smile to her face, I winked. "Today anyway. I'll let you know when I do."

But she didn't reply with one of her quips. My teasing barely got a smile. She nodded and returned to her desk.

After a few moments, I rose from my chair, opening the door she had pulled partially closed. She was on the phone, glancing up as I walked past her. I dug around in the file cabinet, picking a folder at random, and headed back to my office, leaving the door open. I sat down, opening the file, pretending to study it, while I covertly watched her.

Something was wrong. She was polite and professional on the call, as she always was, but her friendliness was off. Her voice wasn't right. The pitch was wrong. Something had upset her, but I wasn't sure what that was. I knew I was right when she hung up and didn't blaze into my office, informing me not to touch the files or that I was doing her job. She simply began working on the budgets I had given her to go over.

I shook my head at my wayward thoughts. It wasn't my place to wonder what was upsetting my assistant. She was an employee. Everyone had bad days.

I turned back to the design I was working on, pushing away all thoughts of anything else, ignoring the voice that whispered she'd been fine before she'd left to get coffee. Whatever had caused her distress happened in twenty minutes.

It took all my concentration to shut out those thoughts.

At six, Myers came into my office. "Do you need anything else before I leave?"

I looked up, narrowing my gaze at her. She looked like herself, except the polite smile. "No."

"I'll see you in the morning."

The question was out of my mouth before I could stop it. "Myers, are you all right?"

"I'm fine."

Her response was too fast, too short, and too wrong.

"Anything on your mind?" I asked.

"Um, well..."

"Yes?" I prompted.

"I was wondering if I was really required to go to the awards dinner tomorrow."

Her question was innocent enough. It was the way her fingers tangled in the lace of her sleeves, pulling on the delicate trim, that caught my eye.

"Required, no," I mused. "But I thought you were looking forward to it."

"Oh, um, I thought perhaps someone more important, better, I mean, um, more essential to the firm should go."

I sat back, tilting my head. "If you don't want to go, I won't force you, Myers. But as a member of my office, an important one, I would like you there. It's a chance for you to see some of the other people in the industry, other key people here, in a different light. We're up for several awards—you don't want to cheer your favorite boss on?"

"Oh no, of course. I was just, ah, checking."

At this point, I wasn't sure I would ever see that blouse again. Soon, there would be nothing left of the sleeves the way she was tearing at the lace.

"I assure you, I would like you to attend. It would be nice to see a friendly face when they call the name of the award winner and it's not mine," I said jokingly.

"You will win!" she said breathlessly, letting her sleeves go. "Your designs are incredible."

"Then be sure to be there to see it for yourself."

"Yes. Of course." She huffed a breath. "Goodnight, Bane."

She turned and walked out, leaving me puzzled.

Bane. She'd called me that a few times, but I was Mr. Bane earlier. And she always addressed me as such in front of colleagues or other staff members. She was exceedingly professional all the time. She was, in fact, a great assistant.

But why, suddenly, did she not want to attend the awards dinner?

I was going to have to figure out this mystery.

♡♡♡

The next day, Myers was quiet but seemed all right. She worked hard all morning on the budgets I gave her. I attended meetings, listened to clients, and was grateful when the final phone call was over.

She entered my office, sliding the budgets on my desk.

"Done?" I asked, not looking up.

"Yes."

"I assume you're leaving to get ready for the dinner?" All staff had been told the office was closing at four.

"If that is all right."

I leaned back in my chair. "Since I was part of the decision to allow it, it is."

"Good, then. I'll head out."

"I'm working tomorrow," I informed her. "I have a lot of changes to the Duncan design."

"Oh. Okay."

She headed for the door, and I called to her. "Myers."

She turned.

"Try to enjoy the evening. The speeches tend to be a little long, but the food is good, and they offer a surprisingly good red at the bar."

She smiled. "Noted."

And she was gone.

I worked until six, then took a fast shower and changed into my tux. I straightened the bow tie, slipping on my cuff links and tugging my sleeves into place. The dinner was happening at a hotel only a few blocks from the office, and I strolled over, arriving in plenty of time. I picked up a drink from the bar, shook some hands, and spoke with some other colleagues. As I stood with a group of men, one of them whistled under his breath. "Now there's a stunner."

I followed his gaze to the bar. A woman had her back to us, but her vivid green dress framed her shoulders and the creamy skin of her upper back. The dress flared out from her waist, showing off shapely legs and a set of dainty ankles, encased in low heels that matched her dress. A tattoo of a flower was on the top of her right shoulder blade, and I squinted to figure out what kind it was.

Then she turned, and I almost dropped my glass.

Magnolia Myers was a vision. Her hair was swept into a stylish knot, tendrils dancing around her face and neck. The cocktail dress crisscrossed her breasts, hanging off her shoulders, showing the rest of the tattoo that was etched into her skin along the front and back side of her shoulder blade. I recognized the flower now, the magnolias stunning on her skin.

She was curves and softness, encased in emerald green. She was exquisite.

Our eyes met and locked. I couldn't force my gaze from hers as she lifted a glass to her lips and sipped. She was a throwback to another era, her choice of dress as eclectic and stylish as the clothes she wore into the office. She was elegant, beautiful, and classy—and she took my breath away.

"Jesus, I'd do her."

"She's taken," I snarled, surprised by my own words, tearing my gaze from her.

"You know her?"

"Yes. She's engaged." Why I was telling him that lie, I didn't know.

"Oh. Shame. Still, I'd have a go."

"Grow up," I snapped and walked away, not caring about the shocked expressions.

I headed across the room, faltering as another staff member, Rylee, joined Magnolia. The two of them hugged, and Myers tugged a shawl over her shoulders before they walked away together. I asked for another scotch, then leaned against the bar, observing the room, my gaze finding Myers time and time again.

She was easily the most captivating woman in the room. She sat down with Rylee, draping the shawl over the back of her chair. I strolled toward my table, choosing a seat that gave me a clear view of her. Despite her smile, she was tense. I could see it in the set of her shoulders, the way the smile didn't reach her eyes. Rylee said something to her, and she shook her head with a rueful smile and a shrug. I wondered what they were discussing, my thoughts interrupted as my tablemates joined me. I talked with my partners and their wives, grateful the extra seat at our table was being used by Lawson's mother and not some stranger or one of the staff. Looking over, I watched as other assistants and employees filled our remaining two tables. I stood and got another drink, standing in a shadowed alcove at the back of the room, shamelessly eavesdropping. I found it interesting how people acted outside the office when they thought no one was listening. Often, their true nature showed. Two women stopped close to me, gossiping, bad-mouthing outfits and people. They didn't notice me, and they became especially nasty, focusing on some woman, disparaging her outfit, calling her names, all while wearing false smiles on their faces. I was admittedly shocked at their venom.

"I hope she's fired after tonight. What a whore," one of them muttered.

My eyebrows shot up at that remark. I scanned the room, unable to see who they were discussing.

"I bet the color of her hair isn't even real," the other responded.

"Oh, the fake red is definitely from a box. And that outfit. Does she buy all her clothes from a thrift store?"

"I'm sure he is so embarrassed he'll get rid of her."

"She acts so high and mighty. I hope the fall back to earth hurts."

"Does she really think she can get away with wearing that dress? She is way too heavy for it. She looks like a sausage. She thinks the green suits her with that dyed hair? Please."

An announcement was made for dinner to start, so I slipped away, sliding onto my chair.

Their remarks bothered me. Not only were they tearing apart someone they obviously worked with, I had a feeling their cattiness went far beyond the outfit. I watched as they joined Rylee and Myers, sitting in the two empty chairs by Rylee. I recognized them from the office but couldn't recall their names. That was confirmed when I asked Lawson, who identified them as being in the assistant pool. "Verity has subbed in for my PA on occasion," he said. "She's fine pinch-hitting, but I'm always grateful when Giselle returns."

His wife crossed her legs. "Not my favorite person," she

murmured, catching my eye. "I'm quite certain a job isn't all she wants at the company." She lifted one brow in hidden meaning. She leaned forward. "Catty," she said quietly. "She'd be nasty when cornered, I think."

I frowned as I raised my glass to my lips, observing the table where Myers sat. She had gone quiet again, her smile absent. I thought of the remarks I'd heard, and I studied all the women at the three tables. Only one who would pass for having red hair. One who dressed differently. One pretty woman who was wearing green.

And suddenly, I was furious.

The light and sunshine Myers liked to spread dwindled, faded, and was finally burned out before dessert. Every time she spoke, one of the women I had overheard earlier talked over her. Their laughter was louder than anyone else's when one of them would make a comment. At times, they were the only two laughing. Myers picked at her dinner, barely sipped her wine, and she looked uncomfortable. She had slipped on her shawl before dinner was served, and it seemed to me she grew smaller each passing moment, shrinking into the cover-up as if trying to disappear. I saw the way Rylee tried to act as a buffer. Yet time and again, one of the women would lean over and say something to Myers that slayed her. I was certain she was the "whore" they had been discussing. The urge to stand and take Myers's hand, leading her to my table, was so strong, I had to curl my hands into fists on my legs to stop myself.

I headed to the bar to get another drink, needing to distance myself. Rylee Jenkins appeared beside me, requesting a fresh glass of wine. I forced myself to smile at her and be calm. "Enjoying yourself?" I asked.

"It's fine," she replied.

"Is Magnolia all right?"

She met my gaze, hers frank. "Do you care?"

"Yes."

"She isn't having a good time, no."

I glanced over my shoulder, seeing Myers had her back turned to the two women and was in conversation with someone else at the table.

"Are they on her a lot?" I asked quietly.

She picked up the wine and met my eyes again. "They're horrible. Total bitches. Usually, it's behind her back, but I guess tonight they're enjoying themselves." She sighed. "Everything is said with a smile or a laugh, but the meaning is clear."

"Why hasn't she come to me?"

She blinked. "You'd have to ask her." She took a sip. "Would you do something?"

That was the million-dollar question. I never got involved in office politics. Relationships.

Ever. Everyone knew that.

"Yes," I repeated.

She nodded. "Good."

I sat, fuming, unsure what to do. I had pulled Rylee to the side in a quiet spot, and she'd confessed to what had happened the other day. The horrid things Myers had heard them say about her. Me as well, but I didn't care about that part. I recalled Myers's hidden distress. How she carried on, working, refusing to quit, to give in to the hurt I knew she felt.

She was incredibly brave and strong.

All through the awards, I stewed, jolting in surprise when my name was announced as the winner for a project I had worked on for over a year. My partners clapped me on the shoulder, and I went to the dais to accept my award. I kept my remarks brief, never enjoying the spotlight. But as I stood there, my gaze flitted to Magnolia again. She was smiling at me, for the first time this evening looking like herself. She was so pleased for me that it made me smile. And I suddenly decided I had a few words to add.

"So, my gratitude to everyone involved, especially those at Balanced Designs. And one last thank-you, if you'll permit me. Although you weren't with me at the time, a special mention to my assistant, Magnolia Myers. You have done exactly what you promised to do at your interview. My office has never run so seamlessly. I would, indeed, be lost without you. Your work is above excellent." With a quick nod, I left the stage amid the polite applause. Walking to the table, I looked over. Myers was in shock, Rylee winked at me, and the two bitches were speechless. I'd go so far as to say furious.

Deciding my job was done, I shook a few hands, tossed back the last of my drink, and left.

But I wasn't done.

Not by a long shot.

CHAPTER EIGHT

Bane

I was busy the next morning when a throat clearing at my door made me look up. Myers stood in the doorway, coffee and a bag clutched in her hand.

"What are you doing here?" I asked.

She came in, sliding the coffee my way and opening the bag, presenting me with a muffin. It was huge, studded with blueberries, and the aroma of it was sweet and lemony.

"I thought you might need some help." She pushed the muffin closer to me. "And sustenance."

"I don't eat store-bought muffins as a rule."

"Good. This is homemade." Another small push my way. "And still warm."

I stared at it, then her. Her hair was in a ponytail, and she was dressed casually again in leggings and a T-shirt. Another too-big flannel shirt topped her outfit.

I pulled the muffin close and broke off a piece, chewing. It was dense, sweet, and delicious. I closed my eyes as I swallowed the treat.

"You made this?" I asked, opening my eyes.

"Yes."

I broke off another piece as she sat down, rolling up the sleeves of her flannel shirt.

"Tell me, Myers. Do you use these as bait in your lumberjack-hunting? Is some poor man wandering the park, dazed, looking for his shirt?" I asked lightly. The truth was, I hated seeing a man's shirt on her, and I had the burning desire to know who it belonged to. "Or is your boyfriend some hulking construction worker who lets you raid his closet?"

She laughed, the sound odd in my office. It was low and sweet, making me long to join in her amusement. Instead, I ate another piece of the delicious muffin.

"The shirts belonged to my dad. They're soft and comfortable. I like casual on the weekends."

That news relaxed my shoulders for some reason. "Ah," was all I said. "Your boyfriend doesn't mind then, I suppose."

She met my eyes. "No boyfriend."

"Ah," I repeated.

"Um, Alex, I mean Bane, I mean Mr. Bane..." She stumbled over her words.

I frowned. "Bane is fine, Myers. What are you so eloquently trying to express?"

She drew in a deep breath. "Thank you for what you said last night. It was very kind of you to include me in your speech even though I didn't work with you at the time you did that design."

"You work for me now."

"I know, and I like it here. I'm trying to do a good job for you."

"Your efforts are noticed."

For a moment, we stared at each other, a warmth growing around us. Her rich brown eyes grew larger, and her breathing picked up. Fascinated, I watched the pulse jump at the base of her throat. Saw the flush on her cheeks. She felt this as well.

I shook my head to dispel the thoughts that had crept in and cleared my throat.

"Your work is fine, Myers. As for helping today, perhaps you can work on some of the 3-D forms on the printer."

She blinked. "Okay. Do you always do that for a client?"

"No, usually the 3-D images on a computer are good enough, but this client is very picky and likes a mock-up that they can stand and look at. He and his wife will move things around and tweak at times. This is their third resort, and they pay big for the concept model and display it under glass once it's done. We have it fully finished for them once everything is set. They say it's always a great draw in the lobby."

"All right."

"Luckily, the buildings are done already. Now, I add the flourishes." I indicated the table at the other end of the room where the model was set up. It had been delivered after she'd left last night, and I planned on starting the time-consuming work of printing and placing the gardens, trees, and pathways.

"I can do that."

"Great."

♡♡♡

We worked for a while, the only sound the printer as it carved out the trees and plants. None of them were huge, but each piece took between ten and twenty minutes. The larger ones, I would print during meetings or after hours.

I kept watching her. She had removed her flannel, and her T-shirt was tight across her breasts as she leaned over the printer, watching or removing one of the pieces being printed and cured. I found her as fascinating to observe today as I had all week.

She brought me a sandwich, this one ham and cheese on sourdough, and I devoured it. I drank the foamy coffee, still not ready to admit I liked it better than the black I'd always preferred. I wouldn't want her to think she was getting the upper hand. After I finished the sandwich, I ate the rest of the muffin from the morning.

I studied her as I ate, not bothering to pretend to be working. I didn't have to. She was busy enough for us both. Last night, she had been stunning. Sexy. A siren. Today, she was plain, simple. And I felt an even stronger draw to her than before. Her clothing covered her more than her usual skirts and blouses, yet she was effortlessly sexy.

And I had a feeling she didn't even know it.

I returned to the document I was trying to work on, impatient when I couldn't access some information on the server. Frustrated, I barked out her name. "Myers!"

She came over, shaking her head. "No need to bellow. I'm right here."

"Why can't I access some of the HR documentation on the server?"

She frowned and came around the desk, indicating for me to move my chair. I pushed back, and she stepped in front of me, bending slightly. Her fingers moved quickly over the keyboard, while my gaze was glued to her ass. Right there. In front of me. Round, perky. Beckoning. My fingers twitched to touch it. Cup and stroke it. The sudden desire to touch her everywhere hit me. I wanted to know if her skin was as soft as it looked. How her hair felt fisted in my hand. If she smelled as sweet as I thought she would at the base of her neck. If her skin would blossom for me if I bit down and left a mark.

My mark.

My cock roared to life, and I almost groaned as yearning swamped me. I wanted her. I wanted to hear her whisper my name again. Not Mr. Bane, not Bane.

Alex.

I wanted to hear her moan. Whimper. I needed her fingers clutching me. Touching me. I longed for her lips on mine. Her tongue in my mouth. I wanted to see that tattoo again. Trace its shape with my tongue. I pushed away, standing just as she straightened. She stumbled back, and without a thought, I wrapped my arm around her, pulling her back to my chest. For a moment, neither of us moved. I felt her against me. Soft to my hard. Cool to my heat. Trembling to my heavy breathing. My cock was trapped between us, evidence of my state of mind.

It took everything in me not to turn her in my arms and kiss her. Sweep everything off my desk and lift her there, settling between her legs and giving in to the overwhelming passion I was feeling. But my gaze drifted to the file folder she had accessed for me. HR.

Jesus, I was her boss, and I was planning on breaking every rule and fucking my assistant on my desk. That was an HR issue ready to explode.

I stepped back, dropping my arms. "Watch your footing, Myers."

"Sorry," she whispered.

"You can go now. We've worked enough."

She hesitated.

"Go, Myers. *Now,*" I growled.

She nodded and edged her way past me. She hurried to my door, shutting it behind her. A moment later, I heard the outside door slam.

I dropped to my chair, cradling my head in my hands.

What had I almost done?

Did she know how she affected me?

How was I going to face her on Monday?

I rolled my shoulders. Nothing happened. Nothing would happen.

I would make sure of it.

Then I turned my attention back to the task at hand and forced her out of my mind.

Which would have been easier if I couldn't smell her everywhere. Taste her fragrance in the air. If the project I had decided to undertake wasn't mostly for her.

Fuck it, it was all for her.

Dammit.

Magnolia

Monday, I was unsure what to expect. His unexpected praise on Friday—in public, no less—had left me reeling. I had no idea what had come over him, unless he was drunk. But his gait was steady, his eyes clear, and his voice firm when he spoke. He left before I had the chance to ask him. At the table, Rylee looked pleased with herself, while Verity and Rhonda were almost gnashing their teeth. I was certain if they could have gotten away with it, I would have been stabbed with their butter knives. They had to settle for dirty looks and some whispered words, no doubt cursing me. Then they left, two dark shadows in an otherwise pleasant night.

"What was that?" I breathed out, sitting back in my chair. *"I think I need a drink."*

Rylee grinned. "That was your boss backing you up."

Then another staff member joined us, and I never got a chance to speak to her alone again.

Saturday, I knew Bane was working. I got up and baked some of my best muffins, made sandwiches, then headed to the office. He was surprised to see me, but he accepted the muffin and waved off my thanks. His words warmed me, though. We had worked well for a few hours, but something felt different. Easier. I caught him staring at me more than once. Felt his eyes on me often. His voice wasn't as clipped. His requests were polite. Nicer.

Until the moment he needed help on the server and I moved in front of him. The sensation of him behind me was overwhelming. In the tight space, his knees pressed against my thighs. I could smell his cologne. When he stood and I stumbled back into him, I felt everything.

His muscled chest. Strong arms that banded me tight to his body. His sinewy forearms that were taut and warm under my fingers. I felt his breath stir my hair, and I swore I felt his lips press to the crown of my head.

And trapped between us, I felt *him*. Hard. Rigid. Huge. For a moment, neither of us moved. All I wanted was to turn in his arms and kiss him. Feel his mouth on mine. Fan the desire coursing through my body.

Until he ordered me to leave, his voice strained with tension. It broke the spell I was under, and I rushed away, fleeing the office as if the hounds of hell were chasing me. I took the stairs, not waiting for the elevator. Panting, exhausted, and confused, I sat on the cold concrete steps of the main floor, catching my breath and wondering what had just happened.

He'd been on my mind the rest of the day, starred in my dreams that were vivid and hot. I woke up Sunday, wet and aching, his name on my lips. He was everywhere the rest of the day, overshadowing anything I attempted to do. I was grateful for a change when my dad slept through most of my visit. I was having trouble concentrating.

And now, standing outside the office building, I had to face him.

Would he be cold and indifferent again?

Address what had happened?

Pretend nothing had occurred?

I drew in a long inhale of oxygen.

There was only one way to find out.

He was already there, his head bent over his laptop, his door partially closed. I sat down, scanning emails, then went to get his coffee. I made a black one, unsure how he would react to one of my "foamy" concoctions. I had a feeling he liked them more than he admitted, only pretending to be upset when I brought him one.

But I wasn't testing anything today.

I walked into the office, grabbed my notebook, squared my shoulders, and knocked on his door.

"In," he snapped.

I pushed open the door, approached his desk, and set down his coffee, flicking on the mug warmer. He lifted his gaze to me, then dropped it quickly.

"Morning," I said brightly as I sat down.

He grunted in return, then spoke. "I have a meeting with HR this morning at nine. Push everything back for a couple of hours."

"I had already cleared your schedule, so you're good."

That got me another grunt.

"If you can keep working on the printing, I would

appreciate it. I got more done, so refer to the list."

"Of course. Anything else?"

He sat back, meeting my gaze. The ice was back in his eyes, and although he looked tired, his voice was clear and the blue was cold. "I apologize for Saturday. That was totally inappropriate."

I swallowed and decided to play dumb. "Asking me to work? I offered."

He narrowed his eyes. "For grabbing you."

I stood, shaking my head. "I stumbled, you caught me, which I'm grateful for. Nothing else."

He met my eyes, and I kept my gaze steady.

"If you say so."

I flashed him a bright smile. "What else could have happened? Now, if you will excuse me, I have the last of your expenses to go through, and then I'll get back to the printing."

He nodded. "Fine."

He was in and out all day, and Laura and Jessica from HR were in his office more than once. He had a meeting with his partners and was terse and impatient. He rushed through his lunch and drank way too much coffee. I had no idea what was going on with HR, but I had an uncomfortable feeling it was about me, and I wondered if it had anything to do with what didn't happen on Saturday.

The flowers that showed up that afternoon were lovely. Larger than the others I had received and fragrant. This time, there was no card. I traced the petals of the pink rose in the middle with my finger, wondering how long I would keep receiving the weekly flowers. I had to admit, I would miss the brightness and scent of them on my desk, but it was bound to happen. One day, the mysterious Ty would stop sending the lovely flowers. Until then, I would enjoy them.

Bane seemed irked as usual when he saw them, but all I heard was a grunt as he walked past, shutting his door.

Tuesday was much of the same behavior from Bane. Unless it was business, we hardly spoke, and whatever he was so deeply entrenched in was taking up all his free time, which was hard to come by as it was.

Wednesday afternoon, I heard a commotion in the hall, and I looked up, recognizing Bane's mother's haughty voice. I stood, rounding the corner of my desk. I met Bane's gaze, confirming that he, too, had heard his mother approaching. He looked annoyed, heading to his door.

"Get rid of her," he hissed. "I have enough shit to deal with today. And I don't need a lecture on what a disappointment I am."

I nodded, grabbing the doorknob to shut it.

"Under no circumstances let her in my office, Myers. Whatever you have to do, do it. If she gets past you this time, you're fired."

I swallowed. "I'll take care of it."

I stayed in front of Bane's door, glad when I heard the lock engage. Short of breaking in to the office, his mother couldn't gain access to him. Now, I had to figure out how to get her to leave without causing a scene. I grabbed a pile of files and my phone to use as a prop, pretending I just happened to be in front of the door.

She came through the outer door, her face set into a scowl. I wondered if she had another expression—I had certainly never seen it.

"Oh, hello, Mrs. Bane—I mean Mrs. Johnstone. I wasn't expecting you today."

"I don't need an appointment to see my son. Step aside."

"I can't do that."

She drew her already straight shoulders even straighter. "And why not?"

"He can't see you right now."

"I'll wait."

"No, that won't work either. He's tied up all afternoon."

"Ridiculous." She tried to get to the door handle, but I stepped in front of it, shaking my head.

"I can't let you go in there."

"Can't or won't?" She narrowed her eyes. "Tell him I am here."

"I can't do that either."

"And why not?"

My mind raced. Telling her he didn't want to see her was useless. She would park herself in front of my desk and wait. Admitting if I let her in I would be fired would do no good either. She wouldn't care.

"He isn't in his office."

"You're lying. I can see the light under the door. I heard his voice when I was in the hall."

I sighed, desperate, unsure what to do. Except I had to get rid of her. I needed this damn job.

"He is in there," I admitted. I heard a low growl, and I knew he had heard me. The bastard was on the other side of the door, waiting to see what was going to happen. "But he can't see you. He's, ah, dealing with a *personal* situation."

"What sort of personal situation?"

I was at a loss. Most people would take the hint and leave, but not this woman. Two ideas quickly developed. Both unacceptable. But I panicked and said the first one that came to mind.

"He sent me out for lunch today. I got him street tacos." I met her eyes, widening mine for drama. "Bad idea."

"I don't understand."

I leaned closer as if sharing a secret. "He has explosive diarrhea. He can't stop shitting himself."

She reared back, the horrified look on her face priceless. "I beg your pardon."

I shrugged. "It's horrendous. The last blowout was excessive. I've called maintenance, but we're still waiting for cleanup and to unclog the pipes. It's a good thing he keeps extra suits here, if you get my drift. But surely you understand he needs his privacy right now."

My phone buzzed, and I glanced at the text.

MYERS

I sighed, hearing his anger in the use of my name. Maybe because it was in bold. Capitals. But he wasn't happy. I shrugged in resignation, committed to getting rid of this woman who upset him so much. "I wouldn't wait. I suggest you try again some other time. When the air is clearer." I waved my hand. "The smell," I whispered. "Like something died."

She turned and walked away. Almost ran.

I sat at my desk and replied.

She's gone.

A moment later, he replied.

My office. NOW, MYERS.

I looked around in sorrow. Shame. I was starting to enjoy this job.

I knocked and waited. I heard the lock unclick, and I heaved a sigh. I brought my notebook with me, unsure why, except I felt better holding it. As if I was going into his office to get instructions, not meet my demise.

I walked in, turning to shut the door after glimpsing his face. Tornado Bane came to mind for this expression. Purveyor of Death was another.

Either way, it wasn't good.

I drew in a much-needed calming breath and crossed the office, not meeting his eyes. I sat down, opening up my notebook, prolonging the inevitable. For a moment, there was nothing but the sound of our breathing. Mine rapid, his deep, no doubt readying to torch me with his words.

I dared to look up. His gaze was enough to incinerate me. He began to tap his finger on his desk, another sign of agitation.

"I need you to assure me that I was having an out-of-body incident, perhaps a stroke, leading me to imagine you told my mother I was 'shitting my pants with explosive diarrhea.' I couldn't possibly have heard that." The tapping increased. "You *did not* use the words blowout and clogged pipes."

"Um," I said hesitantly. "Would you believe me if I said that, yes, you had a stroke? I'll call your physician."

"Myers."

I threw up my hands. "You said by any means possible! It was the best of the two ideas I had!"

"Telling my mother I shat my pants was the best idea?" he roared.

"She left, didn't she?"

That made him pause. He rubbed his eyes, muttering. I frowned. He was anxious, tapping the desk and shaking his head. All signs of high stress for him. Plus, the muttering. He might have a stroke yet. I wasn't sure if that was a bad thing right now or not.

He dropped his head to the back of the chair with a low groan, covering his eyes. "God give me strength. I meant for you to tell her I was in an afternoon meeting or on a client call that would take hours. Something business-related. Not—" he waved his fingers "—that."

"Oh. I did tell her you were busy, but that didn't work. She is difficult to deal with."

He dropped his hand and sat up. "I know."

"So, should I clean out my desk?"

He met my gaze, the electric-blue of his eyes mesmerizing. They didn't look as angry as they had when I first sat down.

"Maybe I'll tell Pete downstairs that the next time she shows up, to call ahead. You can hide," I offered.

"I'm a grown man. I do not hide."

"Um, the locked door and *'get rid of her'* from earlier begs to differ, Bane."

He scowled. "I'll leave my office so you can be honest and say I am not in."

I nodded. "You can hide in the supply closet or somewhere."

His finger was shaking as he pointed to the door. "Out."

"For good?" I asked, worried.

He sighed. "I'll let it go this once. You did get rid of her."

"Thank you, Bane. I mean Mr. Bane. I'll be more circumspect next time."

"See that you are."

I stood, and he looked at me with curiosity. "What was your other idea?"

"I was going to tell her you had an STI."

He gaped at me. "What the fuck?"

I nodded. "No mother wants to walk in on her son playing with his knob like some high schooler with his first Nintendo joystick. I've heard those STIs are itchy." I risked winking at him. "I planned on telling her that I informed you the two Brazilian strippers weren't a good idea at the bachelor party you'd planned on the weekend, but you refused to listen."

He stared, his mouth open, and I wondered if he had indeed had that stroke.

Then he swallowed. "Get out of my office."

I shrugged. "It was either shitting your pants or pulling on your Long John Silver to relieve the itch. I went with the classier one. Either one assured her leaving."

"My long—" He pointed to the door, his voice sounding odd. "Out. Now."

I walked out, beginning to shut the door when I heard it. It was the oddest noise. I turned and poked my head back in the door, making sure he wasn't choking on his tongue. I would have been less surprised at that than the sight that met my eyes.

Alexander Bane was leaning back in his chair, covering his mouth, and laughing.

He was actually laughing.

For a moment, I watched him, fascinated. He was incredibly sexy as he chortled, wiping his eyes and sitting up, only to start chuckling again. I shut the door quietly and returned to my desk.

A hundred points to me.

I made sure to behave on Thursday and Friday. I didn't want to push it. I purposely let all his mother's calls go to voice mail, though.

Bane didn't bring it up—not once. But I had a feeling I would hear about it again at some point.

Friday, an unplanned staff meeting was announced. After some trivial items were addressed, Mr. Lawson stood and discussed the awards, thanking everyone for their hard work and dedication to the company. He indicated Bane, clapping him on the shoulder. "And of course, the man of the hour."

There was a round of applause, and to my shock, Bane stood. "Thank you again. Now, I rarely speak at these meetings, but today, I have something to say. I have been in early talks with HR and my partners, and I want to bring everyone up to speed on a new protocol that will be implemented at Balanced Designs." He paused, looking down at the wooden surface of the boardroom table, his hands closing into fists on the top. His voice deepened as he looked up, his face and voice serious. "Nothing bothers me more than a bully. Than people using their position, their words, or their attitude to make another person feel less. Here at Balanced Designs, we discourage any conduct of that sort, but it seems there are those who engage in that exact behavior."

He cast his ice-cold gaze around the room. "It will not be accepted. A committee is being formed and new anti-bullying protocols will be set in place. Every staff member will attend a series of anti-bullying seminars that will be mandatory. You will not be employed here otherwise." He drew in a long, deep breath. "That we have to do this sickens me. That people refuse to grow up and leave high school behind is a frightening thought. But again, it will not be tolerated here. You bully someone with words, gossip, belittling, you will not work here. And no one is immune to this." He picked up his phone. "I will leave HR to finish up. Any and all questions can be put in writing and directed to them and the committee we have created. I will be the head of it."

And he walked out.

Bane

I stared out the window, leaning against the back of the sofa. The office was quiet since I couldn't be bothered printing anything right now. I sipped some whiskey, the glass a heavy weight in my hand. It was unusual for me to imbibe during the day, but the last week had been hell. From the moment I realized it was Myers those women were disparaging, I had been livid. I despised any sort of person that talked down to others. That made someone feel less. I was upset enough to know a group of women were doing that in my company, but when I knew their target was Myers, it was no-holds-barred. I spent hours going through our HR manuals. Talking with Lawson and Anderson. Laura and Jessica in HR. Our lawyer. When I informed them I wanted this new policy in place and offered to head it up, they were surprised, shocked, but supportive. They, too, disliked the idea of adults still acting like spoiled teenagers.

There was no place for it here.

I swallowed the last of my whiskey and set down the glass. I was restless, upset, and edgy. I needed to go home, hit the gym, then come back tomorrow and finish the model. They would be here next Thursday, and I wanted some time for tweaks. It amazed me once I saw a concept model the number of small changes I would make. Wearily, I rubbed my eyes. I needed something else, but I couldn't have it.

My door opened, and Myers came in, shutting the door behind her. I met her eyes in the reflection of the window, watching her approach me. She was lovely again today, her hair down, a pretty blouse setting off her coloring.

She stood in front of me.

"You should have come to me," I informed her.

"I can handle myself. I don't care what they say about me."

"I do."

"Why?" she asked quietly.

I knew what she was asking.

"Because no one should feel less." I let out a long sigh. "Especially you, Myers."

I held her gaze. "I know I'm not an easy boss. But you can come to me about anything. I'll listen. And I apologize if I have been unkind or mistreated you. I know I can be...hard to handle."

She smiled, her eyes crinkling. "I kind of like you hard to handle. You make me laugh."

I chuckled. "I had no idea."

She nodded. "I keep track when I do."

"Keep track?"

"In my notebook. When I make you laugh, when you make

me laugh." She leaned closer, lowering her voice and shooting me a wink. "I'm winning."

I shook my head. "You're an odd girl, Myers. But I rather like that."

For a moment, there was silence, our eyes locked on each other. I felt the heat grow between us, warm and pulsating. The urge to kiss her, hold her, grew.

"Why?" she asked again.

Bravely, irrationally, stupidly, I raised my hand, stroking it down her cheek. "Because it's you."

I didn't know who moved first, but suddenly, she was in my arms, our mouths fused together. I plunged my tongue inside her sweetness, tasting her. A tortured groan escaped my throat at the feeling of her in my arms. I bent, lifting her, setting her on the back of the sofa, standing between her legs. I wound one hand in her hair, deepening the kiss, devouring her. The other hand rested on her perfect ass, and I ground against her.

It didn't matter that I was her boss. That she irritated me daily. I didn't care that she was my assistant. The desk and the coffee incident didn't matter. Her hilarious way of getting rid of my mother was brilliant. She shocked and beguiled me at every turn. Every day was something new and different. Often outrageous. I had never felt so alive. She was the woman I thought of constantly. I was becoming obsessed with her. I couldn't deny it. I wanted her.

She whimpered as I dragged my lips across her cheek, kissing my way down her neck.

"Myers," I groaned as she dug her fingers into my shoulders.

The slam of a door in the hall brought our passion to a startling halt. I straightened, meeting her panicked eyes.

What the hell was I doing? Ravishing my assistant—in my office during business hours. Jesus, I was her boss. Her superior. I needed to get a grip.

Sadly, I drew a finger across her cheek, rubbing my finger on her wet lips.

I stepped back, tugging her off the sofa.

"That was inappropriate. I apologize."

She stared up at me, eyes large, lips swollen, and her hair in disarray. She had never been more lovely to me.

She reached up, touching my cheek. I captured her hand and kissed the palm.

"Inappropriate? No. Interrupted. Yes," she whispered.

Then she left.

I missed her before she even shut the door.

CHAPTER NINE

Magnolia

Bane was on my mind all night. Every time I shut my eyes, I remembered what it felt like to be in his arms. The weight of his body pressing into mine. The feel of his mouth working mine.

I had been kissed before. Many times. But not by Alexander Bane.

His mouth on mine was magic. He licked and bit at my lips, nipping the bottom one and soothing it with his glorious tongue. The lips that could spout such venom were soft and full against mine. He explored me, his tongue seeking every part of my mouth. He went deep and passionate. Light and sweet. Dipping, teasing, touching. Taking, sucking, demanding. His embrace was tight, and his hand wound around my hair felt divine. We were a flame, drawing heat from each other. I never wanted it to end.

Until we were exposed to a harsh reality. He was right to draw back. To put an end to what was happening. The office was still open, people coming and going.

It wasn't the time for us to be coming with each other.

But it would happen. I knew it as sure as I knew my own name.

Which I totally forgot when his mouth was on mine.

I was up early, unable to sleep. I baked more muffins and made sandwiches. I boarded the bus, absently digging through my purse for a mint. My fingers encountered a small bag, and I recalled the bridal shower I had been at the previous week. All the guests had been given one. The bus was fairly empty and no one was behind me or beside me, so I opened the bag, peeking in. It held some candy, a gift certificate to an adult shop, a tiny bottle of lube, and a lipstick. Curious, I took off the top, realizing too late it was a mini vibrator. I giggled as I put it back in the bag. I dug in the bottom, my eyes going wide when I saw the candies were actually rainbow-colored condoms. One was labeled "glow-in-the-dark." The others were pink, purple, and green, and I dropped them back into the bag with another laugh.

Maybe I would be able to use them one day. Soon.

I walked into the office, already hearing the printer going. I knew Bane wanted this done today, and although I hadn't told him I was coming, I wanted to help. I had stopped and gotten coffee, and after tapping on his door, I went in.

"Morning," I said with a smile.

He looked up from the printer, surprised. "Myers," he said with a quizzical smile. "I wasn't expecting you."

"I thought I could help. I brought coffee."

"Muffins?" he asked, his voice sounding hopeful.

I held up the bag. "Yes."

He crossed over, stopping short of me. He lifted his arm then dropped it, but he smiled. "Come in, then."

We had coffee, and he ate his muffin with no remarks about store-bought this time. "What's in the other bag?" he asked.

"Sandwiches."

"You've already been to the deli?" he questioned.

"No. I make the sandwiches."

He stopped eating, frowning at me.

"You make the sandwiches," he repeated. "The ones I eat every day?"

"Yes."

"Why?"

"Deli meat has all sorts of nitrates and preservatives. My dad's doctor told me how bad they are for you. All that stuff is linked to Alzheimer's and other diseases. I roast the meat, and I make all his sandwiches." I shrugged. "And I make yours."

He studied me. "That's what all the meat in your freezer is for?"

"Yes."

"How are you getting paid for these sandwiches?"

"I'm not. Really, it's not a problem. I make them for my dad. I make one for myself every day. One more is no big deal."

He stared, not speaking. Then he shook his head. "It is to me."

Our eyes met and held, his gaze warm and direct. I had never seen his eyes so blue. They were always intense, but the way he looked at me, they were lit up. A burning cerulean, so clear, they were bottomless. I felt the warmth flow between us, circling and strong.

It took everything in me to drop my gaze as I picked up my coffee. He cleared his throat.

"I see you're prepared for lumberjack-hunting again," he said, a teasing note to his voice.

I laughed. "Whatever, Bane."

"Alex," he said quietly. "When we're alone, it's Alex." He paused. "Magnolia."

"Maggie."

"Maggie," he repeated. "It suits you, but so does Magnolia. I rather like it. It's unique—like you."

I wasn't sure what to say. I wasn't used to a kinder Bane. So I smiled, making him grin.

"You're blushing."

I could feel the heat in my cheeks. "You're embarrassing me."

"I'd stop, but you're very pretty when you blush."

"I think we need to get to work."

That got me another smile. "Okay...Magnolia."

Bane

I had hoped she would show up today. It had taken all my willpower not to call her last night. Not to show up unannounced at her place and continue what we started. Even to have the chance to ask her if she wanted to continue.

When I looked up and saw her in the doorway, something in my chest flexed. Eased. Her shy smile and her sunny greeting made me smile. I walked closer, desperate to touch her, then thought better of it. We had to talk first.

Her quiet confession of making the sandwiches herself caught me off guard. I didn't think anyone had ever made me something. Not even Sally—and she had been with me for years. No one had ever expressed worries over what I was consuming. I found it touching. I would make sure Myers was paid well for her thoughtfulness, even though I knew that wasn't why she did it.

There was something different between us today. Something tangible and real. I felt it. I knew she did as well from the high color that infused her cheeks.

She confounded me. I didn't like sweet, shy, adorable, mouthy, or accident-prone.

She was all of the above.

And yet, I liked her a lot.

More than I should.

I glanced over, watching her remove a finished tree from the printer. I took it from her, placing it in the model. We worked silently for a while, the piece almost complete. I studied it, looking at it from different angles, pursing my lips.

"Write down what I do," I instructed. "Every change, no matter how small."

She grabbed her ever-present notebook and listed what I told her as I moved a few shrubs, then stood back. "Something. I need something."

"Um," she breathed.

I looked at her. "What?"

"Oh, nothing."

"Tell me," I demanded.

"I don't know much about trees or landscaping."

"But you know what you like. What pleases you visually. Tell me."

"This corner." She tapped an area just off a path. "It's on a hill, right?"

"Yes."

"A couple of lovely shade trees and some flowers with a seating place to read would be perfect here." She paused. "I think."

"Yes," I said. "That's what it needs. It's off-balance here."

I headed to the computer, bringing up the design. Myers disappeared, returning a few moments later with more coffee.

She went back to her desk, working as I touched up the design. I sat back with a pleased nod. It was what was missing. Something simple yet perfect. I glanced up, seeing Myers at her desk.

Magnolia.

That summed her up. Simple, but perfect. The yin to my yang.

And I had no idea what to do about it.

It didn't take long to print the additions. Magnolia watched over the printer as I updated the final design, and I sat back, pleased with the project.

"How have your designs evolved?" she asked.

I went to the concept model, tracing my finger back to a building behind the main hotel. "Everything you see here is self-sufficient. There is no freshwater system for keeping the gardens blooming. The gray water from the resort feeds all the plants on the grounds. All recycled. The system we put in will keep everything alive and fed. It's designed specifically for this purpose. It's gaining more and more popularity."

"All the used water?"

"No—not kitchen or toilets. Nothing where bacteria can build or harsh chemicals are used. The system filters out the impurities from the other areas, and it is run using solar panels—another cost-saver and good for the environment."

"And you design all that?"

I nodded. "I don't just dig in the dirt, as my mother thinks. I spent years earning a lot of degrees and gaining knowledge. I keep up with all the current innovations."

She frowned. "Is that what she thinks?"

"My grandfather, her father, was a lawyer. My father was as well until he died. My mother has her degree, although she no longer practices. Her current husband is a lawyer. And so is my stepbrother. He was and is the golden child as well. That is what is acceptable. Being a landscape architect is not. I haven't lived up to my potential, according to my mother. The fact is that I never will."

"Oh," she said with a frown.

"I tried." I barked out a laugh. "I was forced to try. I found it dull and boring. I have been fascinated by plants and how things grow for as long as I can remember. My mother hated it when I would dig in the ground or spend hours with my nose in a book about horticulture. My father thought it was amusing. He was very different from my mother. Quiet. Unassuming. He always told her to relax, that it was simply a phase."

She settled on the back of the sofa, looking at me. "But it wasn't."

I had no idea why I was telling her this. I never discussed my personal life. Ever.

"No. It was my passion, and I think my dad understood. He was the only one. He died when I was young. I had huge fights with my mother that grew worse after my dad died. He was a successful lawyer, yet still a gentle man, from what I recall of him. She always had visions of grandeur. Of being more than we were. I remember disagreements between them. She wanted him to spend his inheritance, but he refused." I laughed dryly. "It wasn't a huge amount, and I think my father knew it would be gone in a hurry. He was saving the money for their future. When he died, she tried to get her hands on the money and failed because my father left it in trust for me, the way his father had left it for him. She wasn't happy, which, coming from her, was the norm, really. I think she thought life with my father would be different than it was. More...opulent. When she met Doug, she saw that opportunity and grabbed it. She married too fast after he died. Changed her name. Wanted me to change mine, which I refused to do. That was another mark against me on a very long list." I ran a hand over my face. "Her refusal to accept what I wanted to do, the only thing that brought me any sort of happiness, was another one of the many arguments that tore us apart."

"You don't get along at all."

"No. We strike sparks. She hates my job. Hates my single status. Hates I'm not in the headlines the way my stepbrother or stepfather are."

"But your reputation..." she protested.

I shook my head. "Isn't enough. I am never enough for her."

"That's why you avoid her."

I sighed, running a hand over my hair and pushing it away from my face. "We argue constantly. Always have. We're like chalk and cheese. Nothing is enough. Right now, all of her friends have weddings they are planning for their children. She wants me to give her that, so she is constantly trying to set me up on dates with the 'right' sort of woman. One who will *make me see sense*. I refuse. We argue. She leaves." I lifted an eyebrow. "And the cycle begins again. She shows up, tells me everything I'm doing wrong, how much of a disappointment I am, a letdown to the family, we argue..." I lifted a shoulder. "She is all about reputation. Presenting a united front. Upper-class BS I want nothing to do with."

She grimaced. "No wonder she was so horrified by my

story of why you couldn't see her."

I began to chuckle, and I moved in front of her, resting my arms on the back of the sofa, caging her in. "I would have given anything to see her face when you said that, Myers. I can only imagine the appalled expression."

Myers frowned then contorted her face into a mock scream of terror. Then she grinned. "Kinda like that."

I laughed again, lowering my head and letting the amusement escape. Good God, she was funny. I lifted my head, meeting her dark eyes. They were dancing in amusement.

"You are too much," I whispered, feeling the heat begin to build between us again. I pushed a long strand of hair off her face, twisting it in my fingers. I lifted it to my nose, inhaling. "You smell so good."

Her breathing picked up. "Yeah?"

"Yeah." I eased closer. "The first day you were in the office, I wondered how you'd smell here." I traced the delicate skin of her neck, making her shiver. "Here." I touched the lobe of her ear. "Here," I added softly, letting my finger ghost down to the vee of her shirt. "Especially here."

She licked her lips, her tongue pink and wet. "Why don't you find out?"

I glanced toward the door.

"The outer office is locked. There's no one else here." She met my eyes. "Just us."

"I won't kiss you while you're wearing another man's shirt. I don't care who it belongs to."

She rolled her shoulders, the plaid shirt falling away. She tugged the sleeves off, exposing her tight tank top. Her hard nipples pressed through the soft material.

I slid my hand up her arm, feeling the goose bumps that

erupted on her skin. I made my way to her neck, brushing the thick hair to one side. I lowered my head to the soft skin of her nape, inhaling.

"Oh, Magnolia," I murmured, my voice raspy. "It's even better than I thought."

Then I claimed her mouth.

CHAPTER TEN

Magnolia

Oh my God. His mouth. He might grunt, shout, and yell a lot, but when he kissed, his mouth and tongue were talented. Erotic. Addictive. He kissed me like I was his oxygen and he needed me to breathe. Deep and carnal. Exploring, licking, sucking, nipping. He held my head between his large hands, tilting me one way, then another. Kissing me until I was dizzy. Drunk with desire. Filled with a need only he could meet. Then he slid his hands down my sides, clutching at my ass, a low, pleased rumble in his chest. He pulled me tight to his chest, and I felt the muscles under the polo he wore. Firm, sculpted, hard. He trailed his hands along my thighs, lifting my legs and wrapping them around his waist, bringing our lower bodies flush.

That muscle was hard. Thick. Pushing into my core, making me want to feel more of it. Of him. He ground against me, and I whimpered at the exquisite sensation. I wanted more. I tugged at his neck, gripped his shoulders, slid my fingers through his hair, feeling the way he reacted to my touch.

As if he was starved for it.

Recalling his mother and the way he held himself away from people, I wondered if perhaps he was.

I held him tighter, and he melted into me, his heat

surrounding us. His kisses became deeper, slower, intense. I tugged on his shirt hem, and he eased back, his chest pumping rapidly.

"You want it off, Magnolia?"

Hearing him say my name in that low, raspy tone made me brave. "Yes."

He grasped the back of it, pulling it over his head and dropping it to the floor. I let myself stare at him. The muscles, the power. His pecs and toned arms. The veins running down his forearms. The light dusting of golden hair on his chest. He was a beautiful specimen of a man.

He fingered my tank. "Do I get the same?" he asked.

I felt the flutter of nerves, and he frowned, stroking my cheek. He leaned down, bracing his arms on the sofa, once again caging me in. "Would it help get rid of those voices in your head if I told you I think you're the sexiest woman I have ever seen? That the mere thought of you makes me hard? Do you want to know I wake up with my hand wrapped around my cock and your name on my lips?" He pressed his mouth to my ear, tracing the shell lightly. "That I shout your name as I come, wishing I were buried inside your tight, sexy little body?"

I whimpered.

"I love how you look."

"I'm not skinny."

He smoothed his thumb up my inner thigh. "Nope."

"I'm short and, ah, curvy."

His thumb went higher, making my breath catch. "Yep."

"I'm not really pinup material."

"I don't want to pin you. I want to fuck you. Taste you. Hear you cry out my name. Then I want to watch you come." He pressed against my center, making me moan. "And then we'll start again."

"Oh God."

"No," he growled, grabbing the bottom of my tank. "Alex. God has nothing to do with what I'm about to do to you."

And he yanked my top over my head.

I waited for his reaction. The cooling of his ardor. It didn't happen. The blue of his eyes was fire. Bright, burning, alive. He took my hand, placing it over the bulge in his pants. "Does this feel like anything but desire?"

I shook my head, unable to speak. He was hard as granite. I stroked him, wanting to see him. Really feel him. Our eyes locked as I pulled down his zipper, the sound of the metal teeth coming apart loud in the room. I slipped my hand in, my eyes widening.

"Commando?"

"It's the weekend, Myers. I wear what I want," he said with a wink, throwing my own words back at me.

He undid the button, pushing at the waistband, and his pants fell to the floor. He was thick, hard, and swollen. The tip glistened. A long vein wound around his cock, and I wrapped my hand around him, my fingers not meeting. He made a low, guttural sound as I explored, letting his head fall back and his eyes shut as I dropped to my knees and took him in my mouth.

His hand flew to the back of my head. "Magnolia," he groaned. "Oh fuck, Maggie."

I worked him, using my tongue, lips, and fingers. Stroked him. Sucked and licked. Teased the engorged head, flicking my tongue over the slit and making him groan. I gripped his tight ass, running my hands over the taut swells, sliding my nails over the skin. He grunted in pleasure.

I played with his balls, cupping them, taking one side into

my mouth, then the other, driving him crazy. He cursed and moaned. Praised and begged. He gripped my hair, lifting my head. His eyes were wild, burning and intense. "You have to stop."

I sucked harder, and he came, our gazes never faltering. His body was rigid, his breath coming out in short bursts, and he whispered my name as I swallowed around him.

Then his head dropped, and he was silent.

I let him slide from my lips, running my hand up and down his thighs.

He opened his eyes, narrowing his gaze as he stared down at me. The intensity was still there, the fire stoked lower but ready to explode any second.

"Took the edge off?" I asked innocently.

He bent, gripping my elbows, and pulled me up. He dragged me into his arms, kissing me again. His hands were everywhere. Cupping my breasts, stroking, pinching, and teasing my nipples. Yanking at the waistband of my leggings, pulling them down until I was bare in front of him. Then he lifted me, carrying me to his desk. He made a detour past his door, and it slammed shut, the lock clicking into place. He deposited me on his desk, pushing off the files, his empty coffee cup and warmer, and anything else in the way. I blinked, looking at the mess. Bane liked it neat. Apparently, Alex didn't care.

He pulled up his chair, sitting down and staring at me. I wanted to cover myself, but I knew he wouldn't let me. His eyes roved over me, and I felt them like a lover's touch caressing my body. He lifted one foot, kissing the ankle and up my calf to my knee, then did the same with the other. He placed them on the arms of his chair, opening me to him. He stood, bending and kissing me until I was a mass of pleading need and desire under him. Then with a wicked grin, he drew away, easing me onto my back. Exhilaration, nerves, and want kicked up as he stood between my legs, staring down, tracing his fingers over me lightly. Teasing. Touching.

"Alex," I whispered. "Please."

His gaze flew to mine. "Keep saying my name, Maggie darling. I'm going to make you come so hard, you'll forget yours."

Then he dropped to his chair and pulled me to his mouth.

Bane

Every filthy dream I'd had about Myers was lying on my desk in front of me. Her creamy skin was on display, the occasional crop of freckles decorating the smooth flesh. I planned on licking every one of them. Tracing her tattoo with my tongue. Discovering every sweet spot on her body. What made her gasp. Groan. Whimper.

I trailed my fingers over her splayed legs. She was almost panting in her desire, and my cock was throbbing at the sight of her sensual beauty—laid out like a feast for my eyes and mouth. She was wet—erotically so—glistening and inviting under the lights. Pink and tempting. I touched her with one finger, gently stroking it up her folds, hearing her sharply indrawn breath. I turned my head, pressing a kiss to her thigh, slowly drawing the skin into my mouth and sucking. Her hands fisted on the wooden desk as I turned and did the same to the other thigh. "Everything between these marks is mine, Magnolia. Do you understand me?"

She made a strangled sound, and I frowned. She was still

tense and trapped somewhere in her mind. I wanted her with me, the way she had been when she was on her knees giving me the best fucking blow job I'd ever had. I had never felt this level of passion and need for a woman. For her to want me as much as I wanted her.

"Maggie darling," I murmured, the endearment slipping from my mouth so easily. "Do you not want this?"

"I'm scared," she admitted.

"Has no one..." I let the words trail off, rubbing soothing circles on her legs.

"Not often. And the last time, ah, it didn't end, um...well." I felt her swallow. "He said I was frigid."

"You didn't come?"

"No. Frankly, he was like a dog with his face in a water bowl. Slurping and shaking his head. He, ah, never, ah...found the right spot."

I tried not to laugh, but I couldn't help it. She was fucking adorable when she was shy.

"He didn't know what he was doing," I murmured, drifting my finger up and down her wetness, barely touching her, smiling as she shifted closer to feel my touch better. "I promise you won't be disappointed."

"I don't want to disappoint you," she replied.

I lifted my head. "Hey." I waited until she met my eyes. "Not possible. But tell me you want this. You want me."

"More than anything." She sighed. "And I'm on birth control."

"I have condoms. We're covered."

"Please," she whispered.

"Say it."

"Please, Alex?" she asked.

"Tell me what you want. Say it out loud for me."

"Your mouth on me."

I reached for her hands. "Hold tight, darling. I'm about to blow your mind."

She was everything I wanted. Wet, hot, sweet, and musky on my tongue. Soft. Her clit was a small nub I suckled, feeling it harden and swell under my touch. I licked her top to bottom, over and over. Feasted on her. Felt her relax and lose herself with me the way I wanted. The tension drained from her body, changing to an entirely different type of posture. Her hands left the desk, burying into my hair. I palmed her breasts, pulling and pinching the nipples. I nipped at the sensitive nub, listening to her gasp of pleasure as I sank one, then two fingers inside her. I skimmed her tight ass with my pinkie, stimulating the little knot. I pulled her closer, draping her legs over my shoulders, lifting her off the desk and taking her with utter abandon. She gasped my name, moaned in pleasure, her sounds an aphrodisiac. She whimpered and begged. Tugged at my hair, her cries getting louder. I added a third finger, sending her over the edge, and she came hard, filling my mouth with her honey, spasming around me, her body a live wire that sparked and shook.

I nuzzled her as she came down, reaching over and grabbing a condom from my drawer, grateful I had thought to put one there last week. My cock was already hard again, desperate to be buried inside her heat. I stood, wiping my mouth and looking at her. I pulled her to the edge of the desk, not giving her a chance to recover, and, with a snap of my hips, buried myself inside her.

Her dark eyes went wide as I started to move. I lifted her, once again draping her legs over my shoulders and gripping her hips. I lost all control as I pounded into her, almost bending her in half as I took her. She lifted her arms, holding on to the edge of the desk, meeting my thrusts, our bodies taking control. She clutched at me like a vise, her muscles fluttering around me. She was breathing hard, her skin flushed and damp, her hair torn from her ponytail and spread across my desk.

She was every fantasy I'd had my entire life come alive. With a shout, I scooped her into my arms and sat down in my chair, her surrounding me. She gasped at how deeply I sank into her. I groaned at the feeling. "Ride me," I commanded.

She held on to the back of my chair and began to move.

"Fuck yes, Magnolia. Like that. Harder."

She leaned back, gripping the desk, and moved. Up. Down. Faster and faster. Quick, hard movements that were sending me over the edge and racing toward completion. The chair creaked, the leather protesting. My desk was getting scratched as the chair slammed into the edges. I didn't care if we destroyed the entire office.

Her eyes rolled to the back of her head, her body shaking. I pulled her to my chest, covering her mouth with mine as she orgasmed, her scream smothered by my lips. My orgasm was intense, burning through me. I clutched her tight, letting the sensation light me on fire. Every muscle, nerve, and sinew exploded, and I was certain I would be reduced to a pile of ash on the floor.

But what a way to go.

Slowly, we stopped, slumping in exhaustion. I held her close, our breathing ragged, skin damp, and bodies sated. I pressed kisses to her hair, forehead, anywhere I could reach. She had her face tucked into my neck, and I slipped a finger under her chin, lifting her face to mine and kissing her.

"Magnolia."

She opened her eyes. "Is that my name? I had forgotten."

I laughed, hugging her close. "My work here is done."

She smiled, looking mischievous. "Oh, I hope not."

I bent, capturing her mouth and kissing her. "No, not by a long shot."

"We're, ah, a bit messy."

"We'll clean up. Then I'll drive you home."

"No driver today?" she teased.

"No. On the weekend, I chauffeur myself around unless I have an event to attend. So maybe you'll invite me in."

"Maybe."

I nuzzled her neck. "You smell like me."

She sniffed. "Like sex."

"Like us."

I lifted her to the desk. "Wait here."

I disposed of the condom and returned to her with a warm cloth. She blushed as I cleaned her, and I kissed the end of her nose. "After all that, now you blush," I teased. I tossed the cloth into the hamper and returned to my desk, pulling her back to my lap. She curled against me as if it was the most natural place for her to be.

And I wondered if, perhaps, it was. I gripped her tighter.

The chair creaked loudly, and I chuckled. "I think it's protesting being ill-used."

She giggled. "It's not the only one."

"I plan on ill-using you again. Soon."

She looked up. "Um, here?" She shifted, and there was another loud creak. "This chair—"

"Wasn't meant for acrobatics like that. In fact, I'm surprised—"

I spoke too soon. Too late, I heard the crack, grabbing at the desk as the chair broke, spilling us both to the floor. I managed to cushion us, but I winced as we hit the floor, a mass of arms and legs entwined together. We looked at each other with shocked eyes, surveying the damage around us. Gingerly, I helped her off me, making sure she was okay, then I rose to my feet. She touched the desk. "Oh my God."

I looked behind her. "Wow."

She followed my gaze. "Holy shit."

Papers were strewn everywhere. My coffee warmer was broken, the surface cracked. Pencils and pens were scattered. Gouges were dug from the drawers where the chair had smashed into the wood repeatedly. The chair was in pieces. The model was intact, but draped over the hotel were her lacy panties I had thrown, not caring where they landed. My laptop teetered on the edge of the desk, mercifully unharmed.

I blinked at the destruction. Then I looked at her, shaking my head. "Only with you, Myers." But there was no bark to my voice. It was impossible to be annoyed with her.

I had to laugh. I had no idea how I was going to explain this away to maintenance. To anyone. Magnolia stared at me, then at the desk, and she began to giggle. Then she laughed, covering her mouth to hide the snorts.

I pulled her into my arms. "We'll get cleaned up, then figure this out." I tipped up her chin. "Tell me you don't regret it."

"Not a bit. Especially the orgasms."

I kissed her smiling mouth. "More where those came from." I swatted her bare ass. "Now, shower."

CHAPTER ELEVEN

Magnolia

His office shower was luxurious, compared to the little old one in my apartment. Tons of pressure and hot water.

"I don't think my breasts are that dirty," I mused as he soaped them repeatedly.

"I disagree. They're filthy."

I tried not to giggle and failed. "I assume you're a boob man."

"*Your* boobs," he conceded. "They're spectacular."

We finished and dried off. I felt shy suddenly, heading to the office and gathering my clothes off the floor, clutching the towel around me tight in my hand. In the bathroom, I turned, tugging my leggings on, unable to find my underwear. Bane came in, watching me for a moment, then slid his arm around my waist. "Are you hiding from me, Myers?"

"Um, maybe."

He pulled me tight to his chest, cupping my breasts in his large hands. "Don't. You're beautiful." He kissed my shoulder. "Every single inch of you."

"Thanks," I mumbled.

He laughed low in his chest, pressing his lips to my head. "Your skin is like silk. I love touching it. Touching you. Your curves drive me wild. Every fantasy I ever had about you didn't do us justice. The way you felt around me." He lowered his head, his lips resting against my ear. "The way it felt to be inside you. Perfection. You are incredible. Understand me?"

"Okay," I squeaked.

"I'm going to clean up the chair and go get one from the supply room downstairs. Then I'm going to take you to lunch."

"I'll tidy the office a bit. But, ah, I cooked some meat earlier. I could make us more sandwiches."

"Mmm. I can't resist one of your sandwiches." He pressed another kiss to my head. "We'll finish here and go." He paused. "Magnolia..."

He waited until I met his eyes in the mirror. "Beautiful. You are incredibly beautiful. Don't forget that."

Then he was gone, leaving me to dress in private.

I looked in the mirror. I looked like me, although my lips were swollen and my hair was a disaster. I had a smile on my lips, and my eyes looked different. Relaxed.

I traced my mouth with my finger. I wasn't used to sweet Bane. His compliments were genuine. His voice was low and the way he looked at me sincere. He really thought I was beautiful. I had to admit, while we were together, he made me feel that way. There was no doubting his passion. His need.

I cast one last look in the mirror and finished dressing. I pushed my bra into my bag and found my underwear swinging from the hotel on the model. Blushing, I added it to my bag, then commenced gathering up the papers and desk items. We had caused quite a mess. I had never felt passion so strongly before. The need for someone as intense as I had for Bane. I tried not to giggle as I straightened things up.

He appeared, pushing a chair and an empty box. Our eyes met, his blue soft and tender as he looked at me. The change in his expression caught me off guard. It was warm and open. His lips were curled into a smile. The dimple I saw so rarely was on full display. He was intoxicatingly handsome.

We were quiet as we cleaned up, and soon, all traces of what had occurred were gone.

"What will you do with the, ah, chair remnants?"

He chuckled. "I'll tell maintenance I leaned back too far, the chair broke, and I gouged the desk as it did. They'll fix it, I'll get my incredible assistant to order me a new chair, and no one will be the wiser." He stroked my cheek. "And I'll smile every time I run my fingers over the marks or look at the top of my desk. I'll never forget the sight of you splayed out on the top, wet and begging me."

I looked away, and he chuckled. "Myers, have I discovered another trait? Talking about sex makes you uncomfortable?"

"Talking about sex with you does," I admitted. "It wasn't expected today."

He cinched his arm around me, drawing me close. "But enjoyed."

"Yes."

"And something that you want to do again?"

"Yes. But, Bane—"

He silenced me with a kiss. "We'll figure it out. Now, let's get out of here."

"Okay."

Bane

I sat on Myers's love seat, looking around in curiosity at things I hadn't noticed last time I was here. There was a sewing machine in the corner, a basket of material on the floor beside it, lace spilling over the top. Vintage curtains hung in the windows, and the floor was covered with old rugs.

She came in, carrying two plates, handing me one. I was starving, and I picked up a thick sandwich, biting down and chewing. "You make the best sandwiches, Myers. I mean, Magnolia."

She grinned. "You can call me Myers. I'm used to it."

"It might be easier, so I don't slip up at work," I agreed.

She frowned, eating her sandwich, looking worried. "I don't know exactly how to ask this..." She trailed off. "I'm not used to... I mean, I don't know how..."

I swallowed my bite and leaned over, tracing her cheek with my finger. "You don't know how to act when you and your boss have sex for the first time?"

She tossed her hair, the light behind her catching the reddish tints. "I don't know what it meant to you."

"I don't either, except it meant something." I thought about her words as I chewed another delicious bite. "You're an excellent assistant, Myers, probably the best I've had. And I can't deny the attraction I feel for you. But they're two separate things. We have to keep them that way."

"I agree. I don't plan on running up and down the hall, yelling about our private matters."

"Good plan."

"So, we keep our private lives private. In the office, we're Myers and Bane. No more, ah, chair-breaking accidents."

I had to laugh. "But we can break things here or my place?"

She rolled her eyes. "Whatever, Bane." Then she became serious. "You went to bat for me last week with those awful women. I don't want to give them a reason to come back at you, saying you were doing it because we're, ah, screwing around."

"I would never allow them to do so. I value both our reputations. I agree, we need to keep it business in the office."

"Okay. So, no touching—or anything else during business hours."

"Agreed. Outside is a different matter."

She took a bite, the worry still on her face. "You want that?" she asked.

I put down my plate, sliding closer to her. "Yes, I do. Today wasn't a one-and-done. I like you. You make me laugh. I feel... different around you. I want to see where this goes." I studied her. "As long as you do."

"I do."

"Then we're in agreement."

"You can't treat me differently."

"I can't promise that. I feel very differently about you than anyone else." I paused, rubbing my lip. "When I realized it was you those women were disparaging at the dinner, I almost lost it. After Rylee told me what had happened in the lunchroom, I was furious. Angrier than I could ever recall feeling." I barked out a dry laugh. "And that is pretty angry. Usually, my mother holds that spot. I have never felt the need to stand up for someone else the way I did for you. The need to make sure you were shielded from them was intense."

She smiled. "No one has protected me that way since my dad got sick."

I returned her smile with one of my own and leaned close to kiss her cheek. "So I will try to be the boss during business hours. But if someone comes after you, I can't promise anything."

"The same goes for you."

I grinned. "Yeah, Myers?"

"I'll go up against your mother for you again."

"Oh God," I said, widening my eyes. "What story will you tell her next time?"

She laughed, and I loved the sound of her amusement. It made me want to laugh with her.

"I'll think of something."

"I'm sure you will. Try to keep it PG this time."

"I can't promise anything. My mouth does get me in trouble at times."

I traced her full lips. "I'm rather fond of this mouth."

"Yeah?" she whispered, kissing my finger, teasing it with the end of her tongue.

"Are you done with that sandwich?" I asked, my question coming out on a low growl.

She nodded, sliding her plate on top of mine.

Seconds later, she was on my lap, our mouths fused together.

I reclined back on the love seat, Myers a snuggled ball of warmth on top of me. As we'd discovered, her love seat was a lot sturdier than my office chair. Our kisses led to touching, then to our clothing being discarded carelessly once more. Luckily, I had another couple of condoms with me I'd grabbed from my private bathroom at the office, and I had the pleasure of watching her ride me again, this time the act happening leisurely with a sea of pillows around us. I pulled a blanket over us once we were cleaned up, and I discovered how much she loved to be held. She made the softest noises in the back of her throat as I stroked her neck and spine, tracing my fingers over her tattoo.

"When did you get this?" I asked.

"When I was twenty-one. I was named after my grandmother, and she died just before my birthday. I got it in her memory." She tapped her shoulder. "The date is here."

"Ah," I said, pulling her back down. "I'm sorry, Maggie darling."

She snuggled closer. "I like it when you call me that."

"Tell me about your grandmother."

"My mom died when I was very young. I barely remember her. We came to live with my gran. In this house."

"What?" I asked.

"I grew up here."

"Why are you living in the basement?"

She sighed. "After Gran died and Dad got sick, I knew I had to sell the house. I needed the money to make sure he had a safe, nice place to be looked after in once I couldn't care for him myself. The government-run homes are terrible. I wanted him to have a place where he'd be happy." She paused, and I felt the emotion coursing through her, so I held her tighter.

"How long ago was that?" I asked.

"Four years. The disease really took hold last year, and his memory is almost gone."

"I'm sorry."

"It's an awful disease. He's here, but he isn't. I see the dad I love. He sees a stranger most of the time. Especially now."

Her voice was low as she spoke. "When his memory started to fail, once the doctors gave him a diagnosis, we sat down and talked about the future. He was accepting, still having the capability of knowing he was forgetting more and more. We toured homes and both liked the place where he is now.

He balked at the cost, but I knew what I would have to do for him to be placed there. Once I could no longer leave him home alone, he went there and stayed in the ward until the house was sold and I could move him to a private room. I furnished it with pieces from the house, and he was comfortable. He knew me still, and visits were filled with recollections of his life." She was quiet for a moment. "Gradually, he forgot about me, living in the past. Some days, he doesn't communicate at all, lost to a world I don't know. Those are the hardest days. I miss him so much. His guidance. The laughter we shared."

"You were close," I stated, hearing the love she had for him in her tone.

"Yes."

"And you've been alone all this time?"

"I'm not alone. I sold the house to friends, with the arrangement I could live down here at a fixed rate. Gran used to rent this space for extra income and it worked well, so I became the extra income for Grant and Lily. Grant does financial planning, and he helped me invest the money so most of the interest pays for Dad's care. I only have to draw on the capital when needed, and it should last as long as Dad is alive. My salary pays my rent and living expenses."

I couldn't help the swell of pride I felt as I looked at her. I thought she was incredible. Strong and resilient. Brave. I touched her cheek, feeling the dampness of her skin.

"Does it upset you living here?"

"No. I like it here. I have so many things of my gran's around me, it still feels like home. I didn't need the huge space upstairs. I would have rambled around all the time. They let me store stuff up in the attic too, and if I want to go in the backyard, I'm welcome. I have dinner with them and see the space often."

I looked around, the eclectic pieces making more sense to me. This was her history. Pieces of her life she kept close.

"My gran was a bit of a fashion plate, and I always loved her clothes. Some of the blouses I wear were hers. Others, I pick apart and sew into new ones. But I loved that period. The lace and silks. The elegance." She shrugged, peeking up and looking self-conscious. "I know people think I dress funny, but I like it."

"I like how you dress," I assured her. "It suits you, and you're incredibly sexy. You're more covered up than most of the women in the office, yet you're a siren, Myers. Some days I can barely concentrate."

"Oh," she replied, looking pleased.

"I'm not sure how I'll concentrate now that I know what the lace and silk are hiding." I grinned at her. "Never mind the lumberjack outfits."

She laughed and I joined her, kissing the end of her nose. "Ignore the haters. They're unhappy, so they want you to be as well."

"I never thought of it that way."

"My mother is never happy. Ever. Even when she gets what she wants. It took me a long time to understand she was trying to make me unhappy too. Now, we just argue, and I go on living my life. She broods and schemes. She tires me," I admitted. "I try not to let her, but she knows how to push my buttons. I see her as little as possible."

"What about your brother?"

"Stepbrother. He's a social climber. He's seen with the right women. Has the right connections. We meet on occasion at a function. Shake hands and smile. That's about it."

"What about holidays? Birthdays, that sort of thing?"

"I'm alone."

She looked stricken, worrying her lip between her teeth. "You?" I asked.

"I go see my dad. He doesn't remember me most of the time now, but I still go see him."

"What else do you do?"

"I have dinner with friends. Christmas, I volunteer at one of the soup kitchens, feeding people."

"So, you're alone too," I summarized.

"Not as alone as you."

"You think there are different degrees of being alone? I think in the end it's all the same."

"I'm not sure. Maybe."

"Or maybe not," I granted. "But we're not alone right now."

"No, we're not."

The air had gotten heavier. Deeper. More personal than I expected. I rarely spoke of my estranged family. No one ever asked me what I did on holidays. Or my birthday. And no one ever looked at me the way Myers did. Her dark eyes and expressive face said so much. For some reason, I disliked the thought of her being alone. And she disliked the fact that I was. We had more in common than I had thought.

Still, we were getting in too deep. Too private. I needed to break the conversation.

"Any chance of another sandwich?"

She smiled and sat up, her breasts pink and rough from rubbing against my chest. I reached out, stroking a finger down one heavy curve. Her nipple hardened, and I looked up to see her watching me with hooded eyes.

"Or maybe," I murmured, leaning close and sucking the nipple into my mouth. "We should try out your bed."

She whimpered, holding my head close as I teased her with my tongue. "Oh," she moaned.

"Or here," I groaned as my cock thickened between us.

"Here is good. Bed after."

I grinned as I slid my hand between us, finding her already wet. "I like how you think, Myers."

CHAPTER TWELVE

Magnolia

I spent Sunday the usual way—errands, groceries, cleaning the apartment, and visiting my dad. He didn't know me, but he was pleased to meet me, telling me about his wife and little daughter. He assumed I was a worker since I brought him sandwiches. I sat with him as he ate a roast beef one, thick with meat and mayo, exactly the way he liked it.

"You won't be in trouble, sitting with me?" he asked, wiping his mouth.

"No. I'm finished for the day."

"You must work in the kitchen," he mused. "Best sandwich I've had here. Not as good as my wife's. She'll be along later, and I'll tell her."

I nodded, my throat thick. I would never get used to him not knowing me, or thinking he was simply here for lunch and was waiting for his wife. Some days were better. A few, he knew me, but those were rare. But he was treated well here, and it was worth every penny, knowing he was getting good care. At least on days like today, he spoke. Even if he didn't know me, hearing his voice helped.

I shook his hand as I left, knowing today wasn't a good day to ask for a hug. I stayed busy with laundry, blushing a little when I found Bane's missing sock from yesterday. I sat down, looking at it, recalling having him here. Eating sandwiches and talking. Having sex on the love seat, in my bed, even the small shower. The man was highly inventive.

I wasn't sure how I would react the next morning when I saw him in the office. We agreed to be professional and keep our personal lives separate.

But now, I knew what was under his expensive suits. The way his muscles rippled as he thrust inside me. The sound of his voice, low and rough for an entirely different reason than yelling. I knew how his mouth tasted and how it felt to be surrounded by him.

I hadn't heard from him today, and I was a little sad about that, yet not surprised. He was a busy man, independent, and his life was mapped out. He had kissed me sweetly before leaving last night. Part of me wanted to ask him to stay, but when he stood in the early evening, saying he had to go, the words died in my throat. Instead, I watched him dress, laughing as we searched for the errant sock. He tucked the other into his pocket, kissed me, and departed. With him, he took all the happiness I had been feeling, and the doubts and worry set in.

I had slept with my boss. Had wild, crazy sex with him in the office and again here. More than once. I didn't recognize the brazen woman I was with him. I hadn't known sex could be that good, and once I got a taste of it, I wanted more. I wanted him.

I was going to have to maintain my distance. It would be difficult, but knowing Bane, he would lead and I would follow. I was sure he would have a far easier time separating the two issues.

Recalling what he said about the way I dressed, I got ready with extra care, wearing an outfit I hadn't worn before. I looked in the mirror, unsure, then remembered how Bane had described me. Sexy.

No one had ever called me sexy before. Cute was the norm. Pretty on occasion. Chubby or full-figured was used. But sexy... Only Bane. And he had proved it a few times on the weekend.

I wondered if he would like this outfit.

I picked up my bag containing the sandwiches I had made and left for work.

I guessed I would know soon enough.

Bane

Lawson and Anderson walked around the model, nodding in appreciation. "It looks amazing, Bane," Lawson murmured. "Between our buildings and your landscaping, it's another winner."

I leaned against the desk, my ankles crossed, arms folded over on my chest. "I think so."

Anderson laughed. "The client will as well." He looked my way. "You know they're already planning resort number four?"

"Where?"

"Banff area."

I whistled. "Big bucks. Land there is scarce and expensive. Tons of environmental issues and guidelines."

He mimicked my stance, leaning on the back of the sofa. I tried not to think of the last person who had leaned on the sofa. Myers had looked far sexier doing so. I blinked to clear my mind.

"They've bought an existing resort. They want to overhaul it, bring it up to today's standards."

I chuckled. "Even more expensive."

There was a knock, and I looked up to see maintenance hovering in the door. "Mr. Bane, I'm here to look at your desk?"

"Oh. Right." I indicated the damage.

"What happened?" Lawson queried.

I stuck with the story I had come up with. "I was working, leaned back too far, and the chair broke. Sent me crashing down, and the wood got damaged."

"You hurt?" Anderson asked with a frown.

"No, just my ego. Scared my assistant. She came running in to see what happened." I chuckled convincingly. "She thought I'd knocked myself out."

"She was working on a Saturday?"

I nodded, keeping my face neutral. "She's been a big help on the project."

"So Laura is gonna have to pay up soon?"

I joined in his laughter. "Yep. I picked a great assistant."

Todd from maintenance picked up the box the chair pieces were in with a shake of his head. "I can fix the desk later. I'll patch it up. I'd be careful with that chair you picked out. It had issues as well."

"Myers is going to order me a new chair."

"Good plan. I'll be back later."

He left, and a moment later, I heard the door open again. I braced myself, knowing it would be Myers. It was after eight, and she was later than usual. She stopped by her desk, appearing in the doorway, breathless and looking worried. "I apologize, Mr. Bane. I missed the bus."

I waved my hand. "It's fine, Myers. But I need coffee. Black." I looked at my partners. "You two want anything?"

They both said no, and she hurried off. I heard the closet

open, and I knew she'd stopped to take off her coat. Then the outer door closed, and she was gone.

Anderson laughed. "It's barely after eight, and she's late? I'm lucky if Annie shows up by nine."

"Like I said, I'm very pleased with my choice." I kept my voice cool.

We talked a bit more about the model and the meeting tomorrow. The door opened, and Myers appeared again, carrying my coffee. I had to look away, locking my body down as she walked toward me, set down my coffee, and headed back to the door, pausing.

"Anything else, Mr. Bane?"

She was wearing pants. Black, slim ones that hugged her ass. Her choice of a tweed vest was form-fitting, and an ivory silk blouse with lace at the cuffs and neck made it perfectly acceptable. Feminine. With her hair up and flats on her feet, she was the perfect assistant. Poised, professional, and ready to work.

Every inch of her was covered from neck to foot, yet she screamed irresistible. Sexy. Provocative.

And I wanted her naked and alone.

Now.

Screw everything else.

It took everything in me not to react. I lifted my coffee and took a sip, barely smiling. "I need the numbers for the Baylor file. ASAP."

"Of course."

She headed to her desk, and I set the mug on the desk, not trusting my hands to remain steady.

"You'll be at the meeting tomorrow?" I asked my partners.

"Of course. Eight-thirty, right?"

"Yes. They have a plane to catch, so they requested an early meeting. I'll have Myers look after refreshments."

We shook hands and they left. I stayed at my desk, drinking my coffee, watching Myers. She was busy, her head bent over her keyboard, typing, her lips moving as she tapped the keys.

She lifted her head, our eyes meeting. She frowned. "Do you need something?"

"Yes."

She came into my office, bringing with her the notebook. Always ready. Always professional. She sat down, her pen poised.

"What can I do for you?"

"You look lovely today."

"Oh."

I ran a finger over my bottom lip as I studied her. "Very fetching." I paused.

She frowned. "Oh."

"Something wrong?"

"We said professional," she whispered.

"That was before you wore pants."

"Pants?" she echoed.

"You're much too sexy to be working in this office today, Myers."

"You think my pants are sexy?" She looked bewildered.

"I think the way they hug your ass is sexy. It reminds me of the way I held it—"

She jumped up, shaking her head. "Stop it."

"I want to peel those pants off and have you on this desk again."

Her eyes widened. "Bane," she protested.

"Alex."

"Bane," she repeated. "I am wearing pants like many other women in this office. It's not a big deal." But she looked happy with my reaction, and I had a feeling she had chosen her outfit hoping I would notice it. It was impossible for me not to notice it, or her, now.

"It is on you. And I told you to call me Alex."

Her eyes flared. "When we're intimate. Which we are not going to be right now. It's business hours, Bane. I am not calling you Alex. It will only encourage this behavior."

I leaned closer, stroking my finger down her cheek. "Okay, Magnolia, have it your way. But come closing time, all bets are off. So are pants. And I'll be watching you all day."

She glared at me and shrugged. "I can solve that problem."

She turned and walked away, giving me an eyeful of the way the pants hugged her ass. She pulled the door shut behind her. "Watch that, Bane," she called.

I began to chuckle. Today was going to be interesting.

I went through my emails, addressing the ones Myers had left for me to handle. There weren't many—she was too efficient at her job.

I sent her a request for refreshments for the next day. She promptly replied, telling me it was already handled. I sent her a fast response.

Excellent work, Myers.

She didn't reply. I waited a while, then sent another message.

I need lunch. And coffee.

Even with the door shut, I heard her sigh. But I also heard her leave to go get my coffee. I sat back, waiting. A few moments later, she came in carrying a tray and slid it on my desk. "Your lunch."

"You didn't knock."

"You didn't knock," she mimicked. "Of course I didn't. You told me you wanted lunch."

My eyebrows shot up, and I stared at her. The action no longer made her quiet.

"You can't do this. Be hot and cold. Come here. Go away. Nice ass. Knock on the door. Decide which of your personalities is in the office and hold on to it, Bane. I'm not jumping."

"You're being rather brave today, Myers," I drawled. "Talking back."

"I talk back all the time—you just don't hear me."

I had to agree. "I bet you do."

"Enjoy your lunch, Mr. Bane."

She started to walk out, and I called to her. "Wait."

She turned around and I smiled. "Thank you for lunch, Magnolia. I'm sure it'll be delicious."

She returned my smile. "You're welcome."

I heard the outer door open, and she groaned when she saw who it was. "Again?" She walked into the office. "Take them back. I do not know a Tyler. And I don't want flowers from—" There was a pause. "Oh, aren't they pretty?"

She sat down at her desk, and, curious, I went to the door. Today's flowers were pale pink roses and baby's breath. Small, delicate, and fragrant. She touched a petal, smiling and looking up at me. "I keep telling them to stop, but they keep arriving."

I had noticed the other flowers at her place on the weekend. Small little bouquets slowly starting to die, yet she kept them.

"Someone wants you to have them. Might as well enjoy," I huffed.

"The delivery guy won't even take my tip. Says it's been looked after."

I didn't say anything, returning to my lunch. Her mysterious flowers arrived every Monday, but I had no time to ponder them. The rest of the day, I watched her. Listened to her talking to people. Heard her low laughter. The polite way she dealt with clients on the phone. Other members of the office. Never short or condescending. I liked her voice. I liked how she represented me and this office. The bottom line was, I liked everything about Magnolia Myers. Probably more than I should. I had already crossed the line. Blew past it, even. Thrown out every rule I had ever set for myself. There was nothing in our policies about dating within the office, but I had always steered clear of anything personal in my business.

But as I discovered, it was impossible to remain impersonal with her.

She came in around six, handing me some files and sliding another sandwich on my desk.

"What is that?"

"I heard a rumor that you always work late the night before a presentation. Tweaking, adjusting, making sure it is perfect."

I sat back. "Maybe."

"Well, *that* is dinner."

I looked at the plate, knowing it would be better than any takeout I ordered.

"I've arranged for an added bonus in your checks to cover the cost of these."

She frowned. "You didn't have to do that."

I walked around to where she was standing in front of the desk, taking her hand. "Magnolia," I said, pausing so she knew I was talking to her, not my assistant. "Not a single person has cared about me, or what I ate, for years. That you do, and you make these incredible sandwiches for me, plus your damn tasty coffees, means more than I can say. My company can afford to make sure you are compensated. So please accept it." I stroked her cheek. "That's my way of taking care of you."

Her expression softened, her eyes becoming liquid chocolate. "Okay," she whispered.

"Okay..." I lifted my eyebrows in expectation.

"Okay, Alex."

I smiled. "Good girl."

Then I pulled her close and kissed her the way I had been wanting to do all day. She whimpered as she kissed me back, winding her arms around my neck and melting into me. I loved how she felt pressed against me. Warm and soft, her curves aligning themselves to my harder planes. I groaned, gripping her nape and cupping her ass. "You have been driving me wild all day in this outfit," I growled against her neck. "I want it off."

I slid a hand between us, tugging on the small brass buttons of her vest. I covered her mouth with mine, swallowing her sighs as I hitched her leg around me, grinding into her. I wanted inside her again. I wanted to feel all of her against me. Her bare skin rubbing on mine. Her scent in my nose, her taste in my mouth. She made me lose control faster than any woman before her. She had from the first moment I'd met her, although I had held back.

I began to lift her when the outside door opened. Instantly, she was on her feet. I rushed to my side of the desk as she dropped into the chair, grabbing her notebook.

"I need those tomorrow, Myers," I instructed, my voice still raw with desire.

"I'll order them," she said as Lawson walked in, carrying a takeout bag.

"I brought supplies," he said cheerfully. "Oh, am I interrupting?"

Myers stood, regret in her eyes but a firm smile on her face. "No, we were just finishing up." She picked up the sandwich. "You won't need this. I'll put it back in the refrigerator." She met my eyes, and I hoped she saw the disappointment I was feeling. "Have a good night, Mr. Bane." She smiled at Lawson as she went by. "You as well, Mr. Lawson."

My cockblocking partner sat down in the chair she vacated. "I got Chinese and some scotch. Much better than a sandwich. I thought we could eat, and I would leave you to your puttering."

I smiled and nodded, not able to say what I was really feeling. I would rather have spent the evening nibbling on a sandwich and Magnolia than eating Szechuan with him and sipping scotch.

Magnolia would be much more delicious.

We would have to try again tomorrow.

CHAPTER THIRTEEN

Bane

The next morning, I opened my front door, freezing when I saw my mother on the other side of it. She wasn't preparing to knock—she was simply there.

Like a vulture waiting until their meal least expected to be pounced on.

She crossed her arms as if to say "Gotcha." Obviously, she had learned trying to get around Myers was a fail, so she lay in wait for me where I least expected. My home.

I'd be impressed if it weren't for it being my mother.

"I don't have time for you this morning. I have a meeting," I said, attempting to brush past her.

"I'm not taking no for an answer this time," she snapped, pushing past me into my condo.

I wasn't leaving her alone in my condo, so I glanced at my watch. "You have ten minutes, Mother. I have a huge presentation for my company this morning."

She rolled her eyes. "Your little plants and flowers," she huffed.

Her snide remark hit its intended target. She thought I played in the dirt and what I did was meaningless. It still bothered me what she thought, although I never allowed her to see my reaction.

"What do you want?"

"There is a function a week Friday—"

"No," I snapped.

"Lisa Summers will be there. She is the sort of woman you need to set you on the right path."

I rubbed my eyes. "Mother, I am not attending. Nor am I interested in meeting one of your socialites to improve my so-called image. I like my life. I love my career."

"It's nothing. You're nothing!" she cried. "Your brother—"

Again, I cut her off. "Stepbrother. And he is a clone of you. Heartless and hungry for power and status." I shook my head. "Do you realize that I could buy and sell you? All of you?"

She scoffed. "I doubt that."

I smirked, liking the slight look of doubt on her face. "The money left in my trust fund was invested and tripled. Then again. And again. I make a great living 'playing in the dirt.'"

"You need to marry well. Get in with the right people. Your brother—"

"Again, stepbrother. I'm sick of being compared to Terence. He's a lawyer with a bad reputation, a penchant for whiskey and women way too young for his age or bank account. How you rank him so high in your favor, I will never know." I paused. "Or care. I am not now nor ever interested in being compared to him. I had enough of that growing up."

"I pushed you to reach your potential."

"You pushed me to be what you wanted. Terry might have liked the attention, but I didn't." I shook my head. "Your second husband and *his* son have always held more affection in your heart than I did. Being *your* son wasn't enough. I had to be what his son was. And while I couldn't say no as a child, I can say no now." I met her eyes, the anger evident. "You want a big society wedding and grandkids to show off? Ask Terry."

"He could have his pick of eligible women. He's a catch," she insisted.

"Then let him get caught." I held open the door. "Now, leave."

She brushed past me, her head held high. "Such a disappointment you are."

I nodded. "That goes for both of us."

The sound of the door slamming between us was loud.

"Can't we go faster, Darryl?" I barked from the back seat.

"Sorry, Mr. Bane, there's an accident ahead."

I looked at my watch. Thanks to my mother's unannounced visit, and the moments I'd required to calm down from her caustic words, I was already late. I'd wanted to be in the office ahead of everyone. To make sure the model was perfect, the refreshments laid out, and everything in its place. I had worked too hard on this for it to fall apart at the last minute. I dialed Myers, upset when the call went to voice mail. I shut my eyes and counted to ten. I looked at the blocked road ahead and did some fast calculations in my head.

"Let me out. I can run faster. Call Myers and tell her I'm on my way."

He stopped the car, and I got out, racing down the alley. By cutting through the back ways, I could shave off time and make it. Five minutes later, I was rushing through the front doors of the building. I managed to get into an elevator before the doors closed, and I checked my reflection. I looked windblown, and my tie was crooked. When the doors opened, I raced to my office, hearing voices.

Myers was waiting, her eyes wide. She handed me a damp cloth and, without my asking, straightened my tie and ran her fingers through my hair. "Darryl called," she whispered. "I told them you were delayed with traffic. They only arrived a few moments ago themselves," she informed me. "Isn't running into the office late my thing?" she teased, making me smile.

She wore a pretty navy-and-white polka-dot dress, tied at the hip with a flirty bow. There were frills at her waist and hem, and she looked cool and professional. Her hair was down, hanging over her shoulders in soft waves. My fingers itched to touch her hair and to find out if that flirty bow was real or simply for show. But I shook my head to clear it. I had to concentrate on this meeting.

"Is everything ready?"

"Yes."

Without thinking, I grabbed her arms and pulled her close, pressing a hard kiss to her mouth. "Thank you."

Because of Myers, everything was perfect. Coffee and her homemade muffins were laid out. The model was covered and the office pristine. I greeted the clients, smiling as they gushed over the muffins and what a treasure my assistant was. They held foamy coffees in their hands, the art on the top more of Myers's handiwork. I drew in a deep breath, smiling as she came in, handing me a coffee, then sat by my desk, her notebook at the ready.

I sipped my coffee, giving everyone a chance to finish their morning treat. Joanne grinned at Myers. "I need to hire you for the resort. These are the most delicious muffins I have ever eaten."

Myers laughed, shaking her head. "I'm quite happy here."

"I'd make it worth your while."

Myers smiled. "I'm honored. It's my grandmother's recipe, and I'm happy to share it with your chef. I have family obligations here."

"Of course. I'll be in touch about the recipe. And if you change your mind, let me know."

Myers inclined her head, gracious and silent. I was glad that subject was closed. She wasn't going anywhere.

Then I went to the model, waiting for my partners to join me. "Ready?"

Joanne and Randy nodded, eager. I watched as their eyes widened and the look of delight spread on their faces as the model was revealed. I went through it step by step, describing in detail everything built into the plan they couldn't see. When I was done, we all answered questions about the entire concept.

I peeked at Myers, surprised to see tears in her eyes. She mouthed "I'm so proud" at me, and I threw her a subtle wink, making her smile.

Suddenly, everything else faded away. The disappointment of being interrupted last night vanished. My mother's snide words no longer mattered. Myers's opinion, my client's reaction, were all I cared about.

And I would hold on to those.

The whole meeting went well. Randy and Joanne loved everything. They were excited and informed us they were offering us their next project without going to tender.

"You've shown us your best," Randy said. "Every time, you've hit it out of the park. We want your stamp on the next one. You have our business."

Lawson, Anderson, and I all exchanged triumphant glances.

Myers slipped out of the office, and we sat discussing the next project. They were as big on conservation as I was, and when they described the next hotel complex, my mind was already firing. All of us were scribbling notes since we worked hand in hand, my landscaping complementing the buildings they would create and/or refurbish. I was in the zone, hyped up on the success and enthusiasm of the people around me. As usual, I kept my emotions in check, but I was pleased. More than pleased.

After the clients left, my partners stayed behind, and we went over ideas and plans. Myers brought more coffee and muffins, staying in the background. As she slid the tray onto the desk, I eyed the bow at her hip again. She met my eyes, rolling hers as if guessing my train of thought.

Once we were done, my partners insisted on going out to lunch to celebrate, and I couldn't get out of it. I wanted to stay at my desk and begin sketching. Eat the delicious sandwich Myers would give me. Talk to her. But I agreed to go, stopping at Myers's desk to tell her I was out for the afternoon.

"Take it off," I whispered.

"I beg your pardon?" she replied, her eyebrows shooting up.

"The afternoon," I replied. "I know these two. I'll roll them into a taxi around three, and then I'll come back here and work. Finish what you're doing and head home."

"Thanks," she said.

I left, feeling oddly bereft. I should have told her I wanted to stay there with her. Listen to her talk, tease her about charming the clients, looking so sexy. But I stayed silent.

It was well past three when I walked back into the building, dodging the rain that was falling. Myers's desk was empty, and I stared at it, recalling the other people who had sat there. None of them had done half the job she did on a daily basis.

I entered my office, shocked to find her leaning on the back of the sofa, staring out the window. Her coat and purse were on the cushions, and she was twirling a lock of hair. The office was dim, the lights off, and the clouds casting shadows through the windows.

"Myers?" I asked. "I gave you the afternoon off. Why are you still here?"

She didn't move. "I know. But I had some things to do. I was waiting for the rain to stop."

I stood beside her, mimicking her stance. "It should be soon. It was only going to rain for a while."

We were silent.

"Were you really waiting for the rain?" I asked. "Or me?"

She didn't answer but laced our fingers together. I looked down at our linked hands, astonished at how intimate it felt.

"You were amazing today," she said quietly, nudging my shoulder. "So knowledgeable, fervent on the subject. So in the zone."

"You had tears in your eyes," I responded. "Why?"

She sighed, turning toward me. "You hold yourself back all the time. You keep your emotions locked down. But when you're discussing something you're passionate about, you open

151

up. Your voice changes, you use your hands. It's as if you're bursting to share your information. Your insight. You make those around you feel that passion. That drive. It was amazing to watch. I love seeing that side of you."

"I agree it doesn't happen often."

"No, it doesn't."

We stared at each other. The air around us began to bubble with the heat between us. "I feel that way when you're close," I confessed.

"So Saturday wasn't only scratching an itch?"

"Not even close. And yesterday only made it worse."

Our eyes remained locked, my body beginning to tighten. The high I had been on all day rushed through my system, my blood pumping fast, my heartbeat picking up. Myers breathing became faster, her hand curling at her side.

"I was wondering all day about this bow," I murmured, fingering the material.

"What about it?" she asked, her voice tremulous and low.

"If it was real or just for show." I tugged on it gently. "What it was hiding."

"Why don't you find out?"

I tugged harder. "I intend to."

The bow gave way under my impatient fingers, revealing creamy, smooth skin. Lace. I pulled her close, dragging my lips up her neck. "You have a thing for lingerie, Maggie darling?"

She shivered. "I like pretty things."

I nipped at her skin. "I like you. There isn't anything prettier in my eyes."

"The door," she whispered, a plea in her voice.

I had the doors locked and was back in a flash. She was relaxing against the sofa, her dress gone, nothing but blue silk and lace over her full breasts. Nowhere else.

I stood in front of her, narrowing my eyes. "Have you been bare under this sexy dress all day?"

"Yes."

I lifted her to the sofa, standing between her splayed legs. I traced my fingers over the lace, snapping the front closure open, her breasts spilling out into my hands. I groaned at the feel of her hard nipples on my palms. I bent and sucked one, then the other, Magnolia whimpering as I slipped my fingers down her torso to where she was wet. Her clit was a hard nub under my thumb, and I strummed it, listening to her soft gasp as I slid my fingers inside her.

"Alex," she groaned.

"Yes, darling, say my name," I murmured, shrugging off my jacket and getting rid of my shirt and tie as quickly as possible. She fumbled with my belt, and the sound of my zipper in the room was a low hiss as it opened. I moaned as she wrapped her hand around me, and I covered her mouth with mine, needing her taste to ground me. We kissed as the last of my clothing was discarded, and I fell to my knees, covering her with my mouth, licking and lapping at her. She was perfect. Sweet, tangy, musky on my tongue. She wound her hand into my hair, tugging, whispering my name, begging me for more. More tongue, more sucking, more fingers. She started to shake, her grip on my hair tightening. She pushed her hips forward, repeating my name as she climaxed. I gentled my touch, standing, and kissing her again. She flung her arms around me, holding me tight, feeding me her tongue and exploring my mouth.

"I want you, Magnolia," I pleaded. "I need to have you."

"Please."

Then it hit me. "I don't have a condom."

"Your bathroom?" she asked, hopeful.

I shook my head, touching her cheek with affection. "I used the few I had here. It's not like I've ever had sex in the office. The ones we used the other day were all I had."

She looked sad, then her face brightened. "Oh, I have one!"

She reached over, digging in her purse, and held a small package high like a trophy.

"I knew they'd come in handy one day."

Then she dropped to her knees. "First, I need to say hello."

The feeling of her mouth on me was indescribable. Hot, wet, teasing. Her tongue traced the lines and ridges lightly, then she nuzzled the head, kissing the tip. Passion, a hot, heavy need for her, rushed through me, and I couldn't wait another moment. I groaned as I caressed her head.

"Save the rest for later. I need to be inside you."

She rolled on the condom, and I pulled her to her feet, kissing her hard and deep. I lifted her to the back of the sofa and settled between her legs, snapping my hips and driving myself deep inside her.

She cried out softly, holding my shoulders. I moved in shallow, rapid strokes. The feel of her clutching me, her heat surrounding me, turned me on even more, and I lifted her higher, her legs wrapping tight around me. It was incredible. My entire being was on fire, my body glistening in the low light. Our skin slid together, the noises between us erotic and constant. I felt tingles around my dick, small prickles of sensation I hadn't experienced before. I wasn't sure I liked them, but I couldn't stop. I was too lost in the moment.

And then, I was too hot. The sensations happening were no longer tingles of anticipation and pleasure. It was uncomfortable. My cock felt odd, burning. Aching. An itch started in my balls, fanning out and up along my shaft.

Something was wrong.

"Magnolia, I'm burning," I gasped, stilling.

"I'm on fire for you too," she replied. "Don't stop, Alex. I'm so close."

"No, I mean badly. My dick hurts."

She frowned, opening her eyes and meeting mine. "It hurts?"

"It's burning. And beginning to itch." I set her down, pulling out, horrified to see my cock swollen and red, almost glowing through a purple-colored condom.

"Where did you get the condom?" I gasped.

"At a bridal shower."

"I need to get it off. Now," I panted. I had been so caught up, I hadn't checked the package. I was allergic to latex and spermicide. Chances were this condom contained both.

I pushed away, heading to the bathroom. The head of my dick was swelling more, and the uncomfortable tightness of the condom was getting to be too much. My balls itched and were turning redder, beginning to swell as well.

Myers appeared beside me, looking at my cock. "Oh God, that looks painful."

"It is," I snapped. "I need it off."

But despite my desire having deflated, my dick was still swollen and getting bigger every moment. The pain grew as the inflammation spread. I tried to get the condom off, but my cock was so enlarged the condom was beginning to cut off circulation.

"Should I call 9-1-1?" she asked, sounding panicked. "If that gets any tighter—"

"No," I yelled, thinking of how the gossip would spread. Faster than my dick was swelling. "Don't call 9-1-1."

Myers raced to my desk, then returned, a pair of scissors in her hand.

"What do you think you're doing with those?" I demanded.

"Cutting off the condom."

"I was circumcised as a baby. I don't need to redo that," I replied. "Or end up in the ER with a missing dick."

She shook her head. "Just the end to help loosen it."

I groaned. It felt as if my dick was being squeezed off my body. The burn was getting worse. I couldn't get the condom off, no matter what I tried. I had no choice.

"Jesus, be careful."

"Wait!"

She raced away, returning with, of all things, a spoon and a tube of lip gloss.

"What the hell?"

"I'll slide the spoon under the condom, then cut it. The lip gloss will help."

I had no choice but to trust her. And I was desperate enough to let her try.

"Get. It. Off."

She kneeled in front of me, and I had to shut my eyes. Despite the pain, she was naked, her skin and breasts right there, and every part of me noticed her nakedness. I was a sick, sick bastard.

I gripped the counter, holding my breath, praying no blood was about to be spilled. I felt the cold of the metal press against my skin, slowly easing down the shaft of my dick. Seconds later, I felt the relief of the condom loosening, and she quickly rolled it off. All the sensations that had been muted now tripled. The burning, the itching were intense. My dick was the color of a fire hydrant, my swollen balls a matching set.

I jumped in the shower, turning it on. The cool water made me yelp, but as it warmed, it helped with the immediate itching. I was careful as I handled myself, letting the water get everywhere to wash away the spermicide.

"I don't understand," she said from the other side of the glass. "What happened?"

"I'm allergic to latex and spermicide," I snarled.

"Why don't you have an EpiPen?"

"I'm usually more careful, and I can't be bothered."

She muttered something about learning my lesson, then raised her voice.

"You should have said something."

"I was a little caught up with trying to fuck you," I replied tersely.

She slammed the door on her way out.

I finished and got out of the shower. My dick was red and still swollen, and it hurt to touch. I opened the drawer, finding the antihistamines and swallowing two down, using my hand to cup the water to my mouth. I dried off, walking into the office, heading to my desk. Myers was on the sofa, fully dressed, looking upset.

I picked up my phone and called a friend. He was a doctor, his office was close, and I trusted him.

He answered quickly. "Alex?"

"Sam, you in the office?"

"Yes."

"I need a huge favor."

"Name it."

"I need a shot. I'm having an allergic reaction, and I can't really come there. I'm at the office."

"Reaction to?"

I drew in a deep breath. "Latex and spermicide."

There was silence for a moment. "I'll be there in ten."

I hung up and looked at Myers, who was staring at me, stricken.

"You should go."

"But—"

"He'll be here in a minute. You need to go. Now."

She stood, grabbing her coat and purse. There was an awkward silence, then she hurried away. I shut my eyes, knowing I should reach out, say something. Comfort her. Tell her I would come see her after. But the outside door shut, and she was gone. I hung my head. Once again, my inability to communicate on a personal level had reared its ugly head, and I had hurt her feelings.

I would have to make up for it tomorrow.

If I survived tonight.

The shot took thirty seconds, and Sam waited until it was done before starting the jokes.

"I guess we don't need to have the whole being safe talk. Well, not entirely, but..."

"Ha-ha-ha."

"Anyone I know?"

"Nope."

"In the office, huh?"

"Leave it alone."

He picked up the little bag from the corner of my desk. "None of these will work for you unless you're looking to die. I'm not even sure how much protection they offer."

"I figured that. I'll return them to the lady."

He held up one. "This glow-in-the-dark one might be fun. Now you see it, now you don't. Adult magic. Or, you know, a fun Star Wars game. Where is the lightsaber now?"

"Stop it," I demanded, trying not to laugh. Myers would love that game.

He dug into his bag, handing me a box. "These, ah, will protect your junk. I really don't want to have to look at it again." Then he handed me a tube of cream. "This will calm the exterior itch. You'll be fine in the morning. Ready to rock and roll again. Although you might be a bit sensitive."

"Thanks."

"Maybe check next time. And I suggest, once again, keeping an EpiPen on hand."

I grunted, but I wondered if maybe he was right.

"I was caught up in the moment."

"Obviously."

"You wanna get a beer and a burger?" He grinned. "I mean, obviously, you can't fuck the rest of the night. Might as well catch up."

"Anyone ever tell you that you have the worst bedside manner around?"

"Nah, my patients love me. I'm serious with them, but if I can't have fun teasing my friend over his swollen pecker, what good is being a doctor?"

I rolled my eyes and grabbed my jacket, wincing a little

as the movement brushed my sore dick against the material of the sweats I had changed into.

"What good, indeed? Come on. I owe you."

"Yeah, you do. We agreed never to look at each other's balls years ago."

"Shut it."

"You can look at mine if it would make it less embarrassing. Tit for tat sort of thing. Of course, mine aren't red and itchy or unnaturally the size of baseballs, but still, they're impressive."

I groaned. It was going to be a long night.

The day started like shit, got fabulous, but appeared to be ending on a low note.

I hoped tomorrow would be better.

CHAPTER FOURTEEN

Bane

Myers wasn't at her desk when I arrived the next morning. I wondered if she was still angry with me. She had every right to be. Once again, I had crossed the line with her in the office, and then I had been the one angry. It wasn't her fault. I kept condoms at my condo that were safe for me to use. I usually had a few in my private bathroom in case I was seeing someone. But it had been a while, and I hadn't thought to stock up.

I wondered how Myers would feel if I asked her to order some for me, telling her my preferred brand but letting her pick out the style. Ribbed. Intense pleasure dots. They had a few choices. I wasn't sure about the glow-in-the-dark variety, but she could check it out and we could try the whole adult magic show thing. Or the lightsaber trick. Whichever she preferred.

But first, I had to smooth things over, man up, and apologize.

I was on the phone when she walked in, carrying coffee and a small cello-wrapped package that she slid onto my desk. I watched her from across the room, where I was leaning by the window as I spoke to one of my favorite garden centers about some special shrubs I would need for the resort. She slid the package closer to the center of the desk, then hesitated and pulled the card I could see out of the cellophane and slid it into her pocket. She turned, briefly meeting my eyes before going back to her desk, shutting the door behind her.

She was pale, with dark circles under her eyes. And all the light was gone from her expression. I shut my eyes at the sight of her anxiety. I finished my call and headed to my desk, sitting down. I winced a little as the fabric pulled over my groin. Sam was right, and the area was still rather sensitive. At least all the swelling was gone. Curious, I opened the package, revealing a flower arrangement made from fruit. Melon, cantaloupe, pineapple, and strawberries had been fashioned into flowers, creating an edible feast for the eyes. I shook my head even as I smiled. I pushed the intercom, waiting as Myers answered.

"Yes, Mr. Bane?"

"I need the Clarkson budget and for you to come into my office."

"Yes, sir."

A moment later, she came in, handing me the file. She sat down, opening her ever-present notebook, and waited expectantly. I studied her for a moment. She was wearing one of my favorite outfits, the moss-green lacy blouse and layered skirt in varied hues of the same green, complementing her coloring. Her gaze was fixed on her notebook, but I noticed a tremble in her hand.

"How are you...Magnolia?" I asked quietly.

Her eyes lifted to mine in surprise.

"I owe you a huge apology." I kept talking. "I shouldn't have snapped, and I shouldn't have told you to leave."

"You were angry."

I tilted my head. "I was in pain, and I wasn't thinking straight. It wasn't your fault. We needed a condom, you had one, and I didn't check. I was too caught up in the moment. In you." I paused. "In us."

"I didn't know."

"I know that. And I'm sorry. I should have called you last night, but I was afraid you'd hang up on me."

"Your, ah, friend helped?"

"Yes. His medical office is two buildings down. Sam and I have known each other for years. We met in college and have stayed in close touch. He gave me a shot and some cream, which helped. Then he teased me mercilessly, and we went for a beer." I waited until she met my eyes again. "I told him all about you."

"Oh."

"He thinks you're good for me. Aside from the kill-me-with-a-condom thing."

Her eyes widened. "You could have died?" Her voice rose as she spoke, her horror evident.

"Sorry, I was teasing. Some people have severe reactions."

She gaped at me. "I saw your dick. That looked pretty severe."

Simply hearing her say dick made mine twitch. I ignored it—I wasn't ready for that yet. But hopefully soon.

"It was bad, but it's all fine. *I* am fine." I waited. "Are *we* fine?"

"Yesterday was inappropriate."

"We seem to excel at inappropriate," I agreed.

"I'm not sure what we are."

I sighed. "Neither am I. But I would like to talk to you about it. How about tonight, you come to dinner at my place? We'll order in and talk."

She nodded.

I indicated the edible arrangement. "Thank you for this."

She pursed her lips. "I wasn't sure on the proper protocol when you make someone's dick swell up that way or their balls turn that shade of purple. I already make you sandwiches. Flowers seemed too girly. Fruit felt like the way to go."

I began to chuckle. "Good plan, Magnolia."

She stood. "I'll go back to my desk now."

I rose out of my chair, going to the front of the desk. I leaned against the wood and trailed my fingers down her cheek. "Everything is okay, you know that?"

"Yes."

"I'm fine."

"Good."

"Are you all right?"

"Yes."

"Put the fruit in the fridge, and we'll have some after lunch, okay? I have meetings all day."

"I know," she replied with a roll of her eyes. "I take care of your schedule."

I leaned close and brushed my lips on hers. "You take good care of it."

I felt the tremble of her mouth, and I kissed her again. "Everything is good, Myers," I whispered. "As long as you're okay, I'm okay."

"I'm good." She turned to go, but I caught her hand.

"I want my card."

"Card?" she repeated.

"The one you took from the fruit."

"Oh, it was just the bill."

I pulled her close and slid my hand into her pocket, holding up the small envelope. "Liar."

"Give it back! I decided it wasn't appropriate."

Holding it aloft, I moved back to my side of the desk, sitting down. "And as I said, we excel at inappropriate."

I opened the card, staring at the words.

Roses are red,

Your dick was too,

Sorry about the condom,

And your balls turning blue.

I read them once. Twice. Looked up at her. Back at the card.

She shrugged. "It seemed fitting."

Laughing, I reached over, pulling her close. I kissed her, still laughing.

"Oh, Myers. Thank God I hired you."

Every time I looked at the card, I started to laugh. When Sam called to check in, I read it to him, and his laughter was long and loud.

"I need to meet this girl."

"Soon. We're still navigating this—it's pretty new."

"Your mother will hate her."

"That's an added bonus. She'll stay away."

"Dinner soon, okay?"

"Sure," I agreed easily and hung up.

I kept my eye on Myers. She was still off. Very formal and somewhat skittish. I wasn't sure how else to say sorry. To let her know how much I regretted my harsh tone and words.

At lunch, she brought my sandwich in with a fresh cup of coffee, sliding the tray onto my desk with a plate of the fruit. She'd included a few of the chocolate-dipped pieces as well.

"Grab your lunch and join me," I urged.

"Um..."

"Bring in your notebook. I have some items I need you to look after. We'll call it a working lunch."

"All right."

When she returned, I had moved the tray to the sofa, and I patted the cushion beside me.

"Join me."

She did, and I picked up my sandwich, biting and chewing. "Great turkey."

She hummed, nibbling on her own sandwich.

"Do you make these pickles?" I asked, curious.

"Yes."

"Incredible," I observed. "*You're* incredible, Myers."

I ate steadily, enjoying the food. I wiped my fingers on the napkin and finished my coffee. I picked up a piece of cantaloupe, biting into the juicy flesh.

"Good," I murmured.

"She was cutting it all up when I was there this morning."

I chose a chocolate-covered strawberry, turning slightly and pressing the fruit to her lips. "Try it," I urged.

She bit down, the juice bursting from the fruit. She licked at her lips, chewing slowly, and I ate the rest of the fruit, winking at her. "Myers-flavored."

"Stop it."

"Simply stating a fact."

She opened her notebook, looking at me expectantly. I sighed and rattled off a list of items I wanted checked, some calls I wanted made, and the final question.

"What do you want for dinner?"

"Oh, ah..."

I took her notebook from her hands and set it on the table.

"I'm sorry," I said quietly. "For my anger, for upsetting you."

"I know."

"Why are you still so upset?"

To my shock and discomfort, her lip began to tremble. Her gaze dropped, and her voice was low when she spoke. "You were hurting, and you sent me away. I didn't know if you were all right. I didn't know if I could call or text you and ask."

"Maggie darling," I said, touched by her concern.

Her eyes met mine, bright with tears. "I stood across the street, waiting to see if you would show up this morning. Then I went and got your fruit."

"That was thoughtful." I nudged her knee with mine. "And I liked your creative poem."

"I wasn't sure if I should make a joke of it or if you'd be too angry with me. When I walked in, I decided maybe you were leaning toward anger, so I took it back."

"Your poem was perfect." I slid my hand over hers. "I wasn't angry. I was worried this morning. You did nothing wrong. We were caught up in our passion. You had a condom, and I was so overcome thinking about being inside you that I didn't say anything. So it's on me."

"Did you get some, ah, safe ones?"

"I will. It's gonna be a few days until I'm ready, I think." I grinned, wanting her to smile. I hated seeing her upset. "We can go online tonight and pick some."

Her gaze dropped to my crotch. "And he'll be okay?"

"Absolutely. Sam says no permanent damage."

She blew out a long sigh. "Okay."

"And you can call me anytime, Magnolia."

"Your cell phone isn't monitored?"

"No. We all have our own cell phones. The company pays the bills, but they belong to us. They aren't monitored."

"Mine too?"

I frowned. "I'm not sure, to be honest."

"I have my own as well. I didn't cancel it in case this place didn't work out."

"Then give me that number. I'll know it's my Magnolia calling, not Myers."

"Okay."

I leaned close and brushed a kiss to her full mouth. "Okay now?"

"Yes."

"We'll talk more tonight, all right? And decide what you want for dinner, and we'll pick it up on the way."

"I can cook."

"I don't want you to cook after a long day. We'll grab something."

She pursed her lips, looking stubborn. I had to smile at her expression. "If you want to cook, then you can. But simple. I don't want to lose you for hours making dinner."

She stood. "Okay. I'm going to get back to work."

"You barely ate your lunch. Sit and finish it."

"Later."

I knew better than to argue with her. I reached into my pocket. "Ah, these are yours."

She grimaced as she took the little bag, looking inside. "I think I'll just throw them out." She paused. "Where is the glow-in-the-dark one?"

I frowned, then chuckled. "I think Sam took it. He thought it might be fun for some adult magic."

"Adult magic?"

"You know," I teased. "Now you see it, now you don't? Repeat..."

Her cheeks flushed and her eyes grew round. "Well then," she muttered. "I hope he doesn't have any allergies."

I laughed as she walked out of the room. She was constantly surprising me. In my face and stern one moment, crazy and funny the next. Then shy. I never knew which Magnolia, Myers, or Maggie I was going to get.

And I was surprisingly okay with that.

Magnolia

I was nervous the rest of the afternoon. I hadn't entirely gotten over the whole "the condom I rolled onto his dick almost killed him" issue. He was calm and relaxed today, apologizing and being sweet Bane again. His decision that we would go to his place for dinner and to talk was unexpected, but I was excited to see his home and to make him dinner. Maybe to understand where he saw this relationship going. Assuming, of course, that he thought it was a relationship.

He was older than I was, jaded. I had no idea what his thoughts on us were for sure. I had checked him out on the internet, and his dating history was sparse. The pictures I could find all contained different women. There weren't many, and he didn't look happy in any of them. His brother, on the other hand, was everywhere. It looked as if he loved attention and being "caught" on camera. The only ones I saw of Bane with a smile were business-related, usually with his partners at the unveiling of one of their many successful projects. From the records I found in my desk, he'd had more assistants than girlfriends, and they never lasted long either.

Given his charming personality, it was a mystery.

Then I laughed. Bane was charming—if he let you in. I had a feeling that was rare.

He was in and out for meetings, and I stayed busy with the list of tasks he'd given me to handle. I was working on an Excel document when he walked in, Jessica from HR behind him.

I smiled, although my nerves kicked in. Had someone seen something?

But she stopped by my desk, handing me a memo. "The anti-bullying seminars start next week," she informed me. "We'll have an informal meeting with the outside group Bane has brought in, and then we'll move on to the next step. We're breaking it into two groups, so I need your preference."

I glanced at the schedule and Bane's calendar. "Tuesday is better."

"Great. I'll mark you down." She smiled kindly. "Still doing well?"

"Oh yes. Everything is great."

"Bane mentioned how invaluable you were with the resort project at the partners' meeting. You must be doing everything right."

I laughed. "Not everything, but some things, I suppose."

Bane came out of his office. "She's being modest. Best assistant ever."

Jessica looked impressed. "High praise, coming from you."

He smiled at me. "She deserves it."

"So I guess we'd better get ready to apologize?"

Bane chuckled. "I consider finding Myers lucky. No apology needed, but I am going to let you take us both to lunch."

He turned and went back into his office. Jessica looked at me, her eyebrows raised. "Whatever you're doing, keep it up."

For some reason, those words made me laugh. "I'll try," I managed to get out.

She left, and I let my amusement out.

"I heard that," Bane called from his office. "What are you—twelve?"

I went to his door, still laughing. "Keep it up. I was trying..."

"Don't even go there." He shifted uncomfortably in his chair. But I saw his lips quirk.

"What apology?"

He explained what had happened and the bet they'd made. I laughed even as I shook my head. "So I'm a means to a free lunch?"

He returned my smile, his tone serious. "Maggie darling, you're a means to many things."

"Oh," I breathed out. He was very good at being charming when he wanted.

"Coffee?" I asked, sounding breathless.

"Yes," he replied. "Some of your foamy stuff. I need the sugar."

I picked up the cup from his desk and, unable to resist, bent and kissed him. "There. Sugar for you."

With a low growl, he captured me around the waist and pulled me close, kissing me again. Harder. Deeper. Then he pushed me away.

"Yeah," he grunted. "I needed that. Now, get my coffee."

But now, he couldn't hide his smile.

I was giving myself more points.

CHAPTER FIFTEEN

Magnolia

Bane's condo was close to the waterfront. One of the popular Rabba stores was across the street—a local specialty market—and he followed me, holding the basket as I picked up some things to make a simple dinner. Then we strolled across the street and headed to his condo. The building wasn't tall, but he had a unit that offered a nice view of the water on the top floor with a generous-sized patio. If I stretched over the railing and strained my neck, I could almost see my neighborhood across the park area that separated the two worlds. Not a huge distance in miles, but vast in the differences. The condo was spacious, the kitchen modern and sleek. And, from what I could tell, rarely used. He had an office and a large living room. His bedroom took up a good portion of the space with a private en suite, walk-in closet, and an exercise corner containing a machine I was sure I would never figure out how to turn on, never mind use.

All the rooms were simply decorated, and I was once again struck by the lack of personal items. No photos, few knickknacks. He had some modern paintings that went with the style of the rooms, a massive TV on one wall over the gas fireplace, but little else that showcased the man who lived there. It was neat, tastefully furnished—and blank.

He watched me as he showed me around, then followed me to the kitchen, draping his suit jacket over one of the high barstools at the island that separated the two rooms.

"Wine?" he murmured, reaching into the cabinet for glasses.

"That would be lovely."

I opened cupboards, looking for what I needed, then grabbed a chopping board and got to work. Bane leaned his elbows on the counter, observing me.

"You like to cook."

"Yes, I find it relaxing."

"I'm not a good cook. I work the microwave well, and I'm great with DoorDash," he admitted.

"Never used it. If I'm not in the mood for cooking, I'll grab something on the way home. There are all sorts of little places by the bus stop. Chinese, Greek, Italian, and a great ramen place I like," I replied, sliding the veggies I had chopped into a bowl. "But I prefer homemade."

"Lucky me," he drawled.

I stopped what I was doing, meeting his eyes. He was being sincere, and his gaze was warm. Interested.

"I like seeing you in my kitchen, Maggie." He paused. "Darling."

I felt a tremor go through me.

I dropped my gaze, reaching for the chicken, slicing it quickly and adding it to a bowl with some olive oil and garlic. On the fancy cooktop, I heated the water and got the pan ready to make the sauce in. I slid the bread into the oven to warm. He sat at the island, scrolling through his phone, directing me when I needed something. He helped make the salad, proving his ineptness with a knife, but at least he tried.

Soon, we were sitting down, bowls of my own version of pasta primavera with chicken steaming in front of us. We ate at the island, Bane laughing as I tried to figure out how to climb up on the barstool, clearly made for someone much taller than I was. He gripped my waist, lifting me, then dropped a kiss to my mouth.

"Dinner smells incredible," he praised, filling my glass with more of the delicious, crisp white wine he had chosen.

"I like it. It's not traditional, but it's tasty. I sort of made it up with the things I like."

He took a bite, closing his eyes. "I like it too."

He leaned over and kissed me. "And you," he said quietly. "I like you."

His words made me smile.

I squealed in delight after dinner when he showed me his coffee machine. "This is awesome," I enthused. "Please tell me you have what I need to use it."

"I hope so."

I prepared the coffees as he loaded the dishwasher, assuring me that was one task he could handle. "How did you learn how to make foamy coffees like that?" he asked, watching me create a little flower on top.

"I worked as a barista during the summer for three years. Once you figure it out, you remember. My old boss loved my coffee creations. He used to have me serve them at every meeting. Said it gave him an edge over competitors."

"Joanne and Randy certainly liked them. And your muffins."

"She was very nice. She emailed me, asking if she could buy the muffin recipe."

He crossed his arms. "That could be a good source of income for you if you structure the deal right."

"I was just going to give it to her."

"Nope. She wants it, you sell it. And you get a cut on every muffin they sell."

I blinked.

"I'll help you."

"Okay. Won't that upset her?"

He laughed. "Joanne is a businesswoman. Very wealthy. She didn't get there by giving her recipes away. She'll happily pay, and she'll understand. You have a product she wants for her resorts, and you need to think of your future."

"All right. What else should I be thinking about?" I asked.

He sat down beside me on the sofa, running his hand up and down my leg. "You mean about us?"

"Yes, Bane. About us."

"Alex," he corrected.

"We're not—"

He interrupted me. "You're in my home, having cooked me dinner. I'm beside you, touching you. None of these things has ever happened in this condo. To me, that is pretty damn intimate."

"You've never had another woman here?"

"Aside from my mother getting past the doorman and breezing in a couple of times? No."

"Oh. How long have you lived here?"

He threw back his head in laughter. "A few years. Lawson designed the building with BAM—they're a huge deal in the real estate business here. I worked on the landscaping, and I loved the building. I bought this unit before it was even built. Prior to that, I lived in a high-rise very close to the office. I used to walk to work daily. And before you can ask, I never had a woman there either."

"Why?" I had to ask.

"I've never thought of myself as a relationship person. I don't connect with people easily. I meet a woman, we go out, but there's never been that spark. After a few dates, either they think I'm an emotionless windbag or I find them boring. If there is nothing but sex, it gets old fast."

"So why am I here?"

He smiled, setting aside his coffee and pulling me onto his lap so I straddled him. "Because you, Maggie darling, don't bore me. You make me laugh, which is rare. You challenge me." His voice became softer. "You see me. You care for me. I've never had that—my entire life. You take my good with my bad, and you equal them out. I love that."

I wasn't sure how to respond. "Are you sure it's not just your perfect calendar talking?"

He slid his hand up my arm, bunching it into my hair. "How you run my office is such a gift for me. But how you run me is what I like. The sandwiches. The coffee." He tilted his head. "Your smile. Your soul. The energy you emit. It draws me in. I want to be around you. I can't wait to see you every day." He sighed. "It's a bit disconcerting, to be honest. I've never experienced this until you."

"Oh."

"I've never had a relationship like this. I don't know how good I'll be at it. If I'm capable."

"Why would you say that?"

"Relationships require a lot of emotion. I'm not good with

177

emotions. Caring."

"I think you're better at them than you give yourself credit for."

"There you go, seeing something in me I don't see myself. I need you for that." He paused. "This isn't some torrid boss-assistant affair, Magnolia," he murmured. "I want to try. With you."

"I want that too."

"I like you. I like everything about you." He paused. "Aside from your horrible taste in condoms."

I started to laugh, then covered my mouth. "Not funny."

He shrugged, a playful smile on his face. "Kinda is—now."

"Can I ask how, um, it—you—are feeling?"

He ran his fingers up my leg, stroking the skin under my skirt. "Better."

"How better?"

"Still sensitive, but better."

I wound my arms around his neck. "What if I kissed your boo-boo and made it all better? Softly, slowly, until you feel really, *really* good."

He tightened his grip on my legs, his cock swelling between us. "As long as you tell me you understand something."

"What?" I asked breathlessly.

"You're mine. In the office, you're my assistant. After hours, you're everything else."

"Can you keep them separate?"

He grinned, standing. "I can. Unless you wear pants. Or that black skirt. Maybe the blue one."

I laughed into his neck as he strode down the hall.

"All right."

He set me on my feet by his bed, bending and cupping

my face. He kissed me until I couldn't breathe. Until I was desperate to feel him. He drew back. "Mine."

I grasped his belt, pulling. "Yours."

Bane

Dawn was beginning to color the sky as I lay watching Magnolia. I found her as fascinating asleep as I did when she was awake. I had never had a woman spend the night. Never invited one into my home and had them cook in my kitchen.

Never felt the pang of regret over the fact that I would have to wake her and end the night that we'd shared.

She'd been exactly what she said she'd be. Gentle, sweet, and somehow sexier than ever as she took my cock in her mouth, using her tongue to gently tease me. There was nothing hurried, hard, or insistent about her. Yet she drew out my orgasm as easily as if we were lost in a frenzy of lust. It was her care, her touch, her eyes as she looked up at me that did it. No one had ever looked at me the way she did. I had a feeling no one ever would.

After, I'd lain her on my bed and worshipped her, discovering every nuance of her body. The ticklish spot below her breasts and knees. The way she trembled as I traced my tongue along her tattoo and suckled behind her ear. How she moaned when I stroked her clit. The way she lost herself with me. All these things were a wonder to a man who always remained closed off. It was impossible to be anything but open with her. Even during office hours.

Her fingers flexed and her toes curled as she slowly blinked awake. She met my gaze with a smile then sat upright, panicked. "Oh God. We fell asleep."

I touched her cheek. "It's fine, Magnolia. Darryl will drive you home first, and you can change and come to the office."

"He'll know," she said, looking worried.

"He knew last night, baby. He's loyal and I trust him. He won't say a word."

"Okay. We should go, then."

"We have lots of time."

"For?"

"One of your coffees. A shower...after."

"After?"

I slid my hand up her naked leg. "My cock is so much better this morning. But I think some time spent inside you where it's all warm and wet would make him feel one hundred percent better."

She whimpered as I slid my fingers over her. "Look at you, Magnolia. All set for me. Wet. Hot. Just waiting for my cock." I brushed over her clit, smiling as she opened her legs wider. "Such a good girl, ready for me."

"Do you have...?"

"I do."

"I'm on birth control. If you want to, ah, go without."

The thought of sliding into her bare was erotic. I had never gone without a condom before.

"It's been a long time for me," she whispered. "I'm good."

"So am I. Are you sure about this?"

"Yes."

I hovered over her, lowering myself so we were chest to chest. Her legs went around my waist, pulling me in. My cock nudged her entrance, the feel of it incredible. I bent and captured her mouth, driving inside her. The sensations were almost overwhelming. The silkiness of her. The heat. The wetness. She surrounded me, welcoming me into her body with the gift of trust.

And I wouldn't let her down.

I was buzzed the rest of the day. The euphoria of being inside Magnolia without a condom hadn't worn off. I had never once been bare before. The sensations were incredible. The feel of her gripping me, the velvet heat, and the touch of her—all of it was indescribable. It had been all I could do to keep my hands off her when she would come into my office. I had left my door open all day, often our eyes meeting and holding. I enjoyed watching her become shy, turning her head away. She was incredibly endearing.

I should hate it. Yet, I didn't.

She came in, carrying a slim folder that she set on my desk, and sat down, waiting until she had my attention.

"Your plane reservation. Hotel confirmation. Dinner reservations at the restaurants you requested. The people attending the meals have been sent the information. Your meetings have been confirmed. Darryl knows your schedule, and he'll be here on Monday to pick you up at four. There will be a car waiting at the airport to take you to the hotel and return the next morning for your first meeting, which is at eleven. Everything has been sent to your calendar, but this is your backup, including all the phone numbers if needed."

I opened the file, looking at the precision—as usual, she was perfect.

"I could rearrange your meetings to catch the early morning flight. There's no stop."

"No, I have a busy day Monday. I can relax on the flight and nap. I don't care about a stop." I paused. "I almost wish I weren't going."

She frowned. "You've been looking forward to this trip. Your design is incredible. They're going to love it."

I smiled at her insistence. "You're missing the point."

"Which is?"

I tapped the folder. "You won't be there."

"Oh." Soft color flooded her cheeks. "You can check in daily. I'll handle everything."

I sat back. "Of that, I have no doubt. But no sandwiches. No sass. No Magnolia beside me when I wake up."

She rolled her eyes. "It was only one night."

"Since I plan on taking you home and keeping you until I leave, it'll be more than one night."

"I don't recall being asked."

"I'm not asking. I'm telling."

She lifted her chin, attempting to look haughty. "I'll think about it. And you have a three o'clock in the boardroom. Nothing after that. You can probably go home."

Then she walked out.

I chuckled as she shut the door. She was coming home with me, and we both knew it. If I was leaving early, then so was she.

Magnolia

I couldn't relax. All day, all I could think about was the man on the other side of the wall. All I could remember was how he had felt last night. Then this morning. His words. His voice. His body. And then informing me he was taking me home again tonight and keeping me for the weekend. I wasn't sure how to respond to that. Part of me was thrilled. Part scared.

Today, he'd been Alex for most of the day, Bane hardly showing at all, unless someone else was around. And there hadn't been many of those incidents. I was sure there was plenty of him showing up at the meeting. He'd be grumpier than normal when he returned—he always disliked partner meetings. He insisted they dragged on too long.

"What could be accomplished in an hour takes two and a half," he griped as he stomped out the door. I was grateful this was a meeting I didn't attend with him.

I was going to miss him next week as well, but it might be a good thing. We'd both have clear heads and could make sure we were on the same page. I couldn't deny that with every sweet word, caring gesture, or passionate kiss, I was falling for my grumpy boss. I was almost certain he felt the same way about me, but still, doubts lingered. He wasn't sure he was emotionally capable of a relationship. I disagreed. Despite, or perhaps in spite of, his mother and his upbringing, he had a lot of depth, and he could care. I had seen it.

I blew out a breath, deciding what I needed was a good, brisk walk. Except, looking out the window, I saw the clouds had moved in and it was threatening rain. I shook out my arms, looking around for something to do. Anything to stay busy. Now that I had the office organized, I was always looking for things to occupy myself when Bane didn't need me.

I did a few jumping jacks, trying to get rid of my tension. Then I decided to turn my efforts to the storage area behind my desk. It was the last thing requiring my attention out here. I planned to work on Bane's office while he was gone. His supply cabinet was a disaster, although he insisted he knew where everything was.

I liked music when I cleaned, and it wasn't allowed to be played at any volume, so I slipped in my earbuds so I could listen as loud as I liked, locked the outer office door, and set the timer for an hour and a half. I would see what I could accomplish, tidy up, and be busy at my desk by the time Bane came back. I'd save the major mess for when he was gone.

Pleased with my decision, I opened the doors and started. I sorted through the top shelf, rolling my eyes at the things I found. Empty cartridges, supplies for the 3-D printer, folded boxes with no use. Whoever had filled in after Bane's assistant had left simply piled things up behind closed doors.

I was deep into organization mode when it happened. My back was to the door, and suddenly, I felt someone behind me. Before I could turn, a hand covered my mouth, and without thinking, I spun and kneed my attacker in the groin.

They fell like a dead tree in a forest. I heard the grunt of pain, even with my earbuds playing.

I felt my eyes widen as I took in the immobile form on the floor. I pulled out my buds, gasping.

"Bane?"

Bane

The last thing I expected to find when I returned from the meeting early was the outer door to be locked. Wondering if Myers had left, I used my key and entered, shutting the door behind me. I looked around at the mess behind her desk.

"Myers, what on earth are you doing?"

There was no response, although I could see and hear her. She was singing along—badly—with whatever music she had playing. A folded box flew over her shoulder, and she stepped off the little ladder, coming out of the small area. She tilted her head, studying her handiwork, and nodded in seeming satisfaction. Then she shimmied her hips, her shoulders moving as she danced to the beat of a song she obviously liked. I leaned against the wall, mesmerized, enjoying the show. She had no idea I was there, and she moved freely, making little noises as she grooved. It was sexy, funny, and much too tempting.

I snuck up behind her, covering her mouth with my hand to muffle the startled scream I expected. She jumped, but before I could pluck out one of her earbuds, she reacted.

She spun, lifting her knee and catching my groin. Luckily, it wasn't a hard contact, but given the fact that my dick was already traumatized and still recovering, it was bad enough that I dropped with a low groan. Instantly, she gasped, yanking out her earbuds and kneeling beside me. "Bane?"

"Jesus," I gasped. "Who did you expect?"

"Oh no," she wailed. "Not your dick again."

"Must you keep trying to kill him?" I muttered.

"You snuck up behind me! I thought I was under attack!"

"By whom? An office-supply thief?"

"I didn't know!"

"I called, but you were too busy dancing and shaking your hips to hear me," I snapped. "I could hear your music blaring."

"Whatever," she replied.

I narrowed my eyes.

"I'll get ice."

She scampered away, back into the supply area, and I heard her open the fridge in there. I sat up, leaning against the desk, and she raced back, tripping over the boxes scattered on the floor, falling. I grabbed at her, lifting my legs, catching her arms to break her fall. But she came down anyway, landing face first in my already tender lap. It wasn't as painful as her knee, but it still made me groan.

She looked up, embarrassed. "I got your ice."

And the door opened, Jessica walking in. I looked up, panicked. Myers stared at her.

"I kneed him in the nuts. I'm trying to help him feel better."

The words hung in the air, and Myers scrambled to sit upright. "I mean, I was getting ice! I fell onto his dick—his lap, I mean. His dick is already sore. I mean—"

Jessica held up her hand. She looked between us, and I had a sense of déjà vu floating in my head. My hands on Myers's breasts. HR showing up. Now, her head on my lap, and once again, HR was witness to it.

Jessica laughed. "Oh my God. You two. I can't. I just can't today." She waved her hand. "I was never here. Figure out your shit, Bane. I'll be back in ten minutes."

And she walked out.

I sat at my desk, the ice bag offering me the relief I needed. When Jessica had walked out, Myers scrambled to her feet, horrified and almost in tears.

"Did I break him?"

I got to my feet. "No. Luckily, your aim was a little off. My thigh took the brunt." Then I ran my hand through my hair. "But seriously, Myers—my dick is starting to think he's on your kill list. First, you try to poison him. Now, you try decapitating the little bugger."

She frowned. "He's not so little."

All I could do was take the ice bag and go to my desk.

Then I put my head down and laughed.

Myers came in with a cup of coffee. "What's so funny?"

"I never realized how dull my life was until you showed up."

"What are you going to say to Jessica?"

"I'm going to tell her the truth. I scared you, you kneed me in the balls, then you tripped. She walked in just as the tripping happened."

"Think she'll buy it?"

"That is exactly what happened, Myers."

"She might not believe it."

"I'm not worried. Even if she thinks there is something between us, she'll stay quiet. She dated Anderson for a year before they married. She knows about privacy."

"She's married to Anderson? But her last name is Aldridge."

"She wanted to keep her maiden name at work. But they've been married for five years. I've known her for six. She'll be fine."

Myers looked doubtful.

"Go home," I encouraged. "Get some things for the weekend, and I'll pick you up. We'll go out for dinner."

"Will you be okay?"

"I'll be fine, Myers. Probably safer than when you're around."

She crossed her arms, making me grin. I liked her angry. She thought she was tough, but the truth was, it reminded me of a chipmunk getting territorial when you got too near his hidden food. All noise and nothing he could do about it. Highly cute, but harmless.

Well, my dick might not agree with the harmless assessment.

"Go. I'll see you soon."

She hesitated, then lunged forward, kissing me. I caught her around the waist and kissed her back.

"Go, little assassin. I'll call when we're getting close."

She left, and it made me laugh to realize I hated that she did.

I was truly fucked.

CHAPTER SIXTEEN

Magnolia

I was anxious by the time Bane texted me to say he was on the way. When he knocked on the door a short time later, I let him in, my nerves kicking into high gear.

"Hi," I said.

He stepped in. "Ready?"

"Are you sure you want me to come stay with you?"

He studied me for a moment, then came closer, cupping my cheek. "Totally."

"Are you, ah, is everything okay?"

He pulled me against him, threading his fingers through my hair and kissing me. I gasped at the intensity of his caress, his tongue entering my mouth with no hesitation and taking control. He kissed me until I was breathless, grasping his shoulders for support. His erection was trapped between us, and he ground it against me.

"Doesn't that feel as if everything is okay?" he murmured into my ear. "I want you, Myers. I want you in my space. My bed. If you don't want that, tell me and I'll go."

"I do. I was worried..."

"I'm fine," he assured me with a droll wink. "And I've learned my lesson. No condoms, no sneak attacks."

"I'm sorry," I whispered.

He stroked my face. "No apologies needed. It's done. Now, we move forward. And I want to enjoy a couple of days with you, just being Alex and Magnolia. Okay?"

"Okay."

"Great. I'll get your bag, and we'll start."

Bane

We held hands in the car, Myers—Magnolia—staring out the window as we slowly drove to my condo in the heavy late-afternoon Friday traffic. She was quiet, seemingly lost in thought. I stared at her profile, noting the delicate point of her chin, how tiny her earlobes were. The little mass of freckles behind the one turned in my direction. I would have to investigate both thoroughly when we were alone.

"Amazing how long it takes to get from my place to yours, even though we're really not that far apart," she mused. "I could probably power walk it faster."

"As long as your lumberjack outfit wasn't tripping you up."

She giggle-snorted. "Whatever, Bane."

I tugged her from the window, wrapping my arm around her and kissing her sweet mouth. "Alex," I admonished. "We're Alex and Magnolia."

"Alex," she repeated, her voice breathless.

I bent and captured her mouth, kissing her until we were both dizzy. I wasn't sure I would ever be able to kiss her enough. Her mouth was a temptation I couldn't resist. She was a temptation I didn't want to resist anymore.

Darryl pulled up to the building, clearing his throat. "Have a good weekend, sir."

I slid from the car, taking Magnolia's hand and grabbing

her bag. "See you Monday."

"Of course."

In the condo, Magnolia looked around, still curious. I carried her bag to the bedroom, changing into more casual attire. I found her in the kitchen, peeking into cupboards. I sat on one of the stools, watching her.

"Not much to cook with," she observed.

"I didn't plan on making you cook. Where would you like to go for dinner?" I asked.

"Pizza?" she asked hopefully.

"Really?"

"I love pizza, and it's a treat I don't get very often."

"Pizza it is. There is a little place a few blocks away I like."

"Okay."

She came closer, smiling at me. "I like your outfit. You look very handsome. Casual but stylish."

I chuckled. "I can dress down. I don't always wear a suit."

She frowned. "I was sure you slept in one."

I tugged her close. "You slept with me, Magnolia. You know the only suit I wear to bed is my birthday one."

"Oh, I thought that was a special occasion. I assumed you got up in the morning looking perfect and ready for the day."

I laughed and swatted her ass. "Enough of your sass. Let's go to dinner."

Enzo's was busy, but we got a table near the back. I ordered a bottle of wine, and we argued over pizza toppings, deciding to get two smaller ones rather than one large. I added a salad, and as we waited for dinner, we chatted about various things.

"Will you go see your father on Sunday?" I asked.

"Yes."

"May I go with you?"

She frowned, took a sip of her wine, then met my eyes. "You really want to do that?"

I took her hand that had begun to fidget with the edge of the tablecloth. I lifted it to my mouth and kissed the tips of her fingers. "You start tearing at things with your fingers when you're nervous."

"I always have. I used to tear my napkins under the table or shred a little piece of paper under my desk at school to help me stay calm."

"Why does it make you nervous about me meeting your dad?"

"He might be having an off day. I don't want you to think badly of him. He's truly a lovely man."

The love she had for her father tugged at something in my chest. I could hear her pain beneath her words.

"How about I take you, and if he isn't up to it, I'll go do something else while you visit. If it's an okay day, I'll come in."

Her eyes lit up. "That would be great."

The pizza arrived, and we dove into dinner. I laughed at her combo, teasing her about a total salt fest on her sausage, bacon, olives, and extra cheese pizza. She informed me my goat cheese, ham, and asparagus was snooty. We both tried a slice of the other's pizza, and I grudgingly had to admit hers was better. It tasted like pizza. The one I ordered was delicious but, as she pointed out, a great appetizer, not pizza. She let me finish hers off, deciding mine would make a great snack for later. We shared some tiramisu and sipped lattes, enjoying the cozy ambiance.

She took a sip and I grinned. "You have some foam by your mouth."

She swiped at it, missing it entirely. I leaned closer,

MELANIE MORELAND

wrapping my hand around her neck and pulling her to my mouth. I kissed away the foam, then took her mouth, tasting her latte and the sweet dessert. I sat back, shaking my head in wonder.

"Thank you," I breathed out.

"For being a messy coffee drinker?"

"No. For being you." I lifted my hands, indicating the restaurant. "For this."

"I don't follow."

I took a sip of latte and offered her the last mouthful of tiramisu. After I fed it to her, I licked the spoon and set it aside. I sighed as I gathered my thoughts.

"The last woman I dated was one of my mother's 'suggestions.' This woman was supposedly 'perfect for me.' She was, in fact, the exact opposite."

"How?" Magnolia asked, cupping her face, with her elbow on the table and looking genuinely curious. "I thought I'd be your exact opposite."

"You are—which makes you perfect."

"Explain."

"This woman was a socialite. She wanted the lifestyle that comes with it. She had a job in her father's company. An office she'd been given that she went into on occasion to say she worked, when the truth was, she spent all her time on social media, posting about her hair and clothing. The first dinner I took her to, she suggested the restaurant. The food was passable at best to me, what little of it there was on the plate. But she could be *seen*, and she made sure she was. That *we* were seen. The bill came and it was over five hundred bucks, and I was still starving."

"Ah."

"All she talked about was herself. What she liked. Wanted. Thought. I tried to give her the benefit of the doubt. I thought she was nervous." I shook my head as I laughed. "I was so wrong."

"What happened?"

"I saw her three times over two weeks. Each restaurant was progressively more expensive. More 'visible.' Acceptable by her standards. By the third date, she was basically telling people we were getting engaged. I was planning on telling her I was breaking it off. All she wanted was my money and my name. Not me. I could have been anyone. In fact, I was quite certain, if she had to, she couldn't pick me out of a lineup."

Magnolia rolled her eyes. "That's a stretch. You are far too good-looking for anyone not to notice, Alex."

"She didn't," I insisted. "She was too busy on her phone, not eating the specks of food they put on the plate, visiting other tables, dropping my name, to bother trying to get to know me."

Magnolia frowned. "What did she do when you broke it off?"

"She told me it was a big mistake. That we could help each other. I could give her the lifestyle she wanted, and she would make sure, despite my lack of charm, that I would be one of the A-listers. We could be a power couple." I drained my latte. "She wasn't happy when I told her I preferred to be on my own and unplugged from power."

"Oh dear," Magnolia murmured.

"You're so easy, Magnolia," I murmured. "You talk to me. Listen to me. You want to eat pizza and relax. You don't fill my head with mundane details about other people's lives and how I should be emulating them. You let me be me." I tilted my head, studying her. "And I like the Alex I am when I'm with you."

"That might be the nicest thing you've ever said to me."

I leaned close and kissed her. "I'll try harder."

I kissed her again. "Ready to go home?"

"Yes."

We strolled toward the condo, Magnolia tucked tight to my side. I carried the pizza box in my other hand. It was dark, the air cool, and she shivered.

"Cold?" I asked. "Do you want my jacket?"

"No, I'm fine."

"We'll be home in five minutes, if those little legs of yours can pick up the pace."

She laughed, and we moved a little faster. But she faltered, and I stopped. "What?"

"Did you hear that?"

"Hear what?"

A strange noise was coming from the shadows. It sounded plaintive and sad.

"That. It sounds like... Oh my God! It is!"

I blinked, unsure what I was looking at. From the dark corner of the building, a little object rushed toward us, almost bleating as it came closer.

"It's a kitten," Magnolia exclaimed, bending and making a little clicking noise in her throat. The creature moved faster and, before I could object, launched itself at me, climbing my pants and jacket, right up to my chest, and burrowing into the fabric. It was wet and dirty, and its claws dug into my skin.

"Get it off me, Myers," I ordered.

"No, it likes you," she replied, not at all put out by my tone. She reached up, scratching the cat's furry head. "Where did you come from?"

"Wherever it was, go back," I demanded.

"Stop it, Bane. Obviously, it's alone and scared." She clasped her hands, peering up at me. "And it chose you!"

I attempted to dislodge the cat's claws, pushing the pizza box into Myers's hands. But the cat wouldn't have it, burrowing closer and digging its claws in deeper.

"What do we do now?" I asked, exasperated. "I can't get it off."

"We take the kitten home," she said in a tone that implied I was an idiot for not understanding this course of action.

"No."

She walked away, muttering. "We'll need a few things."

"Magnolia—Myers—stop walking!"

She kept talking and walking. "I'll make a list. You'll have to go to the store."

I hurried to catch up to her, for some reason holding the kitten in place. "We are not keeping this thing."

She looked at me, surprised. "No, we're not."

I felt relief that she understood. "Great."

"You are," she said with a smirk. "The kitten picked you."

And she turned and walked away.

After a moment, I followed.

In the condo, Magnolia faced me, holding out her hands. "Give him to me."

"It's a him?"

She shrugged. "Fifty-fifty chance. I'll find out soon."

I looked down. "He's sleeping." Then I grimaced. "He's filthy."

"Probably covered in fleas too."

"Get him off me."

She chuckled and held up a finger. "Wait."

She disappeared for a few moments, and I looked at the kitten. I couldn't even tell what color it was. The fur was matted and stuck up all over its body in little spikes. He was thin, and when his eyes opened, they were a dull green. Unsure what to do, I used my index finger and tapped his head. "Hi."

The noise it made was strange. It sounded like a tiny squeak, followed by a motor running.

Was he sick? Broken?

The kitten shut its eyes and kept making the odd noise with a little bleat breaking up the constant hum.

Magnolia appeared, a piece of paper in one hand, a towel in the other.

"It's making a funny noise," I informed her. "I think it's sick."

She leaned in and grinned. "He's purring. He's happy."

"Why?"

"Because he knows he's safe."

I opened my mouth to speak, but she interrupted me.

"You have a choice," she informed me. "Bathe him or go to the store."

"How about we put him back outside?"

"Not even funny, Bane."

I plucked the list from her hand. "Fine, Myers. But he's out of here when the shelter opens up in the morning."

"We'll see." She managed to remove his claws from my shirt, and she bundled him in the towel. "There is a pet store one block over. I called, and they're open. They're waiting for you. Hurry."

I looked at the list in my hand. "Seriously? For one night?"

She rolled her eyes. "Accept it, Bane." Then she grinned. "It's me and the kitten—or the socialite and the five-hundred-dollar dinners."

I waved the list. "You owe me."

She grinned. "Hurry. He needs food."

And for some reason, I did exactly as she told me.

I had no idea I lived that close to a pet store. Or that kittens needed so much stuff. The owners helped me out, and when I couldn't answer the questions, I called Myers and she talked to them. As I was waiting, I spied a fuzzy little tepee-looking structure.

"What is that?" I asked.

"For the cat to sleep in. Unless, of course, you have one?"

"No."

"We don't recommend they sleep on a bed. Too high for them. And they like the comfort of being closed in. It makes them feel safe."

Thinking how cold the kitten had felt when I first touched it, I plucked the tent off the shelf and added it to the pile.

Besides, there was only one pussy sleeping in my bed tonight, and it wasn't the little ruffian who had claimed me as his own.

I walked into the condo, hearing Myers cooing and talking

softly.

"Who is such a handsome boy? So cute! Look at that fur!"

I walked into the kitchen, finding her holding the kitten. She met my eyes. "Congratulations, Daddy! It's a boy!"

I snorted. "Not his daddy. And he isn't staying." Then I dumped the bags on the counter. "All this goes with him tomorrow."

She ignored me, pushing the kitten at me. Having no choice, I took him. Even with his fur damp, I could see the ginger color beginning to show. He snuggled into my chest again, making that purring sound. Absently, I stroked his head, mimicking the actions I had seen Myers make. I watched her mix up some mushy stuff and add a bit of horrendous-smelling food from a can into it.

"I think he is about seven, maybe eight weeks old," she muttered, taking him from my hand and setting him in front of the food. "Oh, he is so hungry!" she exclaimed then laughed as he began to eat, supposedly so famished that he set his front paws in the dish, making growly noises as he devoured the wet mess in front of him.

"So much for the bath," I observed, my lips pulling into a grin without my realizing it.

"I can clean his paws." She dug through the bag and got out some other items, then clapped her hands in delight over the little bed. "He'll love it!" She met my eyes. "What will we name him?"

I rolled my eyes. "How about Goodbye? Because that is where he's going tomorrow. I'm going to change my shirt." I left the kitchen, shaking my head.

As if I was going to keep a cat. I had never had a pet my entire life. I had no idea how to care for one or what to do with it.

Now, I simply had to convince Myers of that fact.

CHAPTER SEVENTEEN

Bane

I walked into the guest room, drying off my hair. Magnolia was on the floor, the kitten sitting on her shoulder as she opened a bag of litter, pouring it into a small pan that I had carried home. When the kitten opened his eyes and saw me, he jumped down, running over and climbing up my leg. I hissed as his sharp little claws dug into my skin, and he curled into my chest as I stopped his trek up my torso. He was purring loudly, making Magnolia chuckle.

"He already loves you. He knows you saved him."

"He's going to the shelter. I don't do pets. Or you can have him."

She stood, shaking her head. "The owners of the house have strict rules. She is highly allergic to cats. I can't take him. You have to keep him, Alex."

"I'm too busy to look after a cat."

"Cats are very independent. He'll settle in here where he is safe and quiet."

"And scratch my furniture and destroy my things."

"You can train him."

"Shelter."

She looked sad but stopped arguing.

I walked over to the little tepee thing, lifting the kitten

down and sliding him in the opening. He sniffed around, then curled up, immediately shutting his eyes.

"There. He's safe. You have food for him, a litter thing, and some toys. He'll be fine." I stood, holding out my hand. "Bed. Now, Magnolia."

She walked past me, and I followed.

"Leave the light on," she instructed.

I did as she asked, even though I rolled my eyes. I did stop before shutting the door, peeking at the kitten. He was curled into a ball, seemingly content. I had an odd feeling as I left the room, but I convinced myself it was simply because I felt unsettled at the thought of an animal in my house.

In my room, I heard Magnolia in the en suite, and I lay on the bed, waiting for her. This wasn't how I planned the evening to go. By now, we should be on round two. Maybe three. Not caring for a stray and at odds about its future.

Magnolia came out, wearing a shirt I'd left on the back of the door. I patted the bed. "Come here, darling."

She hesitated but did as I asked and crawled into bed, letting me pull her close. I pressed a kiss to her neck, ghosting my mouth up and down the silky skin. She hummed in pleasure as I flicked her lobe, nuzzling the sensitive skin behind her ear.

"You mad at me?" I whispered.

"Maybe a little."

"Kitten is safe and warm and fed," I reminded her. "They'll find him a home where he is loved."

"He is so cute. And a ginger."

"He looks like a hedgehog. His fur sticks up everywhere."

"I know. It's cute."

"I have a demanding job, Magnolia. I travel. He'd be alone."

"I know."

"I have never had a pet. I have no desire to have one."

"Okay." The one word was laced with sadness.

I sighed, knowing I had just eliminated sex from the agenda tonight. I pulled her close, brushing her hair off her cheek and burying my face into the thick locks. "Your hair always smells so good."

I nuzzled behind her ear, tightening my arm around her waist. "So does your skin."

"You always smell good too," she whispered, trailing her fingers up and down my forearm.

"Yeah?" I whispered back.

"Sometimes, I want to lick you."

"Jesus," I muttered. Between her scent, her closeness, and her simple words, I was hard as a rock. And she seemed open to the idea of being closer. Maybe sex wasn't off the table. "I'm trying to be a gentleman here. Offer you affection."

She rolled over so we were almost nose to nose on the pillow. "You can offer me affection."

"I want to offer my cock too."

She pressed her lips to mine. "Accepted."

I woke up, Magnolia nestled against me. Our fingers were entwined, her back pressed to my chest. I was holding her tight. I lifted my head, squinting at the clock. It was only two, but something had woken me up. Hearing nothing, I relaxed back onto the pillow, shutting my eyes.

Then I heard it.

A plaintive, quiet little meow. Then another.

I carefully sat up, pulling my arm out from under Magnolia. I grabbed my boxers from the floor where I had tossed them earlier, and I went to the guest room, opening the door and stepping in. On seeing me, the kitten raced over, meowing and moving quickly. I dipped, lifting him before he used my skin as a climbing wall. He began to purr loudly, making little noises that made me smile.

"What's up, little man?"

I checked out his area. He still had food and water. His bed was in place. The litter box was right there. The toys I had added that the pet shop recommended were sitting on the floor. Perplexed, I bent, slipping him into the tepee. "Go back to sleep."

I turned to walk away, but he was right there. By my feet, his strangely large paws on my toes. He meowed again, this time louder.

I bent and scooped him up. "I don't know what you want."

I slid him back into his bed and tossed in a toy to keep him company, but a few steps later, he was back at my feet, crying. I tried twice more, but he insisted on following me. Finally frustrated, I carried him into my room and crawled into bed, snapping on the light and waking up Magnolia.

"Magnolia, the kitten keeps crying."

"He's lonely and scared in there," she mumbled and went back to sleep.

I poked her. "Myers." Then again. *"Myers."*

She kept sleeping.

I looked at him and he at me, each studying the other.

"Pee in my bed and I will put you back where I found you," I threatened. "And it's only for a while."

I lay down, and the kitten crawled beside me on the pillow,

burrowing into my neck. He made an odd motion with his paws, almost tapping at me with them, then curled up, purring loudly in my ear. "Don't get comfortable. You're going back in the other room soon."

Magnolia shifted, draping herself over my chest. Her hair tickled my nose. The kitten's fur tickled my ear. I shut my eyes.

When had this become my life?

Magnolia

I woke up, something irritating my nose. I opened my eyes and turned my head, a smile immediately stretching my lips. Alex was asleep, and curled up on his pillow was the kitten. His paws rested on Alex's mouth, and his tail had been on my face. Both of them looked at peace and comfy. Too comfy to wake up.

I recalled Alex's voice in the night telling me the kitten was crying. What I had said, I had no idea, but somehow the kitten had ended up here with us and had slept with Alex the entire time.

I desperately wanted a picture. I had my phone plugged in on the nightstand, and I carefully reached over and grabbed it, taking a few shots.

The two of them were probably the most adorable thing I had ever seen.

Alex would hate it.

My smile died when I thought about what Alex had said about the kitten going to the shelter today. I understood his position, but I still hated it.

As I watched, the kitten stretched, then curled up again, burrowing into Alex, half draped across his face. I had to bite back my laughter as Alex's eyes fluttered open and he looked at the kitten, then me. His gaze fell back to the kitten, and he rolled his eyes.

"Not the pussy I wanted to find on my face this morning," he grumped.

I gasped at his words, then laughed. The kitten jumped, raising his head and looking at me as if to tell me I had disturbed his sleep. He nestled back into Alex, who frowned. "I only meant to let him stay for a few minutes. I must have fallen asleep."

"You two look so cute together."

He snorted. "Don't get used to it."

He rolled out of bed, ignoring the little meow of protest from his pillow, and headed to the en suite, coming out a few moments later. The whole time he was gone, the little kitten perched on the end of the bed as if waiting for him. When he came out, the kitten meowed loudly in greeting, and Alex looked askance.

"What does he want?"

I slid from the bed, attempting to tame my hair. "You."

He scoffed. "He's getting a one-way trip back to his room. I need coffee and a phone number for the shelter."

I picked up the kitten, pleased when he curled into my arms. "I'll make the coffee."

I brushed past Alex and took the kitten to the room next door, showing him the food. He immediately attacked it, and I left him to go make coffee.

Alex appeared as I was pouring, and he took his mug, taking a large sip. "You do make the best coffee." He studied me. "What?"

"Can we at least take him to a no-kill shelter?" I asked, my voice catching.

"What?"

I repeated myself, and he frowned. "So, if no one came to adopt him, they would..." He trailed off.

"Yes."

"But kittens are always wanted."

"If that was the case, we wouldn't have found him outside in the dark."

Just then, the kitten ran into the kitchen, meowing loudly. Alex frowned and bent to pick him up, not objecting when the kitten attached himself to his shoulder, burrowing into his neck. He took his cup of coffee and left the room.

I knew the look on his face. The stubborn, I-will-handle-this expression. He got it at the office several times a day.

I sat on the sofa and drank my coffee. When he reappeared, he was dressed, the kitten held in his hand against his chest, the other hand holding a bag that I knew contained the things we'd bought the kitten. "I found a place."

"Okay."

"I'm taking him now."

I felt the tears building, which was crazy. But I nodded. "I can't—" I whispered.

"I know. Darryl is coming. I'll be back." He paused. "Will you be here?"

"Yes. I understand, Alex. I'm just being—" I couldn't finish my sentence.

He bent and kissed my forehead. "You're being Magnolia. Tender and sweet. I understand too, but I have to do this."

I was silent as he left, letting the tears fall. While he was making calls, I had tried to find someone to take the kitten but got nowhere. I hoped someone would adopt him. He was a crazy-looking little thing with big paws, the orange fur that stood up all over his head, and his big green eyes.

Surely someone would see that and how adorable he was and would adopt him.

Right?

♡♡♡

To stay busy, I made muffins. I had brought the ingredients with me, and I needed to keep my mind off what was happening.

I heard the door open as I was taking the muffins from the oven and heard the footsteps behind me.

"Those smell good."

I drew in a deep breath and forced a smile to my face as I turned. I was shocked to see the kitten on Alex's shoulder. He met my confused look with a small smile.

"I tried, Magnolia," he said with a shrug. "I got to the shelter, and I was talking to the woman at the counter. I explained the situation, and she was very nice. I started to fill out the forms, and I turned my head to look at him—" he paused, swallowed, then continued "—and he licked my cheek, as if he was saying it was okay. But I felt him trembling like the way he did when he found us last night. And the shelter was full of cats and kittens. He was going to be there a long time. I knew it. So I couldn't leave him."

I clasped my hands, letting the tears fall. Alex didn't understand what this meant. It wasn't only about keeping the kitten. It was the fact that he was bonding with him. Allowing himself to feel.

"But you have to help. He's not just mine. He's ours."

My heart thrilled at his words. "I will."

"I leave Monday. You have to stay here."

"Okay."

"Don't let Hedge scratch my furniture."

"What?"

"Don't let—"

"You named him Hedge?"

"Hedgehog Hedgefund, actually. I have a feeling he is gonna cost me. But he is too little for that, so we settled on Hedge."

"Alex, he's a cat."

"You pointed out he looks like a hedgehog. It suits him, and he likes it. Right, Hedge?" he asked, turning his face and speaking to the kitten.

The kitten, or Hedge, opened his eyes and licked Alex's cheek, as if in agreement. I tried not to squeal at the cuteness level. I had a feeling Alex wouldn't like it.

"I need a coffee. And a muffin."

"I'll bring both to the table."

"Okay. I'll put Hedge in his room, and we're going over the rules. I've already had that conversation with him, but I'll reiterate it again later."

I bit my lip. "Um, okay."

"What?"

"You know Hedgy is a cat, right? They don't really understand a list of rules."

"Hedge," he corrected. "And he is very clever." He flashed a grin. "He found me, didn't he? He could have chosen anyone else, but he waited until we were there and he came to us. To me."

Then he strode from the kitchen, quite proud of himself.

I chuckled to myself. This was going to be fun.

♡♡♡

Twice while we had coffee, Hedgy appeared, climbing Alex's leg and jumping to his shoulder. I listened to Alex's lecture on proper behavior and the rules, trying not to laugh but failing when he scolded Hedgy a second time and told him to go to his room and behave.

"What now?" Alex huffed at me.

"Hedgy is a cat, Alex. They don't do rules or understand what you're saying. All he wants is to be close to you."

He plucked Hedgy off his shoulder, placing him on my lap. "He needs to get used to you."

"He will, but he loves you. You saved him."

A strange look passed over his face, but I didn't ask him what he was thinking. I wasn't sure I wanted to know.

"I was going to take you out to dinner."

"That's fine. We'll put him in his room, and when it's quiet, he'll go to sleep."

"I have a little work to do as well."

"No problem. I brought my knitting with me. The hospital told me they need more blankets."

"Blankets?"

"I knit little blankets and beanies for preemies. I'll whip a few up this week and take them over."

He furrowed his brow. "So, you knit, paint, and sew."

"Old-fashioned endeavors, but I like to stay busy."

"You like old-fashioned things."

"I do. My favorite is remaking my grandmother's clothes to wear."

He sat back, letting Hedgy crawl into his lap and stroking his head. "Like your sexy blouses," he confirmed.

MELANIE MORELAND

"Yes. And some of her skirts. She was taller than me, so I have to adjust the sleeves and hems. I got her curves, though."

He leaned over and kissed me. "I like those curves."

I sighed. "The bullying thing starts while you're away."

"Are you nervous?"

"No. The little group is ignoring me and Rylee now, which is a relief. They stay away from us."

"I have it on good authority that Verity may be leaving the firm."

"Oh?"

"Laura told me she had a reference call about her. Her work is fine, so she gave her a positive one. I hope she moves on. I'd be happy to get her out of the office. Maybe once she's gone, the others will grow up some." He tickled Hedgy's chin. "I still think the courses are good for everyone, but it pleases me to think she won't be around to torment you." He lifted his eyes to mine. "You don't deserve that."

"No one does."

"You, especially."

"Why?"

He frowned. "Because of who you are, Magnolia. Everyone likes you. You're kind, conscientious, good at your job. You care for those around you. That should be celebrated, not ridiculed."

I smiled at his words. "Is that your professional or personal opinion?"

"Professional. My personal one is much more...personal."

"Oh?"

He grinned, setting Hedgy on the sofa beside him and pulling me onto his lap so I straddled him.

"You're everything I said before, but also sexy, funny,

211

witty. Exasperating. Sexy."

"You already said that."

"It stands being repeated. I have never wanted a woman as much as I want you. You're on my mind constantly."

I linked my arms around his neck. "Is that a fact?"

He kissed me, nuzzling my lips softly. "Yes, it is. Undisputed."

Our gazes locked, the heat between us building. His grip on my hips tightened, his erection growing between us. He pulled me closer, covering my mouth, stroking my tongue with his. I whimpered as he cupped my ass, then I giggled as a small ball of fur wiggled between us, meowing and purring as he crawled up to Alex's shoulder. For a moment, Alex stilled, his head thrown back as he found his patience.

"Is that what is going to happen from now on? Cockblocked by a cat?" he asked dryly.

I slid from his knee. "I'll put him in his room. Go do your work."

"I'd rather do you."

I winked. "Something to look forward to."

He grumbled all the way to his office. I fed and petted the kitten, but as soon as I put Hedgy down, he raced to the open door, disappearing down the hall, and I heard Alex's admonishing. "No! Down! Hedge, I said—dammit, stop licking my face and making that infernal noise."

A few moments later, I peeked in then left them alone. Hedgy was on Alex's shoulder, his eyes already shut. Alex had given up and was working on his laptop. Hedgy looked happy. Alex looked resigned.

But I noticed he didn't call me to come and take him.

CHAPTER EIGHTEEN

Magnolia

"Have I mentioned you look beautiful tonight?" Alex asked, staring at me across the table.

"Not in the last few moments," I replied with a smile. He had been very vocal since I appeared in the living room, dressed for our date.

"Remiss of me. You are gorgeous. I love the dress."

I smoothed the silk down my arm. "Thank you."

"The color is spectacular."

"I don't wear red often."

"You should. And I can hardly wait to see it on the floor by my bed." He paused with a wink. "If we make it that far. The living room might be as much as I can stand."

"Stop it," I murmured, loving every second of it.

"Where's the zipper?"

"What?"

"The zipper. It's pretty, and I don't want to rip it."

"Left side."

"Gotcha." He picked up the menu. "So, before I get dessert, I need to feed you. What looks good?" He peered over the heavy paper. "Besides you?"

"I think I need protein."

"Great idea. Steak for two, it is."

We were almost finished dessert when a man approached the table. As soon as Alex saw him, his shoulders drew back, and I felt his tension. He'd been holding my hand as we finished our coffee, and his grip on it tightened. His face became expressionless.

The man stopped, his voice falsely surprised. He held out his hand. "Alexander. How nice to see you."

Alex pursed his lips, looking at the extended hand. For a moment, I thought he would refuse to shake it, and then he stood and gripped the proffered hand briefly. "Terry," he muttered.

I stared in surprise. This was the stepbrother.

"Are you going to introduce us?" Terry asked, indicating me.

"I'd rather not. But, Magnolia, this is Terry."

He held out his hand. "His brother."

"Stepbrother," Alex corrected.

I took Terry's hand, trying not to grimace at his clammy palm. He was decent-looking but lacked Alex's finesse and image. His chin was weaker, his eyes too close together, and his suit didn't fit him the way Alex's skimmed his body. His hair was dark but receding, and his skin had a reddish tinge.

"Surprised to see you out and about," Terry said. "Not holed up playing in the dirt."

I couldn't help my eye roll. What was it with his family?

"What are you doing here, Terry?" Alex asked, ignoring his words.

"Having dinner, of course. My date for the evening is in the ladies' room."

"For the evening?" Alex echoed. "Is that all they can stand to be with you?"

Terry narrowed his eyes. "I don't like to be tied down."

I wanted to laugh. Terry looked between us, a gleeful, evil smile pulling on his lips. "Wait. Didn't Mother tell me your new secretary's name was Magnolia? Fucking the assistant, are we, Alexander?"

Alex flung his napkin on the table and stepped close to Terry. "One more word, Terry, and I'll take you out back and teach you a lesson you'll never forget. Apologize to the lady." He paused, his hands fisted into his sides. *"Now."*

"Touch me, and I'll sue you."

"Turn and leave. Or risk me doing more than touching you. Once I'm finished, they'll be burying you in one of those piles of dirt you think I play in." He leaned close and said something.

Terry blanched, stepped back, and shook his head. "Never able to take a joke, were you, brother?"

The two men glared at each other, their animosity evident. I stood. "Alex, can we go?"

He was at my side immediately. "Of course."

We turned to walk away when Terry called out. "I'll tell Mother we ran into each other."

"Shame you didn't run over him instead," I observed.

Alex looked down at me and started to laugh. He tucked me tight to his side. "Ah, Magnolia. Thank you for that."

I snuggled closer. I loved making him laugh.

I slept in the next morning, waking up when the mattress dipped and Alex pressed a kiss to my forehead. "Morning, sleepyhead."

I blinked in the bright morning light. I grinned at Alex, his ever-present hump on his shoulder. "My boys behaving themselves?"

Alex chuckled. "I made coffee. It was shit. I need one of yours." He reached up, tickling Hedgy. "And the kitten is coming to visit your dad with us. I called the facility, and they said he was allowed. You told me once your dad liked animals."

"Oh."

He bent and kissed me. "Same rules apply. If it's not a good day, I'll leave."

"Okay."

I was nervous when we arrived. Dad was sitting in his room, looking out the window. He smiled when we walked in, a rare real smile. "Hey, Maggie Mae."

I threw my arms around him, hugging him, and felt him return my embrace. "Hi, Dad."

I pulled back, trying to tamp down my emotions. I wiped at my eyes. "Dad, this is my, ah..." I faltered, but Alex stepped beside me.

"Hello, sir. I'm Alex, Magnolia's boyfriend."

"Alex," Dad greeted him, far more distracted by the ball of fluff in his hand. "Who is that?"

"Hedgehog."

Dad frowned. "Odd name, but it suits him."

Alex sat beside him, letting Dad stroke Hedgy, who was content in Alex's hands. "That's what I said. Magnolia here isn't impressed."

Dad looked at him. "Takes a lot to impress her."

Alex nodded sagely. "I'm trying. Maybe you can give me a few hints."

My dad laughed. "Son, you need to figure that out on your own." Dad looked between us. "But I think you're doing okay."

Alex met my eyes with a wink. "I hope so, sir."

Dad chuckled. "Enough of the sir. You can call me Dan." He paused, scratching the kitten under the chin. "How did you meet?"

Alex cleared his throat. "At the office." He hesitated. "I'm her boss."

Dad looked between us. "You think so, do you? I always thought I was the boss too. Maggie Mae allowed me to think so."

Alex looked nonplussed.

Dad chuckled. "You'll figure it out. Eventually."

"I brought you muffins, Dad," I said, trying not to cry at the sight of the three of them. By now, Hedgy had crawled onto Dad's lap and up to his chest. Dad was holding him with one hand, stroking him with the other, and Alex was watching them carefully, ready to grab either one if needed.

"Tea?" he asked hopefully.

"I'll go make us some." I stopped in the doorway, looking back at them.

"Now tell me, Alex. What do you do in your office where you're the boss?"

"Landscape architect."

"Impressive. You serious about my daughter?"

Alex glanced my way. "I am."

"Good."

I left them to their chat.

♡♡♡

We had Chinese for dinner. I was quiet as we ate, and Alex reached across the table, taking my hand. "Are you okay, Magnolia?"

"I'm good. Always a little sad to leave him when he is doing well."

He nodded in understanding. "He loves you a lot."

"You were very good with him."

"He's very intelligent and easy to talk to. I'm glad I got to meet him." He paused. "He's older than I expected."

"He was forty when they had me."

"Ah, a late baby."

"I was a bit of a surprise." I grinned at him. "And he loved Hedgy."

Alex laughed. "Hedgy loved the treats Dan kept feeding him. Little traitor can be bought with food."

"What were the two of you talking about so seriously when I took the tray back?"

He grinned. "Private."

I rolled my eyes. "Better than the encounter last night."

He frowned. "I'm sorry about that. Terry is rude and has no manners."

"You dislike him intensely."

"I dislike what he represents. Lies, injustice, and a superior attitude that he is better than everyone." His face darkened. "And I disliked what came out of his mouth."

"I didn't care."

"I did. He's vulgar and crude. He thinks money gives you class. He's wrong. You have more class in your pinkie finger than he'll ever hope to have." He paused. "Not that I'm saying—"

I laughed. "It's fine, Alex. I'm not wealthy. I am well aware of that. I never have been, but I'm happy." I pushed away my plate. "I don't think your wealth has made you very happy."

"No, it hasn't. I saw what it did to my mother. No matter how much she has, she wants more. The same with Terry. Unlike them, I don't judge people on what they possess. I work hard for my money and enjoy the benefits, but it doesn't run my life."

He looked at our hands clasped together on the counter and lifted them to his mouth, kissing my knuckles. "You make me ridiculously happy, Magnolia. More happiness than I have ever known. Without a dime. Your smile alone is worth millions to me."

My breath caught. "Take me to bed, Alex."

He stood and swept me into his arms.

"And that is priceless."

Bane

I opened the hotel door, striding into the suite. It was dark and quiet, reminding me of the days when I opened the door of my condo to the same atmosphere. The past few days, walking into the condo was brighter. Alive.

All because of the presence of Magnolia—and the troublemaker we called Hedgy.

Even I had succumbed to the cute name. It suited the little bugger.

I tossed my suit jacket over the chair and grabbed a water from the fridge, sitting on the sofa and letting my head fall back.

I had only been gone a few days, yet I felt a longing I had never experienced before. It never mattered if I was traveling or home. Each place was the same. A room to sit, a bed to sleep, a desk to work at. But this time, I had someone to miss.

And dammit, I missed Myers. And Magnolia.

Even though they were the same person, to me, they each had a place in my mind and my heart. I missed Myers's presence beside me at a meeting. Her quiet way of handing me the information I needed without asking. Her attention to detail. Her pleasant demeanor. Clients loved her. She was gracious and warm, and she kept me relaxed. Knowing she was there and supporting me was a surprising perk to my working life. She had become indispensable to me. And despite the chaos that occurred on occasion—or perhaps because of it—I couldn't imagine my office without her.

And on the personal side, she was a gift. I hadn't planned on her. She was everything I would have avoided. Sweet, warm, loving. Adorable and endearing. She made me feel things. I laughed more than I could recall ever laughing before over her antics. I worried about her. Missed her when she wasn't around. And I desired her more than I'd ever wanted a woman before her.

I rubbed my eyes, slid my phone from my jacket pocket, and called her. She answered, breathless and sweet.

"Hi!"

I chuckled. "Myers. What are you doing?"

"Hedgy and I were playing hide-and-seek. He's very good at finding me." She squealed, laughing at the same time. "You got me!"

I had to laugh with her. "Put me on video."

We turned on our cameras, and her face filled the screen.

Hedgy was on her shoulder, curled up tight. "He's down for the count," she said with a grin. "I wish I could fall asleep that fast."

"You did the other night," I replied with a smirk. "Once I was done with you."

She rolled her eyes. "Behave. When are you coming home? Did you manage to wrap things up?"

"I will tomorrow morning. Can you change my flights?"

"Hold up."

I watched as she hurried down the hall into my office and sat at my desk. Her face was serious as she tapped on the keyboard, looking at the screen. "There is a flight I can get you on, but again, there is a stopover. A two-hour one in Calgary."

"Still gets me home a day early. Change it. Please," I added.

"How polite."

"Just get me home, Magnolia," I commanded. "I miss you."

There was a pause. "Really?"

"Yes. And book Friday off. I want the whole weekend with you."

"Okay."

"How was the anti-bullying meeting?"

"Very informative. And you were right. Verity gave her notice, and she didn't come to the meeting. Her cohorts were a lot more pleasant."

"Group mentality," I agreed.

"Yes."

Magnolia yawned, and I glanced at the clock. "I have an eight p.m. dinner. You'll be asleep by the time it's over. I'll call you from the airport. I got the new flight information."

"I'm glad you're coming home a day early."

"Me too." I paused. "Be waiting for me."
"I will."

The hours dragged until flight time the next day. The flight was delayed for an hour, and I sipped a coffee and sent Myers a text to pass the time.

> *I hope you're ready for me, baby. I've been missing you something fierce.*

Oh yeah? she replied with a smiling emoji.

> *Yeah. My flight lands at 8. I'll be at my place by 8:30. Be naked and waiting in my bed for me.*

I book your flights, Bane. I know what time you land. No way you'll make it there by 8:30—it'll be 9. I'll get warmed up.

> *DON'T YOU DARE. That pussy is mine.*

I should be affronted at your possessiveness. Yet I am not. I shaved.

> *Thanks for that visual.*

E v e r y w h e r e.

> *Jesus. Now I'm in the airport lounge,*

*sporting a hard-on. I can't stand, or I'll
scare the nice old lady across from me.*

*Maybe she'd enjoy the show. Give her one
of your sexy winks.*

My winks are sexy?

*Everything about you is. I'll prove it when
you get back. I'll make sure my lips are
super smooth. All of them.*

*My cock just jumped and hit the table. I
think the old lady knows you're sexting
me.*

You started it.

And I'll finish it. Naked by 9.

Sounds like a shootout in the O.K. Corral.

*Oh, Myers, there will be lots of shootouts.
Just a different kind.*

Be ready.

CHAPTER NINETEEN

Bane

Due to a storm, my last flight was late leaving, and my layover became four hours. By the time the car pulled up to the condo, it was well past one in the morning.

"I won't need you until Monday," I informed Darryl.

He looked surprised. "You're taking a day off?"

"I am."

He smiled. "Very good. Have a nice weekend."

In the elevator, I was impatient. I opened the door of the condo, struck once again with the odd feeling of knowing someone was waiting for me. I found Magnolia on the sofa, curled up, Hedgy sleeping on her hip. He woke, seeing me, standing and stretching, offering me a little meow. I picked him up, amused how he burrowed into me. I sat on the coffee table, staring at Magnolia. She was in one of my T-shirts, her hair a dark swath on the leather around her face. She had one hand tucked under her cheek, and she looked comfortable.

I had been half hard all the way home, planning on fucking her as soon as I walked in the door. But when I looked at her, a wave of tenderness washed over me. The need to look after her, care for her, overrode any physical desires I had been feeling. I carefully scooped her off the sofa, carrying her to my room and laying her on the bed. She stirred, her eyes fluttering open and a sweet smile curving her lips.

"You're home," she whispered.

I pressed a kiss to her head. "I am. Go back to sleep. I'll be right there."

With a quiet sigh, she shut her eyes. I headed to the en suite and had a fast shower, feeling better once the heat hit my tired muscles. Back in my room, I had to smile at the sight. Magnolia curled up on her side and on the pillow draped over her head, Hedgy.

I chuckled as I slid in beside her, and she nestled against me. The kitten immediately got up, walked over, turned around, and nestled into my neck, purring loudly.

My plans were screwed. Nothing I had hoped for was going to happen, yet I was strangely content. A feeling of home filled me—something I had never experienced before now. It was an odd sensation, but I liked it.

I shut my eyes, letting sleep find me.

I woke in the early morning, my body on fire and the incredible awareness of Magnolia's mouth wrapped around my dick, teasing me.

I reached down, grasping her hair in my hands and groaning her name.

She sucked, licking at my shaft.

"Good morning," she breathed out, making me shiver.

"It is now," I gasped as she took me deep, the suction and feel of her throat around me overwhelming.

I tugged on her hair gently. "I missed you." She swallowed around me, and I arched my back off the bed. "I missed this. Do that again, baby. Please."

She did, and I hissed with pleasure.

"You are far too good at that," I rumbled.

She made a sound, the vibration around my dick highlighting the pleasure.

"Straddle me," I demanded. "I want to play with you."

Without releasing me, she moved, straddling my torso as she kept sucking me. She was wet for me, her sweet center drenched and glistening. I teased her clit, and she moaned around my shaft. I played with her, inserting two fingers, using my thumb to strum her hard nub. She pushed back against my fingers, working herself.

"Take what you need, baby," I praised. "Come for me. Suck me until I come. Like that." I pressed my head into the pillow, arching myself closer to her perfect mouth. "Yes. Just. Like. That."

She started to shake, and I sped up my movements. She cupped my balls, teasing them, taking me deeper than I had ever been, and my orgasm hit me. Powerful. Hard. Exploding through me like a volcano, destroying everything in its path. I came in her mouth, groaning her name, praising her, cursing, gripping her hips, and then as she slowly released me, I pulled her to my mouth and returned the favor. Soon, she was crying out, her musky release and wild noises filling my mouth and the room. I locked her down, pinning her to my chest until she was whimpering, begging me, coming a second time before collapsing.

We were breathing heavily. Messy. The bed around us was a disaster. I had knocked over the lamp, pulled the sheets off the mattress, and I had no idea where a couple of the pillows were.

It was perfect.

"Welcome home," she mumbled.

I pressed a kiss to her curvy ass, drawing in the skin and leaving a mark. Why I liked to do that with her, I had no idea, but I did enjoy it.

"Best homecoming ever," I replied.

She rolled off me, turning and curling up on my chest, meeting my eyes. Her eyes were damp, her hair a mess, and her lips swollen. A small trace of come was at the corner of her mouth.

I traced her lips. "Hello, Maggie darling."

She smiled, the expression in her eyes so soft I could have drowned in them.

"Hello, my Alex."

"I missed you."

"Me too."

"Where's Hedgy?"

"I fed him and shut the door. I came back to check on you, and I noticed you had woken up—or at least part of you had. I thought I'd help you out."

"You certainly did."

"You weren't bad yourself."

I chuckled, running my fingers through her hair. "How about a shower, and I'll take you out to breakfast?"

"I'd like that. But you're sure about the office?"

I rolled her over, hovering. "Yes. We're both taking the day off and spending the weekend together."

"Oh. I thought I'd be going home today."

I bent and kissed her. "No." It took everything in me not to tell her she was home. I wasn't ready for that conversation.

Yet.

She wrapped her arms around my neck. "Okay."

I had never known a weekend like the one I spent with Magnolia. We didn't leave the condo until Sunday, content to simply be with each other. Hedgy provided a lot of amusement, his antics frequently making me laugh. His favorite place to nap was burrowed into my neck, the crook of my arm, or on my chest, and I gave up trying to move him. Magnolia had taken him to the vet while I was away, arranged for neutering, and he was given his first set of shots.

"He was so sleepy after," she told me. "But so good at the vet. Everyone laughed at his name and thought it was cute."

"Told you," I informed her.

I lifted him up, his green eyes meeting mine. "Sorry about your balls, little bugger. But it has to happen."

He studied me, then licked my nose, which made me laugh.

I couldn't recall laughing this much my entire life.

Sunday, we went to see her dad. It wasn't as good a visit as the week before had been. He didn't remember Magnolia, had no interest in Hedgy, and barely glanced my way. I left her with him so she could visit and waited in the parking lot for her. Hedgy fell asleep on my lap, and I answered emails I had been ignoring.

Magnolia opened the passenger door a short time later, sliding in and looking sad.

"No rush to leave," I assured her.

"He fell asleep. Gladys, his nurse, said he's been doing that a lot this week. I'll come visit in a couple of days and see how he is."

"Okay."

"Can you drop me off?"

I turned and looked at her. "Where?"

"My place. I need to do laundry, get ready for work. Roast the meat for sandwiches."

"All of which you can do at the condo."

"I can't stay at the condo indefinitely."

The words were out of my mouth before I could stop them. "Why not?"

She looked at me as if I was crazy. "I don't think we're ready for that. Have you thought of the implications?"

I hadn't, but I found I didn't really care.

"Does it matter?"

She looked thoughtful, sad, and worried all at once. She drew in a deep breath. "To you, maybe not, Alex. If things don't work out, nothing changes for you. You will still have your job, your home, and your life." Before I could protest, she held up her hand. "I, on the other hand, would be unemployed, have no place to go, and my life would be a disaster."

"Do you think I would do that to you?" I asked with a frown. "Fire you, not make sure you were okay?"

"I don't know."

I turned, capturing her chin in my hand. "Never. And nothing is going to happen to break us. I want things to keep moving, Magnolia. We're a great team. You make me laugh. You make me happy. I'm not used to either. I love how you handle me at work and at home." I huffed out a long sigh. "But I understand you want to be cautious."

She had lost a lot in her life. Her parents, her home, her security. I didn't know how to explain to her I wanted to be all those things. For the first time in my life, I wanted to care for someone, to be there for them. I wanted her to rely on me.

"I'm new at this," I admitted. "I don't know how to tell you how I feel. But I want you with me." I paused. "Please."

"What are you asking?"

"I don't know," I replied honestly. "I want more time with you."

"Can we take it slowly?" she asked after a moment.

"I'll hate that." I lifted her hand and kissed it. "But yes."

She chuckled. "Always so impatient."

"Please let me take you to your place and pick up what you need. You can go home tomorrow night after work." I threw out my ace. "Hedgy will miss you too much."

She met my stare with a roll of her eyes, but I won.

"Fine, I'll go home tomorrow night."

I handed her the kitten and put the car in drive. It was impossible to stop my smile, though.

Monday morning, Darryl picked us up, and I tried not to laugh when Magnolia asked him to drop her off two blocks from the office. As we pulled away from her, I looked back, hating the thought she was walking in the gloomy weather. Then I shook my head, realizing she was a grown woman, had an umbrella, and was very capable of looking after herself. Still, I didn't relax until I heard her come into the office. She left briefly, returning with my coffee, which she placed on the desk.

"Your new warmer will be here this week," she informed me. "The back order has finally cleared."

"Good," I grunted, staring at my computer.

"What's wrong?"

"How strict is your no touching during office hours policy?" I asked. She had given me a list of rules this morning after breakfast. No touching, no kissing, no sexual advances during office hours. I didn't like the new rules, even though I knew she was right. "I mean, you're not coming home with me, I only get to see you during the day, and I can't even kiss you?" I deleted an email with a sharp tap of my finger. "Doesn't seem fair."

I heard a low giggle, and I looked up, glaring. "What is so funny?"

She rounded the desk and cupped my face. "You are, Bane. You're acting like a child who had his favorite toy taken away." Bending down, she kissed me, her lips soft on mine. I gripped her hip, kissing her back, the taste of her an aphrodisiac to my senses. I groaned deep in my chest and pulled her closer, but she stepped back.

"The occasional kiss," she relented. "And we'll see each other in the evenings if you want."

"I want all the time," I insisted, reaching.

She evaded my hands. "Drink your coffee. You have a meeting in twenty minutes."

Then she walked away, her hips swaying. She wore pants today, of all things. With the brocade vest and the lacy blouse. The outfit did something to me.

She did something to me.

And I was fucked.

By lunchtime, I was in a foul mood. My meeting this morning had been unsatisfactory and frustrating. The client was adamant about his desires, and the fact was, his ideas were horrible and would never work. Anderson almost lost it when he expressed his "tweaks" to the already approved design, and it took everything in me to remain calm when he discussed his vision for the maze to the side of his office building. Along with his Zen garden in the middle and the types of trees he wanted. None of which would grow in this region of Canada. Plus the fact that he didn't have the space for a maze or a Zen garden. I tried to explain the cost of upkeep alone since one of his desired choices for the plants he wanted would need constant watering, but he refused to listen. The meeting ended with neither side happy and me with an impossible task on my hands. Give him what he wanted without giving him what he wanted. It was a challenge that was going to drain me.

Then the three of us met, going over budgets, staff, office problems, and every other headache running a business entailed. When I got back to my office, I discovered Myers wasn't at her desk. My sandwich was waiting, a fairly warm cup of coffee beside it, so I knew she hadn't been gone long. I hated the fact that I hated she wasn't there to give me one of her smiles or her funny greetings. When she came back, I was busy on the phone with a client, adjusting a budget for them. Myers brought in a fresh cup of coffee, slid a cookie onto the desk beside it, and shut my door, leaving me the silence I needed to think the problem through. A short while later, I flung open my door, throwing a pile of folders on her desk. "Myers, I need numbers," I snapped.

She looked up, not at all perturbed by my tone. It occurred to me she was no longer scared of me. That wasn't good. Everyone was frightened of me, and I needed her to be— at least at the office. I wondered if I could get her back in line, but I had a feeling it was too late.

The corner of her desk contained the usual Monday flowers. Today, they were magnolias, the scent heavy in the air. When they had arrived, I'd rolled my eyes, annoyed.

"Your secret admirer is cheesy. Sending you magnolias?"

She touched a petal softly. "They're beautiful."

"I think Ty is touched in the head. You find out anything new on him?"

"No. The florist is stubborn. I even tried to bribe the delivery guy to find out, but he says the tips are too good and to stop worrying and enjoy them."

I had huffed. "Such sage advice."

She had waved me off. I had a feeling when I turned my back, she flipped me off as well, but I ignored her.

She pushed the files away. "As soon as I finish this email."

"Now," I added with a glare. "Give me numbers, now."

She picked up her pen.

"One pen!" she said in a strange voice. "One! Wah-ha-ha!"

Next came the file folders.

"Three file folders!" she screeched, again in the odd voice. "Three! Wah-ha-ha!"

She fisted something on her desk and opened her hand, paper clips raining down and dancing on the top.

"Who the hell knows?" she warbled. "Twenty-three, give or take. Twenty-three paper clips! Wah-ha-ha!"

I stepped back in alarm.

"Have you lost your ever-loving mind?" I asked. "What the hell?" I leaned over her, caging her against her desk. Why was she imitating Count von Count from *Sesame Street*—badly, I might add? "Are you taking some sort of hallucinogenic drugs?"

"Not the right numbers?" she asked, seemingly confused. "Hmm. You really need to be more detailed when demanding things, boss."

"I need a specific set of numbers, Myers."

"Oh." She paused, a frown wrinkling her forehead. Then she grinned, her eyes dancing. "Sixty-nine."

"What?"

"That's your favorite number, isn't it?" She grinned. "Sixty-nine lashings of your ton—"

I covered her mouth. "Finish that, and you're fired."

She licked my palm, and I had no choice. I gave up, leaning closer and kissing her. "It never takes sixty-nine, does it, Myers? God knows my cock barely lasts six point nine minutes in your mouth," I murmured before kissing her again—hard and fast. That shut her up.

Then I stood. "Crunch the numbers *in the files*. Get them to me fast."

I slammed my door and leaned against it. Then I buried my face into the sleeve of my jacket and laughed until I could barely stand. She had totally changed my mood with a few silly lines and some teasing.

She was going to be the death of me.

But what a way to go.

CHAPTER TWENTY

Bane

I called her that night, smiling when she answered the phone, sounding breathless.

"What are you doing?" I asked.

"Oh, getting the man out of my apartment. My secret admirer finally made himself known."

"Not funny, Myers," I growled. "You had better be joking."

She giggled. "I was sorting through a trunk, looking for a skirt I thought was in there. But it held mostly my grandmother's cocktail outfits." Her voice became soft. "Her wedding dress is in there, plus some photos. I lost track of time looking at them."

"I see. Like the dress you wore to the awards banquet?"

"Yes, that was one of hers."

"How about I take you to dinner on the weekend to my favorite place, and you wear another one?"

"Oh. That would be amazing." She was quiet. "Are you feeling better now?"

I chuckled. "I ate some of your delicious leftovers, Hedgy hasn't left my shoulder, and I think I came up with a design for Mr. Impossible."

"Oh, all great pieces of news."

"He isn't getting a maze, but I figured out a walled sort of garden with his Zen place in the middle. Again, a much smaller version, but we'll see if he is happy."

"Sometimes money doesn't always help with reality."

I chuckled. "He would have needed to have no building, only a small maze. He's building in Toronto, not the countryside. I discovered he'd recently been to England and decided he wanted something he saw at a castle. I hope I can make him see reason."

"And if you can't?" she asked.

"Then we agree to disagree, and he hires someone else. There's always a clause in the contract for me to walk. For the firm to walk, actually."

"Ah."

"Will you come home with me tomorrow?"

"I was going to go see my dad."

"Go do that. Darryl will drive you and will bring you to me when you're ready. I'll have dinner brought in."

"Okay."

"Good. And you'll stay the night."

She paused.

"I didn't sleep well without you, Maggie darling. Please."

"I didn't sleep well without you either."

"Then stay."

Still, she hesitated.

"I know this is all new. It is to both of us," I assured her. "But we'll figure it out. And let's face it. I'm a lot nicer when I have a good night's sleep. Makes it better for everyone."

"Well, when you put it that way," she teased.

I had to chuckle. "Yes. Do it for the sake of the office, Myers. Stay with me."

"Okay, then."

"Night, Maggie darling."

"Goodnight, my Alex. Sweet dreams."

"If you're in them, they will be."

I hung up, looking at my empty bed. I hadn't been lying when I said I didn't sleep as well without her. The bed felt too big and empty, even with Hedgy purring away in my ear. He missed her too, meowing more and looking around as if searching for her.

I would have to figure out a way of getting her to stay more.

A little voice in my head said the words I didn't dare speak out loud.

Every night. Forever.

The next night, Magnolia was quiet during dinner. She had, in fact, been quiet all day. Withdrawn. I studied her over the coffee cup rim, a pit of worry in my stomach.

"You said your dad was better tonight?" I asked.

"Yes, he was brighter. Didn't know me, but we had coffee."

"Okay. Good." I reached across the table, taking her hand. "But something is wrong."

"What makes you say that?"

"You didn't give me any lip today. No sass of any kind. You barely ate your sandwich. You picked at your dinner, and I got you wonton soup—your favorite."

She sighed. "I have a lot on my mind."

"Me, you mean?"

She offered me a ghost of a smile. "Shocking, I know, but I have other issues in my life than a grumpy boss."

"Tell me."

She took a sip of coffee. "Grant and Lily are moving. He was offered a position in their BC office, and they decided to accept. They're selling the house, and the new owners want the basement apartment for their daughter." She set down her mug, her hands shaking a little. "They came down and told me last night after you and I talked on the phone. So I have three months to find a new place."

"Magnolia," I murmured, covering her hand. "I'll—"

She shook her head. "You'll do nothing. There is nothing to be done. I knew there was a chance it would happen at some point. I'll find a place. I'll have to get a storage locker too since I doubt I'll get that much room, and I'll need a place to store the furniture and boxes in the attic. But I'll be fine. I'm simply coming to terms with it."

"I'll help however I can," I insisted. "Why didn't you tell me earlier?"

"Because we are Bane and Myers in the office, not Magnolia and Alex. You were busy, and I was processing."

"If you have a problem, I'm Alex at any moment," I said firmly. "You never have to wait if something is upsetting you."

She smiled. "Thank you."

I leaned forward and kissed her. "Anytime," I reiterated. "What can I do now?"

"Nothing. Being with you helps."

"Good. I prefer you smiling."

She propped up her chin on her palm. "Make me smile, then."

"The last business trip—" I paused, trying to figure out how to say the words. "When I called you to change my flights. I have never missed anyone before, Magnolia. Never been anxious to come home." I traced her lips. "Because of you, this place now feels like home. Knowing you were here, waiting for me, meant more than I can express."

Her eyes glistened.

"And I have never cared about anyone enough to want to take care of their problems. Of them. This is all new to me. You are new to me. How you make me react is new to me."

"Do you hate it?"

"No. It's disconcerting. Bewildering at times, yet somehow exhilarating."

"You say the nicest things when I least expect it, Alex."

"Did it make you smile?"

"Yes."

"Then my work is done."

"Not quite."

"Oh?" I asked. "What else do you want?"

"Take me to bed. Ravish me."

It was my turn to smile. I laughed, picking her up. "Your wish, my command."

A few days later, I walked into the office, glancing at the empty desk. Where was Myers? I wanted to fill her in on how the meeting went with the maze client. I had finally convinced him it was a pipe dream and to look over my designs. After a lot of talking, he agreed what he wanted was impossible, and we were able to find a starting point. Still, the bickering had tired me.

Frowning, I went to my private office, stopping at the sight of a rounded ass sticking up in the air and squirming underneath my desk. It was Myers.

Again.

I approached the desk, kneeling, one hand on the wood, the other twitching to touch that round ass. Stroke it. But we had agreed to keep things professional at work.

Not that wiggling under my desk was professional.

"This again, Myers? What are you doing?" I asked impatiently.

There was a muffled gasp and the sound of her head hitting the wood.

"Ouch."

I shut my eyes, shaking my head. She tripped everywhere. Fell off her chair. Rolled out of the car once when I opened the door for her, trying to be a gentleman. She'd even missed the bed, trying to jump and not succeeding. It was a wonder she managed to still be alive.

"Myers?" I asked again. "Come out of there."

"I can't," she responded, sounding morose.

"Why the hell not?"

"I'm stuck."

"Stuck," I repeated.

"Yes."

"How the hell did you get stuck?"

"I think one of my sleeve buttons is caught on something. When I tried to fix it, my hair got trapped somewhere. I can't seem to get either loose."

It was all I could do not to laugh. How she did these things was beyond me.

She wiggled again. "Help, please?"

Unable to resist, I swatted her butt. "Never-ending trouble," I chastised her. I added another swat for good measure, then rubbed the cheek. That part was for me.

"Coming in," I told her, ducking under the desk, turning on my flashlight. Given the angle of her body, it was tight and I couldn't help at all.

"Lie down."

She grunted and moved, and I slid over her as best I could, first locating the trapped hair. Her clip was lodged between the drawer and the edge, and I managed to tug it off, but it broke as I did.

"Oops, sorry."

"It's fine."

I moved my fingers along her arm, finding her hand and feeling for the snag. "Wow, you got this in the carpet good." I tugged on it, hearing her fast intake of breath.

"Please don't tear it," she pleaded. "It's my favorite."

I inhaled a deep breath, praying for patience. That was my second mistake. I should have backed out and dragged her out by the feet, torn blouse or not. Inside, trapped in the confines of the small space and pressing into her, I could smell her perfume. Feel her curves under me. My cock liked being this close to her. She moved and I groaned. "Stop."

I shifted and tugged on the sleeve as gently as I could. It didn't budge.

"Sorry, Myers. I tried." I grabbed her wrist and tugged. Hard. I heard the rending of material, and her hand smacked the wood. She cried out, I grunted, and a horrified voice behind me gasped.

"Alexander Donovan Bane. What is going on here?"

"Shit," I muttered, moving backward as fast as I could. I hit my head, cursing again, crouching, and turning to see my mother standing, her mouth agape, her normally sallow skin flushed a dark red.

"What—what are you doing?" she cried.

I tugged on Myers's feet, dragging her out. I helped her stand, taking in her disheveled appearance. Her blouse was torn, pulled out from her skirt. Her hair was tumbling over her shoulders, looking as if she'd been in a hurricane. She was flushed, her lipstick smeared. Her breathing was fast.

She looked as if she'd been fucked hard.

I had a feeling I did as well, especially given the fact that I still had an erection, although in the face of my appalled mother, it was rapidly deflating.

She looked between Myers and me, her eyes filled with shock.

"Were you—were you *rutting* her?" she asked. "Your secretary? Under your desk?"

I opened my mouth to tell her no such thing had occurred. But Myers spoke up, slipping an arm around my waist.

"Yes, he was. He *ruts* very well."

The flush left my mother's face, and she became pale.

"Alexander, explain yourself."

Suddenly, I was tired of explaining myself. Defending everything I did, every decision I made, to my mother. Nothing was ever going to be right in her eyes. No doubt she had shown up to discuss her latest idea that a wife would help me see reason.

I decided to give her what she wanted.

"Sorry, Mother. I forgot to lock the door. It happens when Maggie Mae here is around. I can't keep my hands to myself." I turned, pressing a kiss to Myers's forehead. "My fiancée smiles, and everything else disappears."

I wasn't sure who was more shocked by my words.

Me.

My mother.

Or Myers.

❦❦❦

I sat on my chair, hanging my head in my hands. I couldn't believe what I had done. What I had said.

My mother had spewed out a bunch of garbage about Myers not being good enough for me, and I told her to get out. She had stormed away, and Myers had turned to me, calm and steady.

"I doubt she'll be paying another visit soon."

Then she headed down the hall, not even bringing up my word bomb.

I heard her come into the office, shut the door, and the sound of liquid being poured. She leaned on the desk in front of me, running her fingers through my hair.

"Poor Bane," she murmured.

I grunted, leaning into her softness and letting her tickle the strands of my hair and run her fingers along my neck.

"I brought you coffee and Advil."

I sat up, taking the pills and coffee, grateful it was black. Now was not the time for cream and foam.

I took a deep swallow, almost choking on the flavor.

"What the hell?" I sputtered.

"Brandy," she said with a grin. "I thought you needed it."

She wasn't wrong.

"Warn a guy next time."

"Like you warned me?"

I grimaced. I deserved that.

"I mean, calling me that?"

"I know—"

She kept going as if I hadn't spoken. "You rarely call me anything but Myers in the office. Hearing you say Maggie Mae, I almost swallowed my tongue."

I gaped at her. *That* was what surprised her?

Then she winked. "Add in the fiancée part, and I almost expired on the spot." She shook her head. "What were you thinking, Bane?"

I had to laugh. She was ridiculous.

I pulled her between my legs, burying my head into her warmth. "I wasn't thinking. I was reacting." I pinched her ass playfully. "To the 'he ruts very well' comment."

Myers scoffed. "As if we were a couple of farmyard animals."

"I'm sure, to my mother, we were."

"She's one to talk. Pretentious cow."

And once again, I was laughing. I looked up. Myers was smiling, but she looked troubled.

"Why did you say that?" she asked.

"To shut her up," I admitted.

"You better hope she keeps it to herself. Otherwise, you will have a lot of explaining and damage control to do."

"Damage control?"

She shook her head, taking a sip of the brandy-laced coffee and grimacing. "You'll have to let people know it was a joke. Make sure the partners understand. Not sure how exactly you'll explain it, but—"

I stopped her. "What if it's not a joke?"

She frowned. "Pardon me?"

I took her hand and kissed it. "Marry me, Myers."

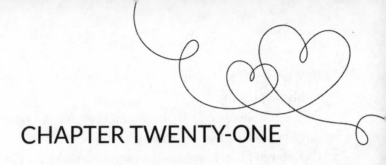

CHAPTER TWENTY-ONE

Magnolia

I stared at him. Then I glanced at his coffee cup. How much brandy had I put in it?

Obviously, the man was drunk.

I tried to tug my hand away, but he held tight.

"I'll get you fresh coffee. The nonalcoholic kind. You've obviously had enough."

"I'm not drunk."

"You must be. You just proposed marriage. In the office. You called me Myers while doing it."

He frowned, releasing my hand and rubbing his chin. "Not the most romantic proposal, I agree. But I meant it." He paused. "Maggie darling, marry me."

I laughed. "Nice try."

He shook his head. "I'm serious."

"You don't want to get married. You've said so many times."

"I said I don't want to marry the women my mother likes. She doesn't like you."

"So that makes me marriage material?"

"Think about it. We get married—my mother will shut up and stay away. You move in with me, your housing problem is solved. You wouldn't even have to work for me or anyone if you didn't want to. You could paint. Craft. Do all the things you enjoy."

"As hobbies. I enjoy them as hobbies. I like working."

"Even better. You can run me here and at home."

I stared at him, aghast. He was serious. He wanted to get married to solve our problems. Nothing about love, a life together, or anything personal.

"It sounds like a business deal."

"Well, I don't usually have sex with business deals, but I'm willing to make an exception in your case." He smirked, looking proud of himself. "We have a cat together, we enjoy each other's company. Sex with you is incredible. I love your sandwiches."

I shut my eyes and counted to ten. Then I opened them, leaned close, and smiled. "Bane?"

"Magnolia?" he murmured, lifting his hand and running a finger down my cheek.

"Suggest this again, and the next time your mother drops in, I'll let her into your office and lock the door behind her."

Then I turned and walked out of the office, shutting the door firmly behind me.

Loudly.

What a jerk.

I sat down, stared at my desk, then decided I needed to stay busy and I needed it to be physical. Everything in this office was clean, tidy, and orderly. Bane's office was organized, although I still wanted to clean his cupboard—I wasn't going in there with him.

I was angry. Hurt.

When he'd first uttered the words "marry me," my heart raced. I was filled with elation. Wonder. The belief that he felt the same way about me as I did about him. This wasn't some office affair. It was something real.

And then he opened his mouth again and ruined it all. He didn't love me. I was a convenience. We could get married and help each other.

He had told me he didn't think he was capable of having a relationship. Of experiencing or expressing real feelings. I should have known better. But given the fact that I realized I was falling for him, I thought he'd felt the same about me. I was an idiot.

Simply thinking about it made me angry again. I rose from my desk, went to the kitchen, and made Bane a coffee. I could still be professional, and he liked a coffee this time of the day. Then I gathered up some garbage bags and tucked them under my arm. I knocked on his door, walking in before he answered. I knew he was alone. I set down the coffee, and he eyed the bags under my arm.

"Are you cleaning out your desk, or are those for my body once you dismember me?"

"I am tidying the supply room in the hall. It's a disaster." I walked to the door, glancing over my shoulder. "Just like you."

In the supply room, I looked around, mentally organizing the room. It blew my mind that with the number of extra assistants they had, no one ever came in here and fixed it. Granted, the room was small—a closet, really, but it could still be tidy. I propped open the door that was known to stick, then opened a bag and got busy.

About an hour later, Bane stuck his head in. "How's it

going?"

"Fine."

He grimaced, entering the room and looking around. "Looks much better."

I snorted. "When was the last time you were in here?"

"A couple of months ago, looking for some printer supplies." He rubbed his neck. "I didn't find any."

"They're on the third shelf now," I informed him, stacking some packages of copy paper. It amazed me, for a paperless environment, how much paper was used and wasted. Bending, I grabbed another cartridge for the printer, stretching up on my toes to try to put it on the top shelf.

Bane was suddenly behind me, taking the box from my hand and easily reaching the top without any problem. "You need a small step stool."

"No room, really."

He bracketed his arms on the shelves, crowding and caging me in. "No, it's a pretty tight fit."

I felt him aligned with me, our bodies meshing with perfection. His hard melding to my soft. He lowered his head, his lips ghosting my neck. He moved his hands, grasping mine, the feel of his skin hot. I inhaled, smelling him. Warm. Rich.

Bane.

"Stop," I whispered.

"You're angry with me. I don't like it."

"I don't like being a convenience."

"You're not, Magnolia. You're so much more." He pressed his lips to my neck. "I'm sorry I hurt you."

I knew Bane didn't apologize. He never seemed to care for others' opinions. But he did care about mine. He cared about me in his own way. Which, most of the time, was wonderful.

"I'm not a tool to keep your mother away."

"I know."

"I'm not a toy. I have feelings."

He slid his arm around my waist. "I know," he murmured in my ear, teasing the lobe with his tongue. I shut my eyes, trying not to whimper. He pulled me closer, and I felt every inch of him. Every. Single. Hard. Inch.

"I love your feelings," he murmured. "They remind me to be human. You make me feel too, Maggie darling. Sometimes it scares me how much I feel for you."

With a little cry, I turned, flinging my arms around his neck. He took my mouth, kissing me with a desperation that had me curling my toes. He kissed me as if he needed me more than life. I kissed him back, shocked at how much he could make me want him so quickly.

"I need you," I whispered as he lifted me.

"Hold on, baby. I got you."

Like a pro, he pushed up my skirt, the lace parting for him as if it was welcoming him in.

"We can't— The door—"

In a graceful move, he stepped to the side, pulling the door shut. I heard the click as he locked the handle, and the automatic light went off, leaving only the dim EXIT light over the door to save us from total darkness. I reached between us, fumbling with his belt, and he groaned as I slid my hand inside his pants, caressing him.

"Hold on to the shelves," he demanded. "Tight."

I did as he instructed, and a moment later, I heard his pants hit the floor. Once again, he wrapped his hands around my thighs, and then my underwear was tugged away. When he slammed into me, I gasped, throwing my head back, hitting the shelf.

"Easy, darling," he murmured. "I need you conscious."

"Fuck me, Alex. Now."

And he did.

I grasped the shelves as he began to move. Hard, tight rolls of his hips kept him lodged inside me as our bodies swayed together. He pushed me higher, opening me wider, and hitting me in the perfect spot, making me see stars behind my eyelids. There was no finesse about our coupling. No sweet words murmured. All I heard were the sounds of us. Our skin touching and gliding. Our bodies meshing, our breathing hard, bursts of air escaping. His low groans. My hushed whimpers. He surrounded me. Claimed me. Made me feel alive like no one else had ever done. Ever would do.

My orgasm hit like a shooting star, exploding me into thousands of tiny shards of light. He kept going, finally stilling as he succumbed, my name a long whisper in my ear. Then he sagged against me, burying his head in my neck, his chest heaving fast. He slid his hand up my torso, cupping my face and kissing me. Softly now. Sweetly.

He stepped back, easing me onto my feet. We fumbled with our clothing, and he reached for me, wrapping me in his arms. "Still mad?"

"No."

He kissed me again. "We'll talk tonight, Magnolia."

"Okay."

"Done arranging the closet for today? Ready to come back to the office? I have things to keep you busy."

"I'm sure you do."

He chuckled and bent, kissing me. "Work-related."

"Okay, then."

He attempted to open the door, frowning. "It's stuck."

"You have to turn it—hard. It sticks."

He tried and failed. Rammed the door with his shoulder, but it didn't budge. He reached for the light, flicking it on. Nothing happened.

"Dammit," he muttered. He crouched in front of the door, grasping the doorknob, turning it. It barely moved.

"I need some light."

"Wait. There was a flashlight up here." I felt around the shelf. "Got it!"

I bent over him, focusing the light. He studied the handle. "It's jammed. There's a little notch. I think if I can fit something in it, I can jimmy it."

I used the flashlight and found a couple of screwdrivers. I handed them to him. "Will these work?"

"Maybe. Shine the light for me."

I crouched behind him, holding the light. "I need it that way," he pointed. "Get in front of me."

I did as he instructed and once again found myself crowded in a small space by Bane. His scent, the scent of us, washed over me, and I turned my head, meeting his gaze in the dim light.

"Stop," he hissed. "I'm trying to get us out."

"We could call someone."

"Do you have your cell? Mine is sitting on my desk."

"So is mine."

"I figured. Aim the light, Magnolia."

I did, ducking my head and steadying myself on the door. He muttered constantly as he tried to open the lock. I was getting warm, my legs going numb.

"I need to move."

He grabbed the doorknob, rattling it, almost snarling in frustration. "Fucking thing. I'm going to break it down."

Except the door opened suddenly, the light from the hall spilling in. I gasped as I pitched forward, Bane on top of me. I looked up into the startled gaze of Jessica from HR. She stared at me, then Bane, who was pushing himself up. My eyes widened at his appearance. His hair was everywhere, his collar undone and his tie loose. He had lipstick on his face. My lipstick. He looked mauled and, frankly, freshly fucked. I knew I must look equally as bad. We had been caught red-handed, so to speak.

"Oh my God," she breathed. "Again? Why do I always have to find you?"

I met Jessica's eyes and blurted the only thing that came to mind.

"We're getting married."

I waited for Bane to return, sitting in his office. Unable to stay still, I opened his cupboard and began reorganizing. My movements were swift, controlled. Sorting, piling up unneeded or outdated supplies. It didn't take long, but the difference was incredible. I stood, brushing off my skirt, frowning at the safety pin holding the lace on the sleeve together. I would have to try to repair the damage—and change the buttons unless I could find the one I lost under Bane's desk.

And I had no plans on looking right now. We were in enough turmoil as it was.

I turned to leave as he strode in, looking surprised to see me. "Magnolia, I thought you'd gone home."

"I was waiting to see if I still had a job."

He leaned on his desk and took my hands with a frown. "Of course you do."

"What did you tell them?"

"That we got locked in and we were trying to get out. I told them how you were cleaning the shelves because you couldn't bear the disorganization any longer."

"They bought that?"

"Jessica saw how clean it was. I may have expounded a little on how hot the closet was, which is why my tie was loose and your lipstick was on my face, because of when we fell out of the room."

"Really?"

"I can be very convincing." He folded his arms over his chest. "And of course, I confirmed we were getting married."

I glared at him, and the bastard just smiled at me. "You're the one who blurted it out."

"I was in shock. You sexed me up in the supply room, and then that happened. I wasn't thinking."

He stood and pressed a kiss to my head. "Well, I was. We'll talk about it at home. Get your things, and I'll call Darryl."

I stared after him as he sauntered away, looking as if he didn't have a care in the world. He was acting very un-Bane-like.

I wasn't sure I approved.

Bane, I could handle. Alex was incredibly hard to resist.

Bane

Magnolia was quiet in the car, staring out the window. But her fingers were restless, tugging on the lace of her sleeves, picking at the buttons on her coat. I could always tell when she was nervous or upset. Her cleaning episodes were certainly a dead giveaway. The supply closet, my shelves, and the cupboard in the office had never been so organized. It was done with almost military precision. Anything I asked for, Magnolia knew where it was.

I hadn't planned on going into the supply closet in the hall to fuck her. But I had missed seeing her at her desk, the office feeling strangely empty without her in it. Walking into the small room, I was, as usual, amazed at her capacity for turning a disaster into an organized space. I wanted to apologize to her, coax her back into the office. I only meant to kiss her, but as usual, as soon as I was close to her, I wanted closer. One thing led to another, and before I knew it once again, my body had taken over my mind and we were suddenly a cliché. The boss fucking his assistant in the supply closet.

Except it wasn't only fucking, and she wasn't only my assistant.

My partners had been surprised when I'd shown up on their floor, asking for an immediate meeting. Their shock at my informing them I planned to marry Magnolia was immense. They had a few questions, and Lawson had asked how long the relationship had been going on.

I shrugged. "A while. It's private." I paused. "Or it was until Jessica saw us together earlier in a slightly less-than-welcome moment." I explained about the closet, omitting the graphic details and skimming over the truth. I informed them I had been kissing her rather aggressively before we realized the door was locked, and we were attempting to get out when Jessica heard us. They withheld their disbelief since none of us wanted to delve too deeply into my story.

Jessica and Laura appeared, and we discussed office protocol. I assured them it wouldn't happen again, and I was extremely grateful for their discretion.

I was also thankful that no one else had an office on my floor or that there hadn't been a meeting going on in the boardroom that took up the other half of the floor—but I kept that to myself.

I glanced at Magnolia, wondering how she would take it when I told her HR had been informed of our new status.

And how she was going to feel when I told her I wasn't backing down. I wanted to marry her. I had a feeling I was in for a long night of arguments.

But I planned on winning.

Hedgy was all over us when we entered the condo. He hated being alone and was effusive with his greeting. Purring, doing figure eights around our legs, climbing my pants to burrow in my neck as quickly as possible.

"Maybe we should get a cat sitter. Or I could bring him to the office."

Magnolia looked over her shoulder. "That would not fly with HR, and I think we're on thin ice there already."

I laughed. "I could put it to a vote. I'd win."

"So cocky," she muttered, taking off her jacket and slinging it over the back of a stool. I sat at the island, watching her move around the kitchen as if she owned it. Which, really, she already did.

"No. Fact. I own fifty-one percent of the company, so I'd always win if pushed."

She gaped at me. "You own the majority share? How?"

I pulled Hedgy's treats close, giving him one and listening to him crunch and purr in my ear simultaneously. I scratched the top of his head thoughtfully. "When we were planning the company, we needed capital. I had it, so I became the majority shareholder. I rarely flex that muscle, but I would if I had to. Lawson and Anderson are great partners. We work."

"Where did you get the money?"

"I told you before. I come from old money. My grandfather was a smart man. The money he left my father couldn't be touched by my mother. It was left in a trust for me that was looked after by someone he could rely on. Tom and I got along, and he stayed in touch, always checking on me. When I was only fourteen, I had done a project at school about investing. I found it fascinating and told him I wanted to help him invest it. He gave me some money to try. I doubled it. He gave me more. I doubled that. I kept going through the years, and when I turned twenty-one, my fund was millions. It's gone up more with my holdings and investments."

"Why do you work?"

"I like working. I also like being able to back projects that I believe in." He grinned. "Some clients who hire me have no idea I have also invested in their venture at all. My mother has no idea of my true wealth. I tried to tell her once, but she didn't believe me. She never believed in me at all."

Magnolia's eyes were sad as she slid her hand over mine. "I'm sorry."

I met her gaze. "You've believed in me since the day you met me. Why?"

"I could see your passion when you talked about your designs. I looked up your work."

"My mother thinks I play in the dirt and need help to find a wife who can elevate me above that."

Magnolia snorted. "Your mother is incredibly shortsighted and unfocused. You don't promote your wealth." She frowned. "You don't wear it like a trophy. You're humble. You'd rather talk about plants and the environment than money."

"But I am wealthy."

"I assumed you were, but not the kind of wealth you're talking about."

I leaned closer. "Does that make the idea of being married to me a little easier?" I teased.

"Not happening."

"I disagree."

"Go look in the mirror and argue with yourself, Bane. It's the only way you win this one."

She walked away, skirting the island so I couldn't catch her. "I'm tired. Order something in, okay, Daddy Warbucks? I'm hungry, and I need a shower."

"I'll order Chinese and come wash your back."

"I want two spring rolls," she called over her shoulder.

But she didn't tell me to stay put.

Win number one for the night.

CHAPTER TWENTY-TWO

Magnolia

I padded toward the kitchen, rolling my shoulders. Alex had done an amazing job washing my back. Plus a lot of other areas he found especially dirty. Two orgasms and gallons of hot water later, I was a great deal more relaxed than I had been earlier. Hedgy was asleep on the bed, his head buried between the pillows.

There was a knock at the door, and I mentally did a happy dance, glad the food had arrived. I had built up quite the appetite, thanks to Alex's wandering hands and mouth.

Alex appeared, heading for the door. "Get the plates," he said with a smirk and a wink. "Unless you want me to eat sweet-and-sour off your naked body."

I tossed my damp hair and rolled my eyes. "Not likely, Bane."

He chuckled, the sound warm and low. "Never say never, Maggie darling."

In the kitchen, I reached for the plates, then stopped, hearing his voice, now pitched low and angry. A female voice was speaking, and my heart sank when I recognized who it was.

"You are doing this to spite me! I know it."

"Get over yourself, Mother."

"You have always done this. Found ways to hurt me.

Belittle the values I hold so dear."

Alex snorted. "The only things you hold dear are money and social status. I'm interested in neither. And frankly, the reasons I'm marrying her don't involve you in the slightest."

"You are going to listen—"

"No. I have no interest in hearing what you have to say. Either of you."

I set down the plates, hurrying to the door.

Alex stood in front of his mother and brother, all three of them glaring and looking unhappy.

Terry spotted me, a lecherous grin crossing his face. "Ah, the little assistant, now fiancée, appears."

I was suddenly aware I was wearing a pair of leggings and one of Alex's T-shirts. No bra or underwear. The shirt came down to my thighs and was loose, the color dark so he couldn't see anything, but somehow, he made me feel as if he did.

"It's fine, Magnolia," Alex said. "They're leaving. And whoever let them up just got themselves fired."

Terry smirked. "Money talks, brother. Mine louder than yours, I daresay."

Alex shook his head. "Whatever makes you sleep better. And stop calling me brother. We are in no way related."

"You cannot marry her," his mother informed Alex, indicating me and looking as if I were a bug she wanted to squash under her shoe. I glanced down, biting my lip to stop from laughing. She had to be agitated. She was wearing two different black pumps. "We came to put a stop to this ridiculousness."

"I'm an adult, Mother. I can marry whomever I choose." He slipped his arm around me. "And I choose her."

"She's no one!"

"She's everything to me."

My heart melted, and I wished with everything in me it was true. I knew without a doubt I had fallen for him. Hard. I only wished he felt the same, but I knew his words were simply uttered to anger his mother.

Terry laughed. "Gone sentimental now, have you, Alexander?"

"I won't try explaining anything to you," Alex stated dryly. "I don't have enough time to break all my words into tiny ones so you can understand."

I bit back another grin, but Terry saw my expression, as did his mother. It only angered them more.

"I will cut you out of my life if you marry her," she threatened.

"Then I'll take her to Vegas tonight and seal the deal. I want no part of your life, Mother. So cutting me out is the best present I could ask for."

"You'll embarrass me. The whole family. Marrying a nobody."

"I won't be in your life, so it doesn't matter."

"Why must you continue to hurt me? You have always been so difficult!"

Alex shook his head, looking sorrowful. "I think your expectations have been the difficult thing."

"She only wants you for your money."

Alex began to laugh. "Which you think I have none of. So, again, no problem." Then he kissed my head. "And since you don't know her, I'll thank you to keep your mouth shut when it comes to your opinion. Magnolia is the most incredible woman I have ever known."

Terry narrowed his eyes. "Maybe you need a prenup. If

her heart is as pure as you say, then it'll prove she's not a gold digger."

"Maybe you need to shut your mouth," Alex snarled. "Or I'll shut it for you."

"Stop!" I demanded, stepping away from Alex. "Stop all of this."

They all stared at me.

"I'm not interested in his money. Alex is amazing. Talented. Warm and caring." I shook my head. "How he ended up that way, given the lot of you, I have no idea, but he is. He must take after his real father." I turned to his mother. "Why must you criticize him all the time? You don't even know him! Do you realize how many awards and accolades he has won for his work on environmental issues? How incredible his designs are? How respected he is? All you care about is your image. Your world. If you knew him at all, you would realize he is exactly the son you should be shouting about. You think a name and money give you prestige? What about honor and integrity? Class and manners? Good God, lady, grow up. All you do is belittle him and nag him. Stop it!"

Then I turned to his brother. "As for you, I have read enough to know why Alex doesn't want you in his life. Your so-called victories in court—mostly defending low-life criminals, your constant revolving door of women. You have no morals! You change law firms more often than I change my socks. No doubt before they fire you, given the stories I've read." I swung my furious gaze back to Mrs. Johnstone. "And you praise him and ignore your biological son! What kind of morals does that show you have?"

I turned my venom back to Terry. "You think being in the papers and the gossip columns is what makes you a man?

Alex is a hundred times the man you are. You might have your stepmother drinking the Kool-Aid, but one day, once you end up without a career, drain all your money away, and start dipping into her accounts, she is going to see you for what you are. Unless—" I snorted. "You can marry some idiot heiress who is as blind as your stepmother." I pointed a finger between them. "You are both greedy, nasty people. Leave Alex alone. Leave us alone. You are not welcome here."

There was a beat of silence, and Alex pulled me to his chest. "I think Magnolia has said everything that needs to be said. Leave. Don't come back. You aren't welcome here or at the office."

Terry's face was almost purple in his rage. His mother's cheeks were flushed a deep red, her eyes almost silver with ice. "I have never been more ashamed of you," Mrs. Johnstone hissed. "Letting her speak to us that way. I will not stand for it!"

"The truth is never pretty, Mother. Magnolia said what had to be said."

"You will regret this."

"I highly doubt it." Alex stepped to the door, opening it. "Get out."

Terry shook his head. "I hope you rot in hell."

Alex smirked. "You first—*brother*," he added sarcastically, looking pleased as Terry stomped out.

His mother stopped, glaring at me. "You caused all this."

I laughed sardonically. "I think you're the key factor here. And you might want to check your shoes when you get home."

She glanced down, the detail I found so humorous sending her over the edge. "You little—" She raised her hand, and in an instant, Alex was in front of me, grabbing her wrist.

"If you dare," he snarled, "I will have you arrested

for battery." He leaned close. "This entire encounter was videotaped, Mother, so you'll have none of your lies to wiggle out of it. How would all your friends and upper-class associates feel about you being convicted of striking an innocent woman in her own home?"

She wrenched her hand away, glaring. "She doesn't deserve to have the last name Bane."

Alex regarded her somberly. "That shouldn't bother you since you were very fast to remarry and change your name after Father died."

"I am still associated with that name. With you. What you do reflects on me."

He narrowed his eyes. "I have done nothing to be ashamed of. Tell me, Mother, can you or Terry say the same thing? Or your sainted husband?"

I thought she was going to strike him, except she recalled his threat and pulled back, stiffening her shoulders. "I no longer consider you my son."

"A good day all around, then," he replied, reopening the door. "Get out, Mrs. Johnstone. You are no longer welcome here. Not that you ever really were."

She flounced out, and he shut the door, his shoulders dropping. He rested his forehead on the wood, a long exhale escaping.

I didn't know what to do. I wanted to touch him. Get him to talk to me. But I wasn't sure if he wanted that.

He straightened, turning to me.

"Dinner and a show," he muttered. "Didn't expect that."

"Alex—"

He held up his hand. "It's fine, Magnolia."

"No, it's not."

For a moment, he said nothing. Then he spoke, his voice filled with wonder. "You defended me. You told them off."

"Of course I did." The words were out before I could stop them. "I love you."

His eyes widened and his brow furrowed as he processed my words.

"You. Love. Me?"

I couldn't stand the space between us. I rushed forward, flinging my arms around his neck and holding him close. "I love you."

It took a moment. Then his arms came around me, holding me so tight I could barely breathe. He buried his face into my neck, breathing deeply. He pulled me even closer, not speaking, not denying my words. He held me as if he needed my touch to hold him together. As if I was what was keeping him upright. He spread his hands open across my back, and I felt every inch of him against me. Solid, strong, yet in such need of my embrace, I knew I couldn't let go.

I would hold him until he felt my love. Until it filled him up and he could stand on his own.

And I would be right beside him, ready to fill him up again anytime he needed it.

Bane

I held her as tight as I could. No one had ever defended me the way she had done. Stood up and yelled at the two people who liked to criticize and tear me down. I had long since stopped caring what they thought and let their words roll off my back, but there was a small part of me that still cringed at their hateful vitriol.

But with Magnolia wrapped around me, none of it hurt. I had her.

And she'd said the words to me.

I love you.

No one had ever said those words to me before today.

I only wished I were capable of saying them back. Of feeling them.

But my mother and her cold ways had long since stripped me of those emotions.

I cared. I truly cared. I wanted Magnolia safe, appreciated, even cherished, but I couldn't love.

However, I could make sure she would never want for anything.

There was another knock, and I felt Magnolia tense.

"That better be some spring rolls," I muttered. "Anyone else, and they're getting a punch in the jaw."

I stepped back, instantly missing the warmth of her against me. Wrapped in her arms, I had the sense nothing could hurt me. She wouldn't allow it.

It was disconcerting, to say the least.

But I liked it.

I opened the door, taking the bag from the usual deliveryman. I tipped him well and went to the kitchen, setting the bag on the counter. Magnolia was quiet, staring at the island, tracing a finger over the design in the quartz repeatedly.

"Hey," I called.

She looked up, clearly distraught.

"They're gone. I refuse to let them take away the evening we had planned. I want this time with you, Maggie darling. Us. Okay?"

She nodded halfheartedly.

"I want Chinese, a movie, and you under me later, groaning my name. Maybe on top too."

A glimmer of a smile crossed her face.

"Is that all you think of?"

"When you're close, yes. Now, if it would make you feel better, I have a key to Terry's place I stole once, planning to play a joke on him. I never did, but we could go hide in the dark and jump him when he gets home. Leave him naked and tied up with the doors open. Call the rags he loves to have his name in and let them find him. Then we could go to my mother's and rearrange her pristine wardrobe so she couldn't find anything. Steal all her matching shoes and only leave her with one of each. That would hurt her more than physical violence."

That brought a grin to her lips. "Did you see?" she said with a giggle.

I returned her grin, handing her a spring roll.

"Once you pointed it out. Which I loved, by the way. She was as horrified by the idea of me shitting my pants in public."

She nodded, sliding onto a stool and taking a bite of her spring roll. "Same thing in her eyes."

"Yep. Great shame on the family name."

"What is with that? She's not a Bane, so why is she so concerned?"

I was happy for her questions. It meant she wasn't dwelling. "The name Bane is still known in the legal world. My dad was a great lawyer, and his reputation was stellar. She still pulls it out as a double whammy when needed."

"Double-dipping."

I chuckled. "She's an expert at it."

I took a bite of my spring roll and chewed. "Doug Johnstone was also a huge name in the legal world. Very well-known and represented the wealthy in a lot of trials. He had a reputation for helping the rich stay rich. His first wife died, and he married my mother about two years later." I paused. "She was very beautiful when she was young, and I imagine she caught his eye. My dad was a good businessman and we were okay financially, but not on Doug's level. He was and is a snob. She was arm candy. Once she married him, every grandiose idea in her head became the norm for her. I was the fly in the ointment, so to speak. I refused to take his name, then later I heard my mother say she was glad I hadn't. So was Doug. Neither wanted me to be a Johnstone. So, she uses Bane when it suits her. She doesn't want either name sullied, and she thinks I have never lived up to my potential."

"She's blind."

I grinned, opening a container and passing it to her. "You know it. Now, enough about my family history. I want you to eat. You're going to need it for later."

"Whatever."

I grinned. "I'll give you whatever soon enough."

She frowned, and I leaned close. "Hey. Leave it. They're gone."

She met my gaze. "I hate that they hurt you."

"Then it's a good thing I have you, isn't it?"

She furrowed her brow but nodded.

We ate in silence for a while. Despite what had happened, I was hungry. Somehow with Magnolia beside me, her words still in my head, nothing my so-called family said had any meaning. I studied her as we ate. I slid closer, feeding her pieces of sweet-and-sour chicken, garlicky green beans, steamed dumplings. I needed her to eat. I refused to allow them into our space.

After dinner, she put away the leftovers and made some of her foamy coffees. We sipped, eating the lychee nuts I had ordered, picking them from the ice bath one by one and enjoying the unique flavor. She nibbled on the fortune cookies, crunching them and laughing over the fortunes.

The sun was setting, and we went out to the patio, watching as it sank, turning the sky a myriad of colors. I sipped a brandy, then stood behind Magnolia, linking my arms around her. She leaned back into me with a sigh.

"Marry me."

"Why? To get back at your mother?"

"Frankly, she has nothing to do with it. I don't care about her feelings one way or another."

"Then why?"

"Because we suit. We like each other. You make me...feel."

"I make you feel. But not enough to love."

"I'm not capable of that."

"I want more," she replied, her voice sad.

"I can't love, Myers. I can care. I can protect. Provide. We can have a good life together."

She was silent.

"It solves so many things. You'll have a great place to live. A partner who will support you in everything. You can do whatever you want with your life."

"Except have a husband who loves me."

"Maybe what we'll have will be better. Desire, affection, friendship, respect. Those things mean a great deal."

"What about children?"

"I don't want kids," I replied honestly.

"Why?"

"Magnolia, I have no idea how to be a father. If I'd make

a good one. My childhood was so awful, I have no clue how to nurture a child." I paused. "If I could even love them."

"I think you could learn. And I think if you open yourself up, you could love them."

"It's not a chance I want to take." I swallowed. "But you want kids, I assume."

"I'm not sure. But I do know I want the option if I decide."

I wasn't sure what to say. "Maybe we could revisit that subject." It was all I could offer. I couldn't see changing my mind, but we could discuss it.

She turned in my arms. "Why?" she asked again. "Why do you want to marry me? You can get companionship with someone else."

"No. Because of your heart. How you care. How you love. I might not be able to do it, but with you, it's effortless. You offer love so freely. In your touch. Your actions."

"And what would I get from it?"

"Security. Wealth. Permanent custody of Hedgy." I paused, dipping down and kissing her. "Of me."

"But not your heart."

"There are other parts of me so much more useful, Myers." I dragged my mouth down her neck. "So much more enjoyable."

She whimpered, and I took the opportunity to cover her mouth with mine, kissing her until she was shaking in my arms.

"Think about it," I begged.

"Okay."

I took that as progress. It wasn't a yes, but I had a feeling it would be soon enough.

CHAPTER TWENTY-THREE

Magnolia

He didn't say it back.

He said he can't love.

He can *care*.

I rolled over carefully, looking at Alex in the dim light of the morning. Asleep, he looked younger, less stressed. Not stern and uptight, but almost peaceful.

The missing scowl and furrows on his forehead helped. So did the kitten curled up by his neck.

Before I could stop myself, I lifted my hand and drifted my fingers over his cheek. Traced his jawline gently. Touched his hair. His skin was rougher than mine, the scruff on his chin scratchy. His hair was soft, though.

As soft as the heart I thought he was hiding.

He did care. But there was more. I saw it when he couldn't let Hedgy go to an unknown future. I saw it when he spoke with my father, careful and gentle.

I felt it when he held me. Every single time.

And I felt it when I held him.

He was broken. Unsure. Scared.

But not unable to love.

He had to figure it out on his own, though, because the one thing I knew without a doubt about Alexander Bane was that he was stubborn.

If I pushed, he would back away. Declare his heart off-limits and refuse to even try.

If I showed him the same patience he showed to Hedgy, there was a good chance he would come to the same realization I had.

He loved me.

How I longed to hear those words from him, but it had to be on his own terms and in his own time.

I could be patient. Show him trust.

Which meant—

The fluttering of his eyelashes on my hand distracted me. I was cupping his cheek, stroking the skin with my thumb. He was awake now, staring at me, the beautiful blue of his eyes warm and sleepy in the morning light. He turned his head, pressing a kiss to my palm.

"I want this," he murmured.

"What?" I asked, confused.

"Waking up to you every day. Having you with me." He covered my hand with his. "I like how I feel when I'm with you."

I glanced toward his hips.

"Erect, you mean?"

He laughed, disturbing the kitten. Hedgy jumped up with a little hiss, his back arched as if prepared to fight. Then he mewled and ran to the end of the bed, jumped to the bench at the bottom, then to the floor and scurried in the direction of his food in the next room.

In seconds, I was pinned under Alex. He hovered over me, his eyes no longer sleepy, his body ready and his gaze intense. "That is a response, not a feeling, darling. And I always have that response to you." He lowered his chest to mine, brushing over my taut nipples with the dusting of hair on his chest. "The response gives me feelings, I admit. Strong fucking waves of feelings."

"Oh," I whispered breathlessly. "You like those?"

"I want tsunamis of them. Daily. At least twice a day."

"You, ah, might drown," I whimpered as he settled between my legs, dragging his cock along my aching center.

"What a way to go."

He trailed his lips up and down my neck. "Tell me I can have it. Tell me I can wake up to you every day. Fuck you every day." He eased back, nudging my entrance. "As my wife."

I shook my head, and he covered my mouth, kissing me hard. It was possessive, deep, and hot. I felt it to the very tips of my feet. He slid his tongue down my neck, sucking on my breasts so hard I swore he'd leave marks. "You're mine, Maggie Mae. You know it. I know it. Admit it and marry me."

"Alex," I gasped as he sat up, pulling me up his thighs and thrusting shallowly. Entering me an inch then backing out. Giving me what I wanted but taking it back. Once. Twice. Three times.

"Please," I begged.

"Give me what I want," he demanded. "I'll give you what you want."

"That's not fair."

He slid in deeper, making me groan. "All of it is yours. All I am is yours, Magnolia. Say it. Say yes."

I couldn't take it. I wanted him so much. The truth was, I wanted to belong to him in every way.

"Yes!"

He slammed into me.

And my fate was sealed.

❤❤❤

Every time Bane looked at me all day, he had a self-satisfied smile on his lips. I wanted to wipe it off, but for some reason, when he would look at me, I would smile back.

We had a quiet day on Saturday. He worked for a while and ran a couple of errands, while I curled on the sofa, reading. It was a relaxing day, and I enjoyed it.

Sunday morning after we ate, he pulled out a strange-looking contraption from a bag. I eyed it suspiciously.

"If you think I'm going to let you truss me up in that like you're Mr. Grey, you can forget it, Bane."

He frowned. "Who the hell is Mr. Grey? And when did he truss you up?"

"Not me. It was a movie."

"A movie where there is trussing? Name, please."

"Never mind."

He stroked his chin. "I never thought about 'trussing you up,' but now you mentioned it..." He let his voice trail off suggestively, lifting his eyebrows in question.

"Not happening."

He chuckled. "It's for Hedgy."

"What for?"

"So I can take him for walks. I thought he could come running with me eventually."

"You do know he's a cat, right? They don't tend to do marathons. In fact, I doubt he'll like walking either. Or the lead."

"I read some cats do very well on a lead. I think Hedgy will love it. The walks will do him good."

I finished my coffee, rising from my chair.

"Good luck with that, Bane."

He snagged me around my waist as I went past him, pulling me close and kissing me. "I got you to agree to marry me, Myers. Teaching Hedgy to walk with a lead will be child's play."

I rolled my eyes and pushed away.

"You haven't gotten me down the aisle yet," I called over my shoulder.

A moment later, I was pressed against the wall, Bane crowding me with his body. "You promised."

"I was being tortured. I agreed under duress."

"You're marrying me. That's final."

I wanted to tell him all he had to do was tell me he loved me and I would marry him today. I would stand beside him forever if he admitted his feelings. But I knew it was a useless cause.

"So romantic."

He studied me with narrowed eyes. "Is that what you need, Maggie darling? Romance?"

I shrugged. "Wouldn't hurt."

"Done." He backed away. "I'll teach Hedgy to walk, and I am going to romance the hell out of you. You'll be begging me to drag you down the aisle."

"Uh-huh."

"Watch."

"Okay, Romeo. I'm going to shower and see my dad and meet Rylee for coffee."

"Since when?"

I shook my head. "Since I told you on Friday. You're supposed to have lunch with Sam."

He furrowed his brow. "Right. Forgot."

"Well, between the marriage demands, the walking lessons, and the trussing, not surprised. You have a lot on your mind."

"You know, you used to be afraid of me."

With a grin, I slid my hand down his torso, cupping his dick. It reacted immediately, growing stiff under my fingers. "That was before I knew how to control you."

He groaned as I dropped to my knees, pulling down his sweats.

"Oh fuck," he muttered as I took him in my mouth. "I'm going to enjoy being married to you."

I hummed around him, and he fisted a handful of my hair. "Forever, Myers. It's you and me forever."

I had to admit, the thought of that thrilled me.

"What's on your mind, Maggie Mae?" Dad asked.

I startled at the use of my pet name and his voice. Dad had been pleased to see me, without remembering me. He happily ate the sandwich I brought him and chatted to me about his wife and little daughter, then fell asleep sitting in the sun.

I looked his way to see how clear his eyes were. He was watching me, understanding coloring his voice. The way he always used to before the disease took hold of his mind.

"Just thinking, Dad."

"About?"

"I met someone," I said, unsure how clear his memory was.

"I see. Is it serious?"

"I love him."

"Is he good to you?"

I sighed, taking his hands. They were gnarled and rough, and I dug in my bag, bringing out the hand cream I always carried. I rubbed the cream into his dry skin, talking as I did. "He's very good to me, Dad. He wants to take care of me."

He grunted. "As he should. You're a catch. Why haven't I met him?"

"You did once," I said carefully, unsure if he could recall the encounter. "He brought his kitten to see you."

Dad frowned. "I remember a cat. A man, no."

I chuckled. "Well, Hedgy is pretty cute."

"Wait. I do remember a man. Tall. He asked me for my blessing to marry you."

I looked down, not wanting him to see my disappointment. He was confusing memories. That happened a lot. Small bits got mixed together. TV shows, movies, past events, all became one memory at times. Incorrect, but I never tried to explain that. It only upset him. And me. I worked on his hands for a moment, then spoke when I knew my voice was steady.

"Well, did you say yes?"

There was no response. I peeked up to see his eyes closed. He'd fallen asleep again. It happened more and more these days. Less time awake, more spent asleep or in another world.

Still, I kept rubbing the cream into his hands until they felt softer.

I sat with him for a while longer, and when he woke up, he politely asked where his wife was, and when I said she was out, he nodded.

"She likes to shop," he informed me. "For herself and my daughter. Have you met her?"

"Yes," I replied with a catch in my voice. "She is nice."

"She's amazing. We are so proud of her."

I nodded, fighting back my sob. "I'm sure she knows."

Rylee patted my hand, her eyes filled with sympathy. "It must be hard," she murmured. "Your dad is in front of you, but not there."

"Yes, it is." I wiped at the tears that kept coming. "Sorry, I can't stop."

"It's okay."

"What about your parents?" I asked, wanting the subject off me.

She shook her head. "My dad and mom divorced when I was young. I lived with my mom for a while, but we never really got along well. My dad remarried and I stayed with them, but they moved to Denmark when I was eighteen. I've been on my own since then."

"Do you get on well with them?"

"Dad and Cara? Yes. She always wanted to move home, and Dad was thrilled for the chance to travel. They asked me to come, but I was deep into tech school. My mom, I rarely see." She grimaced. "We still don't get on."

"Any particular reason or usual parent stuff?" I asked, thinking of Bane.

"She was a model. I am anything but. I don't measure up."

"I see. Her loss, then."

She barked out a humorless laugh. "Maybe if I lost a lot of weight, she'd approve. But I gave up on that a long time ago. She had me on a diet as far back as I could remember. It took me years and years to have a healthy relationship with food. I doubt I will ever have one with her. Even my therapist agrees. She is toxic."

"I'm sorry." I reached for her hand. "For what it's worth, I think you're beautiful. You have amazing eyes and a wonderful smile."

"Thanks." She took a sip of coffee. "And it's fine. I've moved on. Now tell me something fun you did this weekend."

I hesitated, then blurted it out. "Bane asked me to marry him."

She choked on her coffee, sputtering into her cup. "Say what now? He did what?"

I nodded. "He asked me to marry him. Well, sort of demanded, then asked. Then demanded again."

"Well, that sounds like him, but I had no idea..." She let her voice trail off. "You and he have been...?" She lifted her eyebrows in question.

I nodded.

She leaned closer, her eyes dancing. "Oh my God, tell me everything. Since when? The dinner, right? It started after the dinner. I knew he liked you. He was so intense when he asked me what happened. I knew if he could get away with it, he would have pitched those women off the roof to shut them up. He was so angry and protective. I had a feeling about you two even then. He's incredible in bed, am I right? Demanding and controlling? Of course he is," she muttered, answering her own question. "Is it amazing? Is he grumpy at home too or all soft and squishy like a marshmallow? Do the partners know? I mean, there are no rules against it, but what do they think? I mean, it's Bane." She grabbed my arm, almost squealing. "Did you say yes? Oh, please tell me you said yes."

I gaped at her rapid-fire questions.

"Um, yes, after the dinner. And he is wonderful. The partners know, and he is pretty intense all the time. But he is so good to me. We, ah, got a cat together and everything."

"Oh my God," she repeated. "A pet. Bane with a cat? I need to see this." She was practically humming, leaning so far over the table, her ample breasts were resting on the top. "And in bed? How is he in bed?"

"Yes, do tell us how I am in bed." Bane's voice broke in. "I'd love to hear it."

CHAPTER TWENTY-FOUR

Bane

It was shocking how empty the condo felt when Magnolia was gone. I wandered around, then tried to get the harness on Hedgy. He wasn't a fan and kept walking backward as if to try to get it off. Watching it made me laugh. I clipped the leash on and tried to encourage him, but all he did was lie down on the floor and play dead. I dragged him around a bit, tried setting him on his feet and showing him what to do, but he simply flopped back to the floor. I scratched my head. Maybe Magnolia was right.

Finally, I gave up but left the harness on. He'd get used to it, and we'd try walking again later. I left him to his endeavors and got dressed to meet Sam. He had suggested a new place close to the condo, so I decided to walk. I checked on Hedgy, finding him still attempting to take the harness off and not looking happy. I gave in and took it off him. He shot me a look that said it all, then he ran away, ducking under the bed in the guest room. I held it up, Magnolia's words coming back to me. I wondered how sexy she would look tied up on my bed.

Then I shook my head and left to meet Sam. I took a table outside and waited for him. I was a little early. I texted Magnolia, who told me she was having coffee with Rylee soon. I asked about her dad, and she informed me he was alert for a brief time, but it hadn't lasted. I felt her sadness in the short reply and decided I needed to do something to cheer her up. I sipped at my coffee and, for fun, Googled Mr. Grey. My eyes were wide as I read about the books, and I decided I was enough to deal with without adding ropes.

Unless she asked. Then I'd invest in some silk scarves for her.

I moved on to Googling information about getting a cat to enjoy taking walks. Patience seemed to be the key, and the bottom line was, I never was good with that word. Then I stumbled on a backpack you could wear, letting the cat get fresh air and enjoy the walk, while keeping them safe. I had a feeling it would work for my runs too. I wondered how Hedgy would feel. If Magnolia would laugh at my efforts.

Sam appeared behind me, reading over my shoulder.

"A backpack for a cat? What the hell, Bane?" He sat down, plucking the phone from my hand and reading the screen. "Since when do you have a cat?"

I told him the story after the waitress took our orders. He regarded me over the rim of his glass. "You and the condom girl now have a cat," he repeated.

"Don't call her that."

He held up his hands. "Sorry. You and *Ms. Myers* now have a cat."

I nodded, picking up my sandwich and inspecting it. It didn't look as good as the ones Magnolia made me. I took a bite and chewed slowly. It was okay but didn't taste as good either.

"So, you're still seeing her?" he asked.

"I asked her to marry me."

His eyes widened, and he sputtered into his beer. "What the hell?"

"She said yes."

He regarded me with narrowed eyes. "So, the girl who tried to kill your dick then junk-punched you is the one you want to spend the rest of your life with?" He slung an arm over the back of his chair, eyeing me up. "You got some weird penis pain fetish I don't know about?"

I started to laugh. "I have a weird Magnolia Myers fetish."

"You serious about this girl?"

"I asked her to marry me," I repeated.

He was silent for a few moments. "You love this girl, Alex?"

"I care about her. I want to spend my life with her."

"Do you love her?"

"As much as I can love."

He shook his head. "I think you're capable of loving."

"I'm capable of caring. Looking after. Protecting. Providing."

"And that's enough for her?"

"She says she loves me," I admitted quietly.

"How did that feel?"

"Like a gift I don't deserve."

"I think you do deserve it. I hope you feel like that someday. If she is the one, then I hope she makes you see that as well." He paused. "Have you thought about the fact that by denying her your love, it could be hurting her?"

I frowned. "I don't want to hurt her. She knows I care."

"But your care has a ceiling."

"No."

"Then you love her."

He was confusing me and starting to piss me off. I glared at him. "She is the right one. She's the only one. She knows that."

Sam didn't look convinced. "You care, so you put a ring on it," he mused. "Interesting."

I had no idea what he meant by that, but his words made me curse.

"Shit, no. I haven't got a ring yet. The proposal sort of slipped out."

"You are such an idiot." He leaned back, typing on his phone. A moment later, he grinned. "You're lucky. My friend Smithy is a jeweler. He'll meet us in half an hour at his shop."

"Perfect."

"And you're paying for lunch."

I laughed. "Least I can do."

"That's what I thought."

We came out of the shop, the small box in my pocket feeling too light for what it represented. The ring was perfect for Magnolia, and I hoped she'd love it.

"Celebratory drink?" Sam asked.

I looked across the street, a dark swath of hair catching my eye. Magnolia and Rylee were at a table outside of a small café. Rylee was bent over the table and talking a mile a minute. Magnolia was looking shell-shocked.

"How about you meet the lady instead?"

"What?" he asked. "Where?"

"Across the street."

He looked over and whistled. "Buddy, if you tell me your lady is the sexy little blonde with the curves, we're gonna have a problem."

"Nope. That's Rylee Jenkins—she works for me. My Magnolia is the dark-haired vixen."

"Then do introduce me. To both."

We crossed the street, neither woman noticing us. I stood beside the table, hearing Rylee's low demand.

"And in bed? How is he in bed?"

My mouth curved at the immediate flush on Magnolia's face. "Yes, do tell us how I am in bed," I broke in, startling them. "I'd love to hear it."

Both women jerked upright at the sound of my voice. Magnolia's eyes went wide. "Alex, what are you doing here?"

I tutted her and bent, pressing a kiss to her head. "Sam and I had to pick something up across the street. I saw you and thought we could join you." I smiled at Rylee. "If you wouldn't mind."

"Of course not, Mr. Bane."

I shook my head. "You're a friend of Magnolia's, and we're out of the office. Call me Alex." I indicated Sam, who was staring at her. "This is Sam." I nudged him. "Sam, this is Magnolia. And Rylee."

He shook Rylee's hand. "Pleasure," he rumbled. He turned to Magnolia. "The infamous Magnolia Myers."

"Infamous?"

He grinned. "Oh, the stories." He winked. "The, ah, incidents."

Magnolia flushed, unsure where to look. "Don't be an ass," I muttered and sat beside her, pulling her close. "Don't let him get to you."

Sam sat next to Rylee, pulling out the chair and straddling it. "So, Rylee, you work for my friend here?"

"Yes."

"You're an assistant too?"

"I'm head of IT."

"Most brilliant programmer I've ever worked with," I added. "And her systems and security are incredible. I'm constantly fighting off offers to take her away."

Sam looked impressed. "Wow. Aside from the programs at the hospital, I'm not great with computers."

"Well, I can't diagnose an illness. We all have our talents."

Rylee's phone buzzed, and she frowned as she read it. "Maggie, I'm sorry. I have to go."

Magnolia looked disappointed, but she was understanding. "Okay."

"I need to order an Uber."

"I can drive you," Sam offered. "I was leaving."

"Oh. It might be out of your way."

"Nope. It's not."

"I haven't said where—"

He stood, offering her his hand. "It's fine. I'll drive you."

"Um, okay." She accepted his hand and looked at Magnolia. "I'll see you tomorrow."

Magnolia nodded, and I saw the look that passed between them. They were going to be talking hard in the morning. I hoped Magnolia shared. I had no idea what Sam was doing.

They left, and I ordered a coffee. Then I started to laugh.

"What?"

"Sam left. He drove us here."

Magnolia joined in my amusement.

"I think Rylee bowled him over."

"Well, at least not literally, like the way you did the first time we met."

Magnolia rolled her eyes. "Whatever, Bane. I guess you'll

have to slum it on the bus with me home."

"Nope. I can call an Uber, too, you know. Or Darryl."

"Or we can walk. Too bad Hedgy isn't here."

I grimaced. "He wasn't impressed earlier." I showed her the video I had made of our attempted walk. She laughed merrily over Hedgy's antics.

"Maybe he'll get used to it."

"I have a feeling, Maggie darling, as usual, you were right."

She leaned closer and kissed me. "If we're getting married, you better get used to it."

I kissed her back. "I guess so."

But somehow, the thought didn't upset me.

Magnolia

I woke up early Monday morning, Bane sitting on the side of the bed, a tray in his hands.

"Hi," I murmured, sitting up.

He grinned, sliding the tray onto my knees. "I made breakfast. Not as good as yours..."

I smiled at the tray. Toast and coffee. A small container of jam. Some slightly scorched bacon.

"Looks good," I assured him. I touched the pretty roses in the vase. "Nice touch."

"Romantic," he replied.

I laughed, picking up my cup and taking a sip. "Yes, very romantic."

He handed me a piece of bacon, and I crunched it, the salty flavor helping hide the burned edges.

"Crispy," I mumbled.

He grimaced. "A little too much. I got distracted."

"Doing?"

"Taking the thorns off the roses."

"That was thoughtful."

He stared at me, his eyes intense. "I know."

I glanced at the pretty roses, the pink petals soft. I could smell the fragrance. I looked at Bane again. He was watching me, his gaze focused, something in it making me wary. I reached out to touch a petal when I saw it. Between the green foliage was a ring. Sparkling in the low light, simple and elegant. So beautiful, my breath caught.

My gaze flew to meet his. He reached for the flower, letting the ring fall into his palm. Then he reached for my hand, slipping it into place. It fit perfectly, and I stared at it, speechless.

"Alex," I breathed out.

"Sam had a friend who let me into his store yesterday. I saw this ring and knew it was meant for you."

I let out a shaky breath. "It's so lovely."

He took the tray, placing it on the floor and moving closer. "Marry me, Magnolia. I promise to be the best husband I can be." He swallowed. "I asked your dad, and he gave me his blessing."

"What?" I gasped.

"I went to see him on Saturday afternoon. It was good. He recalled meeting me. We talked about you, and I promised to take care of you—make sure you were always looked after. I told you meant more than anyone else ever had or ever would. That I thought you were incredible. He said that was all he wanted, and he agreed."

Tears built behind my eyes. "I thought he was mixing things up in his head. He told me he gave a tall man his blessing."

"No, he really did."

I burst into tears, and Alex dragged me to his lap. He held me close, letting me get it out.

"He fell asleep while I went to get him a cup of tea," he told me. "When he woke up, he didn't remember anymore, but I was okay with that. He thought I was an orderly bringing him the tea. I sat with him for a few moments and left when he fell asleep again."

"He does that a lot now."

He held me tighter. "I know." His voice was low in my ear. "I'll take care of you, Maggie darling. I promise I'll try to be everything you need. I adore you. I want a life with you. Please."

I had already agreed, but I gave him the word he wanted. "Yes."

He kissed me, wiping away the tears. "Thank you."

My flowers were waiting for me when I got to the office. Today was a massive bouquet, so large I couldn't fit it on my desk. Bane walked past me, eyeing the flowers with disdain. "You really have to control your suitor," he muttered. "Do I need to send flowers to compete?"

"No," I insisted. I didn't want more flowers. "Listen, Bane, maybe you could call them. Or better yet, take your intimidating self into the shop and demand to know who is sending them. It's starting to bother me."

"Why?"

"Because a mysterious stranger sends me flowers every week. No other contact. Nothing. It feels wrong—especially now."

"Especially now?"

I glanced at my ring. "Yes, now."

He smiled and lifted my hand, kissing it. "I wouldn't

worry, Magnolia. I read something the other day about various experiments people do. Like sending flowers or friendly cards as part of a social experiment to see how people react and if the offerings change their outlooks. Maybe you are part of one of those."

I frowned. "I never thought of that."

"I'm sure they'll stop soon enough. In the meantime, in the wise words of your deliveryman—enjoy."

He left for his meeting, and I touched the petals of a beautiful lily. He was probably right, but part of me felt a weird sensation. As if I wanted him to get upset over the flowers and throw them away, ranting only he should be sending me the pretty blooms.

But since he didn't love me, that reaction would make no sense.

I felt a little sad as I went back to work.

Later that morning, I sat in the lounge, smiling as Rylee joined me. "You sneaking a break?" she asked.

I grinned, shaking my head. "Bane's in a meeting. I needed a coffee." I hunched closer. "What the hell happened yesterday?"

She shook her head, her eyes confused. "I have no idea. Sam insisted on driving me home so I could get to work on the problem one of my clients has—" She stopped at my quizzical look. "I have a few outside clients I design websites and software for."

"Ah."

"He followed me into my apartment, all serious and curious. He told me I needed a better place to live—somewhere more secure. I told him if he wanted to pay my rent, feel free to make suggestions. Otherwise, it was none of his business."

"Ooh," I breathed out. "What did he say?"

"He got all up in my face, telling me he was looking out for me. I told him I had just met him and to back off. Then he laughed and told me he'd see me soon and left." She paused. "But not before he grabbed me and kissed me."

My eyes widened and I grinned. "Oh, Bane is gonna love this."

She gasped, her eyes going round.

"I have to tell him," I protested.

"No!" She grabbed my hand. "When the hell did this appear?"

"Oh. Um, this morning."

"Magnolia, it's gorgeous!"

"It is," I agreed. "A surprise too." I told her how he asked, and she smiled.

"He's so sweet under all that bluster."

"He is."

She turned my hand various ways, catching the light. "It suits you."

I studied the elongated cushion cut with the pavé band. It glittered and sparkled under the lights, sending bright dots onto the walls. "I didn't expect it."

She stood. "I doubt he expected you."

I had to laugh. "Probably not."

"I have to get back. Lunch this week, right?"

"Sounds good."

She left, and I stared at my ring.

I hadn't expected him either.

CHAPTER TWENTY-FIVE

Magnolia

The following week, sitting at my desk, I frowned at the multitude of changes to the budget Bane had handed me earlier, asking me to update it. This client was frustrating him to no end. Bane was grumpier than usual, which was pretty damn grumpy. He hadn't even commented on the flowers that arrived, the pretty bouquet bright and cheerful. He'd shot them the same disparaging look as usual and ignored them.

His mood was also due to the fact that I refused to move in with him yet, and he was almost surly at times. I wanted to enjoy the time at the house while I could. Spend some evenings with my memories. I loved my nights with him, especially waking up beside him, his strong, warm body next to mine, plus the inevitable, pleasurable sex that happened when he woke up. But everything was happening so quickly, I was trying to make sure I didn't get swept up in the Bane-hurricane.

Besides, I had to admit, I still liked ramping him up. Watching him glower at me as I got ready to leave at night without him, thoroughly enjoying his intense, passionate kisses as he tried to persuade me to change my mind. I also hid my amusement when he would show up at my place, a bag of ramen or Chinese in hand, insisting he had to make sure I was eating. Offering to help pack things up in order to hasten my departure from the apartment. I had agreed during a prolonged and mind-scrambling orgasm to let him hire movers to take all the boxes and furniture from the attic and move it to his storage area the other night. The fact that he'd had it done in twenty-four hours shouldn't have surprised me, yet it still did.

A loud curse interrupted my musings, and I looked up, peering into Bane's office.

"Goddammit," he roared, kicking at the desk.

Curious, I got up and bravely approached the lion. "Something wrong?" I asked.

"This bloody desk," he replied. "I was reaching for something in the drawer, and I got a massive splinter in my hand."

I reached for his hand he was holding, inspecting the "massive" piece of wood. He had a sliver under his skin, the area around it red with irritation. A second piece was beside it, the end sticking out.

Keeping the amusement out of my voice, I instructed him to sit and went to the bathroom, getting out the first aid kit. I sat on the desk, holding his hand under the light. Using the special tweezers I had put in the kit, I probed the area, trying to ignore his squirming.

"This will go faster if you stop moving."

"You're hurting me, Myers," he grumbled.

I bit back a laugh. I had hardly touched him. "Sorry."

I grasped the end of the smaller sliver and pulled. It came out fairly easily, hardly any tugging needed on my end.

Bane grunted in annoyance. "Can you leave my hand intact? I need it."

"What a baby you're being," I admonished. "Big, bad wolf Bane, taken out by a sliver."

"Am not," he muttered.

"Are so," I replied with a low laugh. "Now, sit still. This one is gonna take all my concentration."

I grabbed a needle, and he watched anxiously as I heated it with a match then carefully picked at the skin to be able to get to the end hidden under the top layer. He grumbled and muttered the entire time, gripping my thigh.

"Okay, I'm gonna try to get it now. It should come out clean," I lied. It was deep and the end jagged. I hoped I could get it with one pull.

I looked at him. "Ready?"

"Yes."

"Scream if you have to," I assured him, pressing down around the wood.

"I don't need to— *Jesus fucking Christ, Myers!*" he yelled.

"Got it!" I said triumphantly.

He glared at me, standing from his chair and towering over me. I took his hand, dabbing an alcohol wipe over it, then adding a Band-Aid. "All done."

He kept glaring, and I lifted his hand to my lips and kissed it. "There," I crooned, desperately trying not to laugh. "All better now."

His eyes darkened. "Not quite," he growled and grabbed me, pulling me up to his chest and covering my mouth with his, kissing me passionately. Much too passionately for the office. But as soon as his lips touched mine, I was lost. To his scent, his heat, his mouth. His tongue tangled with mine, and he groaned low in his chest. I clutched his shoulders, gripping him tight, gasping when he pulled back.

"Now it's all better."

I blinked up at him. He smirked down at me.

"I have a meeting to get to, Nurse Ratched. Otherwise, I'd show you how it feels to have something hard driven into you." He kissed me fast. "I'd make you scream too."

"Not at the office," I said, summoning my primmest voice.

He laughed, clearly amused. He bent, pressing his lips to my ear. "If I touched you right now, Myers, we both know how wet you'd be. How ready for me." He nipped my lobe, then stood back, pulling me from the desk.

"Now, back to work on that budget. I need it for two o'clock."

Then to add insult to injury, he swatted my butt as I sidled past him. But I felt his erection.

I had a feeling he was going to be a little late for his meeting, waiting for it to die down. So I wiggled against him, making him groan.

Two could play at that game.

"Enjoy your meeting," I teased.

"You're going to pay for that, Myers."

"I hope so," I replied with a wink.

He began to laugh, unable to stay annoyed. I loved that I had that effect on him.

Bane picked up his laptop, straightened his shoulders, and buttoned his jacket. He walked past me, not stopping. "We're going to dinner tonight," he informed me. "I have reservations. Seven. Wear one of your pretty dresses. I'll pick you up."

Then he was gone, not giving me the chance to reply. I knew he would go to the boardroom downstairs and sit for a few moments, gathering his thoughts before the client and his partners joined him. When he came back, he'd be starving, needing coffee and a sandwich, then throw himself into work before the next meeting.

I wondered where we were going. He rarely asked me to wear something special. I mentally went through my wardrobe, picking out the right dress. No doubt this was part of his romancing the hell out of me. He'd been very attentive the past week and, this weekend, had made me breakfast in bed again. He'd bought me flowers twice, the blooms brightening up the condo. My Monday flowers had appeared earlier, larger than normal, the scent filling the office. He was trying so hard to show me how much he cared, and I appreciated it, constantly trying to tamp down the sadness of the unspoken words. I told him I loved him every day, and he seemed to like hearing me say it—especially when we were wrapped around each other at night. And when I went back to my apartment and he called, he waited to hang up until I said the words. I hoped if I said them enough, one day, he'd say them back.

My biggest fear was that he never would.

My phone rang, and I was distracted as I answered. "Hello."

"Ms. Myers, it's Garden Villa, calling about your father."

"Is he all right?" I asked, panicked.

"He's had a fall and has been taken to the hospital."

"I'm on my way."

I paced the waiting room, anxious and upset. All I knew was my dad was here, the doctors were checking him out, and that he'd fallen in his room and been found, unconscious, by a staff member. I had been told to be patient—twice.

I looked down at my phone, tracing the screen. I wanted to call Alex and tell him what was happening. To hear his voice soothe me and tell me everything would be okay. To let me know he would drop everything right now and come be with me.

But it was business hours, he was in an important meeting, and I couldn't do it. Be that girl who panicked and called her boyfriend—fiancé—to come hold her hand. Until I knew what was happening, I could handle this.

My name was called, and I hurried over to where a doctor stood. He greeted me with a serious expression. "Your father has dislocated his shoulder, broken his arm, and has a concussion. We're going to stitch up his head, fix the shoulder, set the arm, and we need to keep him in for observation." He paused. "It could have been a lot worse. If he had fallen differently, he might have broken a hip, and I'm not sure he'd survive surgery."

I swallowed, my throat thick and the tears threatening. "How long will he be in?"

"We'll reassess in the morning. We need to make sure there's no brain swelling—it was a bad tumble. He'll need watching over when he returns to the home. I'm going to suggest he be moved to a smaller ward with more care."

"Can I see him?"

"He's in pain and very confused. I suggest you wait until after we set his arm, so that we're able to give him something to help with his pain and transfer him upstairs to the ward. We have to be careful due to the concussion."

"Of course."

"Someone will come get you, but it might be a while. We're pretty slammed here. As soon as we know the ward, you can go up and wait there. It will be more comfortable."

"Okay."

He left and I sat down, my legs not able to hold me up. The next level of care in the home was more expensive. Not that it mattered since if that was what he needed, then it had to happen. I would have to contact the home and discuss it with them.

Knowing I was going to be here a while, I slid my phone from my pocket, deciding I needed to call Bane. I paused as a wave of dizziness hit me, and I had to let my head fall on my chest for a moment. I hadn't eaten today. I would rest a minute, call Bane, then get something to eat. A sandwich from the cafeteria would help.

"Magnolia?"

I looked up into the kind eyes of my doctor. Hannah Wilson had been my caregiver for almost ten years. Close to retirement, she had a head full of white hair and twinkling dark eyes.

"Are you all right?" she asked. "Your father?"

I explained to her about Dad, and she nodded as she listened. "Sadly, falls tend to adversely affect those already dealing with memory issues."

"I know."

She tilted her head, studying me. "Are you all right? You're very pale, Magnolia. Is your anemia acting up?"

"Oh, I don't think so. I mean, I had the blood work done a few months ago that you ordered, and you said my levels were good. I'm taking my supplements," I assured her.

She frowned, not looking pleased, picking up my wrist and taking my pulse. "While you're here and waiting, and I'm in between patients, how about we draw some blood and check? We don't want another deficiency happening."

"I shouldn't go far."

"And you won't," she said firmly. "I'll tell them at the desk, and you'll be gone half an hour, tops. I'll do a quick finger jab to check and send away a sample for verification."

"Okay," I agreed, knowing she wouldn't take no.

I followed her down the hall, and she had me sit. "Have you eaten today?"

"No. I got the call and came right here."

She swabbed my finger and jabbed it, taking the sample and testing it. "A little low," she murmured. "But not as bad as I've seen with you. Okay, we'll do a full work-up. Some results will be back right away and the rest in a couple of days. You can come see me, and we'll go over the results." She sat down with a form. "And eat some meat, please."

"Okay," I said with a smile. Bane would love steak for dinner.

"Are you sexually active?"

"Um, yes."

"We'll do a pregnancy test, then."

"I'm on birth control."

"Still, just to be sure. Just another check on the form."

Ten minutes later, I was back in the lounge, the blood drawn. Dr. Wilson had given me a sandwich from the fridge in the doctor's lounge, insisting I eat it, along with a container of milk. "Better than the horrid coffee here."

I sat down and nibbled on the sandwich and drank the milk, feeling better once I had consumed some calories. Remembering I needed to call Bane, I grabbed my phone, groaning when I realized I had no battery life left.

A nurse appeared and told me I could go up to floor four and wait. I headed up, hoping to find a charging station. Before I could inquire, I was allowed to see Dad, and I forgot about everything else as I followed the woman into his room. He was asleep, a nasty-looking bruise covering half his face, the bandage white against the dark discoloration. His arm was casted and in a sling, and I could see other bruises forming on his skin. I sat beside him for a few moments, watching his chest rise and fall in steady, even breaths. I held his hand, feeling how cool his body was, and I went to get another blanket to cover him.

I stayed for a while, then returned to the waiting room, unsure what to do. I was surprised when Dr. Wilson appeared and sat beside me. She looked serious.

"Is everything all right?" I asked, a new pit of worry forming in my stomach.

She took my hand. "I have some results, Magnolia."

"And?"

"You're pregnant."

CHAPTER TWENTY-SIX

Bane

I walked into the office, needing two things. A sandwich and Magnolia's smile.

I was agitated, grumpy as hell, and hungry. Magnolia would describe it as hangry.

She wouldn't be wrong.

But I knew in ten minutes I would feel better.

Maybe a few kisses would help as well. I was certain I could persuade her.

Except, she wasn't at her desk. Instead, one of the temps sat there, flipping through a magazine, not particularly concerned to be caught doing so.

"Who are you?" I demanded.

"Tammy," she replied. "I'm new."

"Where the hell is Myers?" I snapped.

"She had to leave."

"Why?"

"Personal reasons."

I leaned on the desk, glaring at her. She shrank back a little. "What kind of personal reasons? Is she ill?"

"I'm not at liberty to say."

"I'm her boss. And yours. What reasons?"

"I don't know. You'll have to inquire with HR." Then as

MELANIE MORELAND

if to gain favor, she smiled. "She left you a sandwich in the fridge. I'll get it for you." She hurried away, and I went to my desk, already dialing Magnolia's phone. It went straight to voice mail, and I left her a fast message. "Are you sick? What's happening? Why aren't you here?"

I sat down, puzzled. She'd been okay when I left for the meeting. She'd teased me about my sliver and purposely got me riled up. If I'd had time, I would have shown her who was boss fast and hard with my door locked. But the meeting I was attending was important, and the client hated to be kept waiting.

He also loved to hear himself talk and had taken up almost three hours of my day.

And to top things off, Magnolia was missing.

I called HR as I chewed a bite of my sandwich the temp had dropped off. Laura's line went directly to voice mail, and the same thing happened when I called Jessica. Irritated, I called Rylee, interrupting her before she even finished her greeting.

"Do you know where Magnolia went?"

"Hello, Bane," she replied dryly. "No. Is she not at her desk?"

"No. The temp said she left for personal reasons. I thought you'd know."

"I haven't spoken to her—"

I cut her off. "That's HR on the other line." I hung up. "Why is there some stranger outside, and where is Magnolia?" I snarled into the phone.

"Hello, Bane," Jessica said in the same tone as Rylee had used earlier.

"Where is she? I tried calling, but it goes to voice mail."

"Reception is never good in a hospital."

I was on my feet in an instant. "*Hospital?* Is she okay? Which one?"

"Her father fell," she replied. "She had to go be with him. I made sure she got there as quickly as possible."

"Which one?" I repeated.

"St. Joe's."

"Thanks." I hung up and rushed from the office, stopping by the desk out front. "I'm gone the rest of the day. Cancel my appointments and leave. Don't touch anything." I paused. *"Anything."*

"Okay."

I headed downstairs, hailing a cab and giving him the address. "There's a huge tip if you make it fast."

"On it," he replied with a smirk and took off like a bat out of hell.

The whole way, I worried. Why hadn't she called me? Did she think I wouldn't care?

Was she all right? Was she alone? How was her father? I called her again, and it went to voice mail again.

Why wasn't she answering?

What if the fall was serious? How would she handle it?

How would I handle her?

We pulled up to the hospital, and I threw some money at the cabbie and hurried inside.

I was about to find out.

After several inquiries, I found her. She was curled in the corner of a plastic-covered sofa that had seen better days. The waiting room was empty, aside from Magnolia. Her head was down, and I called her name as I approached, shocked when she looked up, her eyes red from crying, her face inordinately pale. My heart sank at the blatant pain in her eyes, and I rushed toward her, once again surprised as she jumped up, throwing herself into my arms. She sobbed into my chest, her tears soaking my shirt, the force of her cries making something in my chest break open. I held her close, sitting down and pulling her to my lap. I made low sounds of what I hoped was comfort, rocking her. She settled quickly, her crying ceasing. I felt her entire body shudder as she melted into me.

"Your dad?" I asked quietly, dreading the news.

"He's okay," she replied, then explained what the doctors had said.

"So, he needs more care now," she finished. "I have to contact the home about moving him."

"I'll handle it."

"No—"

"I'll handle it," I repeated. "You look after your dad and yourself. Let me do this."

Her hesitant acceptance was a small victory to me.

"Why are you so upset?" I said quietly. "I mean, I understand about your dad, but is there something else?"

"No, the shock, and I was so worried."

"Why didn't you call, Magnolia?"

"You were in an important meeting. This was personal, and it was business..." She trailed off.

I slid a finger under her chin and forced her to meet my eyes. "I told you before, I am always Alex. No matter what I'm doing, if you need me, I'm yours. Never doubt that."

Her eyes were filled with turmoil, and I had a feeling there was something she wasn't telling me.

"You could have left a message," I admonished her gently. "Even a text."

She slipped her phone from her pocket. "The battery died. My charger is on my desk. No one had one that worked."

"I'm getting you a new phone tomorrow." My tone brooked no argument, and I was glad she didn't offer one.

A woman I assumed was a doctor stepped into the waiting room, carrying a small bag. She walked toward us, and Magnolia stood, wiping her eyes.

"Dr. Wilson."

I stood, placing my hand on Magnolia's shoulder. The doctor looked at me, her gaze encompassing, then she nodded. "You must be Alex."

I offered my hand. "I am."

Her grip was firm. "I'm Dr. Wilson."

"Dan's doctor?"

"No, Magnolia's. I ran into her earlier while she was waiting for news of her father."

She handed Magnolia the small bag, a look passing between them. "Remember what I said. Eat. Rest. Take the vitamins. Come see me next week."

Then, with another nod to me, she left. I turned to Magnolia, anxiety making me tense. "What is it? What did she give you? Are you all right?"

She heaved a sigh and sat on the sofa. I sat beside her, wanting to grab the bag and find out, but I knew that would anger her.

"I had a bad bout of anemia once. I have to be careful with my iron levels. When she saw me earlier, she noticed I was pale, and she insisted on doing some blood work. She was right, and my levels are low." She shook the bag. "I need some vitamins and to add more iron to my diet."

"Iron. Meat, right?" I asked.

"Yes. And seafood, spinach, nuts, among other things. I've been neglectful."

"I won't let you forget. Why didn't you tell me?"

"Alex," she said gently. "We're just getting to know each other."

"I want to know everything. We're getting married. I need to know how to take care of you."

A strange look passed over her face. But she stood. "I need to go and check on Dad."

I followed her, standing at the bottom of Dan's bed as she straightened his covers and smoothed the wisps of gray hair from his forehead. He had a nasty bruise on the side of his face, and his arm was trussed up in a sling. He looked older and frailer than the last time I saw him.

His eyes fluttered open, and he watched Magnolia for a moment, then covered her hand with his. "Stop fussing, Maggie Mae."

"Hi, Dad," she whispered, her voice thick.

"Hi yourself." He glanced at me. "You again. Alex, right?"

"Yes, sir."

"What's all the fuss about?"

"You fell," Magnolia told him. "Scared me."

"At my age, hardly surprising," he mused, his mind surprisingly clear. He looked back at me, his eyes narrowed. "From the rock on her hand, I'd say you got up the balls and asked?"

"Dad!" Magnolia scolded, making me chuckle as Dan attempted a wink.

"I did. She said yes." I winked back. "Once I convinced her. You were right. Stubborn as can be."

He nodded, then winced. "What does a man have to do to get something to eat?"

Magnolia patted the blanket. "I'll go check."

She left, and Dan indicated for me to come closer. I approached his side, and he looked up at me, his eyes as clear as I'd ever seen them. "You'll look after her, right?"

"Always."

"You'll make her happy?"

"She'll be my priority."

I wasn't lying to him. She was going to be the focus of my world, and I would do everything I could to make her happy.

He sighed and nodded. "Good. That's all I need to know."

Magnolia came in, carrying a tray. "I got you a sandwich, some soup, and tea, Dad."

"Sounds good."

I sat to the side and let Magnolia and Dan talk. Well, she talked and he grunted, not really eating the sandwich, but staring at her, letting her spoon soup into his mouth. She helped him sip the tea, and she fed him bites of chocolate from a bar she had in her purse. He was in and out, his mind slowly tiring and the fog creeping back in. But as she stood to take away the tray, he gripped her hand. "I love you, Maggie Mae. You're the best daughter a man could ask for."

She leaned over and kissed his cheek. "Love you too, Daddy."

He closed his eyes and slipped into sleep. Not long after, a nurse bustled in, checking his vitals and smiling at us. "His vitals are steady. He'll be in and out all night," she said. "We'll wake him every few hours. You should go home and come back in the morning."

Magnolia hesitated, staring down at her fingers entwined with her dad's. Recalling what Dr. Wilson had said, I crouched beside her. "Your dad needs you strong, Maggie darling. And you need to look after yourself. We can go home, eat, and sleep. I'll have you back first thing."

She paused then nodded in agreement. "Okay."

I pressed a kiss to her forehead. "Let's go."

Magnolia was asleep when my phone vibrated on my bedside table. Hedgy looked at me, blinking and sleepy, then padded to her pillow, curling back up as if he knew he needed to move. I slipped from bed, already knowing what I would be told when I answered. I had given my number to the head nurse, asking to be contacted in the night if need be.

A few moments later, I stared down at Magnolia, finally asleep, although not resting well. Her brow was furrowed, and her hand clutched the pillow tightly, as if warding off bad dreams. The worst of which was about to come true when I woke her up and told her that her father had passed a short while ago. Peacefully and in his sleep, the nurse assured me. I doubted that would be much comfort to the woman in my bed. I'd had the strangest feeling while we were at the hospital and he was so clear. It was as if he knew it and was saying a final goodbye to the girl he loved so deeply. I crouched beside the bed, reaching out to stroke Magnolia's hair, surprised to see her dark eyes open and staring at me.

"Hey," I whispered, pushing her hair from her face.

Tears filled her eyes. "He's gone, isn't he?"

"Yeah, Maggie darling. He is."

She sat up, and I wrapped her in my arms.

"I knew it. He was saying goodbye earlier."

"I think so."

"He needed to be sure I was being looked after." She shuddered. "He was tired."

"I know, baby," I murmured, having no idea how to comfort her or what to say. I had little experience with death and grieving. I had been a child when my dad died and had lost my grandmother much earlier. I recall missing them, but not the feeling of adult grief. The understanding that came with the knowledge of losing someone you loved.

"I have to make arrangements."

"I'll help you."

She turned her head to my chest and began to cry. Quiet, subdued tears, unlike the ones earlier.

Somehow, these tears hurt me more.

I held her tight. "I have you, Magnolia. I won't let go."

And I meant it.

The following Monday, I faced her in the bedroom. "It's too soon."

Magnolia shook her head. "I want to come back to work. I'm going crazy sitting around."

"Maggie darling—"

She cut me off. "You need me at the office. I need to be busy. I'm coming with you today."

I stared at her in wonder. She'd been so strong. I'd helped her arrange a small celebration of life for her dad. There had been a good turnout. Many from the office came and paid their respects. Sam came, as did Rylee, and I noticed the friction between them, even though they were polite and stayed away from each other. I met her small group of friends. Many of Dan's friends, who were still alive and able to, had come and shared stories. She laughed as much as she cried. Smiled and shared her own stories. It was touching to watch.

I had all his things boxed up and sent to the condo, ready for when she wanted to sort through them. And then she grieved. Privately, quietly.

Now, she wanted to start living again.

And if I was being honest, I wanted that as well. I missed her desperately in the office. Her smile and teasing. The way she had of keeping me in line. I missed hearing her laughter. I knew she went to her apartment at times, no doubt reliving memories.

"If you're sure," I agreed. "But if it's too much, you can come home."

She smiled. "Really, Bane. I'm sure the people in the temp office will rejoice. I heard you're driving them crazy. You've gone through the lot of them. Twice."

"I have been on my best behavior."

She smiled. A real smile that showed her amusement. "Not what I've been told, but whatever lets you sleep at night."

I held out my hand. "Let's go, then."

In the car, I studied her, noticing the way she played with her ring. It was looser now. She had lost some weight, and although I tried, it was hard to get her to eat.

"Are you taking your vitamins?"

She looked startled then nodded. "Yes."

"You need to eat more."

"I'm trying."

"Maybe some protein shakes if your appetite doesn't pick up."

She slept a great deal, which I put down to grief. Given how often she napped, she still looked tired.

"Have you made an appointment to see Dr. Wilson?"

She nodded, looking out the window. "Next week."

"Okay. Add it to my calendar, and I'll come."

A look of panic flitted over her face. "I don't need you to escort me to the doctor. I'm quite capable of going on my own."

"I'm well aware of that. I have a couple of questions I'd like to ask."

She nodded but didn't say anything. I had a feeling she wouldn't be adding it to my calendar. I also had the feeling she was hiding something. And I didn't like it.

I would have to find out what it was. I needed to help with whatever was bothering her.

No matter what.

CHAPTER TWENTY-SEVEN

Bane

"Myers," I called from my desk.

She appeared, carrying her notepad and pen, efficient as always.

And sad. So sad and trying to hide it.

I indicated the chair. "Sit, Maggie darling."

She frowned but didn't correct my using her pet name at the office.

"You look tired."

She sighed. "I'm fine."

I leaned forward. "Please stop being brave. You lost your father. Obviously, this anemia is worse than I thought—"

"Why would you say that?"

"You're pale. You sleep a lot. Your appetite is off. You're highly emotional—understandably so, but still. You're jumpy." I listed all the things I'd noticed the past few days of careful observation.

"Maybe your overprotectiveness is making me emotional and jumpy," she responded.

"Really?" I asked, amused at her instant anger. It happened frequently.

"Yes. You're always watching me. It makes me nervous."

"That's interesting since, until I said something a moment

ago, I don't think you were even aware I was watching you."

She stood. "You know what? I am tired. You're tiring me today."

"Then maybe you should go home and relax. We'll start again in the morning."

"That's a good idea. I'm going to the apartment."

I rose from my chair. "That's not what I meant, and you know it."

She lifted her chin, defiant. "That's what I want."

I decided not to argue. There was a quiver to her chin, and her eyes, although flashing with anger, were troubled. "Fine. Darryl will drive you."

She turned and walked away, and I heard her getting her coat. I called Darryl, who stayed close these days.

"She'll be down in a few moments. Take her to the apartment." I paused. "Could you pick her up some ramen from that place down the block from her? With chicken and a spring roll?"

That was her favorite, and if Darryl gave it to her, I knew she would eat it. There wasn't much left at her place, and I needed to know she would eat something.

"Of course."

I hung up, hearing the outer door close. I knew she was upset if she didn't at least say goodbye. I sighed, leaning back in my chair and rubbing my eyes. I knew without a doubt I would end up at her place later, too worried to stay away.

Ten minutes later, my phone rang, and I picked it up. "Darryl?"

"Is she coming soon?"

I frowned. "She should be down there already."

"Nope. I was out front when you called, and she hasn't

shown up."

I hung up and checked the app I had on my phone. The new one I'd gotten her let me track her, and although she'd laughed when I installed it, she allowed me to do so. Her light blinked and was slowly moving away, and I groaned. I called her number, and she answered, the background noise affirming what I already suspected.

"Really, Myers? You took the bus?"

"I wanted to be alone."

"You'll hurt Darryl's feelings when I tell him that." I rubbed my eyes. "Only you would want to take public transportation instead of a comfortable town car to prove a point."

"What point would that be?"

"That you're independent and can handle the world on your own. I know you can, Maggie darling. But you don't have to," I added softly, unable to be angry with her.

"Until you stop caring," she replied, so quiet I almost missed it.

I was shocked into silence. *That was what she thought?*

"Magnolia—"

"I have to go. I'll see you later."

She hung up, but I heard the tears in her voice. I stared at the phone, then called Darryl and told him she had taken the bus. He laughed, not at all put out.

"Stubborn," he said. "I'll wait a bit and take her some food."

"Thanks."

I returned to my computer, determined to finish the concept I was working on. But all I could see, all I could think about, was Magnolia. The pain she was hiding. It was more than losing her father. But what it was, I didn't know. I had tried to corner her doctor at her father's get-together, but she told me nothing except to look after Magnolia.

And I was trying, but it felt as if she was pushing me away to prove a point. And the only point I could come up with was to prove she didn't need me.

I gave up and shut off my computer, determined to go and see her and hash this out once and for all. I reached for my phone then recalled Darryl was going to take her food, so I decided to grab a cab. Outside, I walked to the curb, about to raise my arm, when I heard my name being called.

I turned to see Sam heading my way. He took one look at me and grabbed my arm. "Come with me, Bane. You look like you need a drink and an ear. Luckily, both are available."

Sam stared at me after I finished talking. Blathering was more like it. Once I started, I couldn't stop. Magnolia, my worries, my fears, everything came out. Her father's death, the sadness and worry in her eyes, the way I felt she was pulling away from me. Her anemia and how pale she was.

"Who is her doctor?"

"Wilson. Hannah Wilson."

He nodded. "Good physician. She's in capable hands." He took a sip of his beer. "You know, Bane, grief is a funny thing. Everyone reacts differently to it. You've never experienced it in your adult life or been around it. It could just be that."

"It's more," I insisted.

He leaned back, draping his arm along the top of the booth. "And you care?"

"Of course I do."

"Why?"

I stared at him.

"Could it be because you love her?"

His words hit me like a ton of bricks.

I blinked as I repeated the words in my head.

Love her.

Love Magnolia.

I loved Magnolia Myers.

Holy shit.

All of the worry, the questions, the wonder, the joy—all of it made sense.

I fucking loved her.

Sam chuckled. "That was quite the epiphany." He took another sip. "Perhaps you need to tell the lady."

I sat back, still in shock. "I know."

The thought of saying those words made me anxious. Of what they meant to my life, of the power they could give a person.

Except it was Magnolia I would say them to. My Maggie darling.

Suddenly, I wasn't anxious because of the words. I was anxious to say them. To see the wonder on her face. To know I could make her feel the way I did when she said them to me.

Incredible. Invincible. Alive.

"As for the anemia, I'm sure Dr. Wilson has it in hand. Magnolia needs to watch her diet, take her supplements, and get lots of rest."

"I make sure she takes her pills every day. I bought her a dispenser. In fact—" I paused as I dug in my pocket for my phone "—I took a picture of the bottles so I could pick up more to make sure she doesn't run out. I haven't had a chance to look at it," I snorted. "She doesn't even like me to see them, so she keeps them in her drawer." I showed the picture to Sam, who studied it, looked at me, then back at the picture.

"You said she is sleeping a lot?"

"Yes."

"Emotional."

"Yes."

"Has she been ill?"

"Her appetite is off." I frowned. "Why?"

"And Dr. Wilson gave her these?"

"Yes. What is it?"

He shook his head in amusement. "Buddy, I have no idea how to tell you this... She may be anemic, but your girl is also pregnant."

I gaped at him. "Impossible. She's on birth control pills."

"Which is not one hundred percent effective. Even if you wear a condom, plus the pills, she could still get pregnant."

"What?"

He grinned. "The only sure way not to get pregnant is to practice abstinence. Which I know you haven't been doing." He tapped the picture, enlarging it. He showed me the labels. "Along with her other supplements, these are prenatal vitamins. Dr. Wilson would only give them to her if she was pregnant."

I sat frozen. Pregnant.

Magnolia was *pregnant*?

She hadn't told me. Why hasn't she told me?

Sam looked at me, serious. "Did you tell her you didn't want kids? The whole you wouldn't make a good dad bullshit concept?"

"Yes."

"That's why she hasn't told you. Why she's distancing herself. She thinks she's going to have to do this alone."

He studied me. "Is she right, Bane?"

I thought of Magnolia pregnant. Rounded and glowing. Carrying our child. My child.

The intense feeling of protectiveness and need overwhelmed me. I had to get to her.

"Fuck no." I jumped from my seat. "Pay for the drinks. I owe you."

He grinned, waving me off. "Go get your girl."

Her apartment was dim when I let myself in. Quiet. I shrugged off my coat, looking at Magnolia asleep on the chaise. Evidence of her tears was on her damp cheeks. She was clutching a blanket, a frown on her face. The unopened bag of food Darryl had brought her was on the coffee table.

All the way here, I kept going through all the information in my head. The signs I missed. I was horrified, thinking of the thoughts Magnolia must have been having all this time. How alone she must have felt. The insecurity and worry for the future. Add in the grief she was feeling—no wonder she was so emotional and exhausted.

And yet, with all the concern and fear in my head, one thought kept pushing through.

She was pregnant. With my child.

And the idea of it made me so incredibly happy, I could barely contain it.

I bent over her, kissing her cheek, nuzzling the damp skin, tasting her sadness. Her eyes fluttered open, widening when they saw me. "Bane?"

I smiled. "Alex. Only Alex from now on."

"Um—"

"I have a question, Maggie darling. And I want you to tell me the truth. Do you promise?"

"Okay."

I slid my hands under her, lifting her and sitting down, holding her against my chest. I tilted up her chin, holding her gaze.

"Are you pregnant?"

Her chin began to quiver, tears filling her eyes.

"Yes."

I wrapped her in my embrace, holding her close.

"Good."

Magnolia

"Good."

One word. That was all he said, yet it felt as if the weight of the world had been lifted from my shoulders.

Since the awful day my dad fell and I found out I was pregnant, my world had been dark, scary, and uncertain.

I had stared at Dr. Wilson, certain I had heard her wrong. *"How?" I whispered.*

She shook her head. "You're a smart girl, Magnolia. You know the pill isn't one hundred percent effective. Even using a condom doesn't guarantee anything. Is the father in your life?" She indicated my hand. "Is he the giver of that promise?"

"Yes, but he doesn't want kids."

"Well, then you'll have to change his mind. Love has a way of doing that."

I didn't know how to tell her he didn't love me.
He cared. Even adored. But not loved.

When Dad died, Bane had been incredible. Helping me at every turn. Holding me when I cried. Standing beside me, always patient. But I wondered how he would look at me when I told him about the baby.

The baby I would keep, no matter what. With Dad passing, the rest of the money from the house sale could be used as a nest egg. I could find another job, maybe even in the company. Surely Bane wouldn't banish me totally.

I missed my dad terribly. The comfort that he was no longer in pain or forgetting the life he'd had offered me little relief most days. Other days, I clung to it.

I clung to Bane. But every day I didn't tell him, I felt worse. Every day, I longed to blurt it out, and in my greatest fantasy, he would be pleased. Happy. It was reality that kept my mouth shut.

But as I'd looked around my little apartment earlier, half packed up, I knew I had to tell him. No matter his reaction, he had the right to know. And once he did, I would know what I had to do next. For my baby. Myself.

But Bane—Alex—was holding me, whispering soft words of tenderness and care.

I looked up into his blue eyes, shocked at what I saw. Nothing but love. It blazed brighter than any anger I had ever seen.

"I don't understand."

He smiled. "I'm an idiot, as Sam pointed out. I was so certain I couldn't love, I refused to admit what was right in front of my face. You. I love you so much, Maggie darling. I have from the moment you bowled me over and made me laugh. I felt as if I began to live once you were around. You bring everything bright and good into my life." He laid his hand on my stomach. "Including this little surprise."

"You said you didn't want—"

He shook his head. "Like I said, an idiot. I was afraid to have kids in case I treated them the way my mother treated me. I held tight to one lesson she drummed into my head. Not to love. Not to rely on someone. Those were the lessons I should have ignored." He paused, tucking a strand of hair behind my ear in a tender gesture. "You have taught me to love. To be open. I can do better than she can."

"I know."

"Tell me how," he asked, his tone almost pleading.

I cupped his cheek, loving how he leaned into my touch. "You're a good man, Alex. You're intelligent and thoughtful. You take care of people around you without even thinking about it. You treat your partners well. You're a trusted friend. You hide your goodness under a grumpy exterior, to keep people away, but you care about them." I smiled. "You're a deeply beloved fiancé. You'll be a good dad. I know it. I'll make sure of it."

"I won't be like her—I know that now. You would never let me. And I can't be because, unlike her, I *can* love. I *do* love. I love you. I love the nugget."

"The nugget?"

"The baby."

"You pick awful names."

He grinned. "I pick great names. Hedgy, Nugget, and Maggie darling. All excellent choices."

I shook my head, and he lowered his voice. "I love you."

"Really?" I whispered. "You're not just saying that because you feel bad?"

"You want to know a secret, Maggie darling?"

I nodded, the tears beginning to glimmer in my eyes.

"I send you the flowers every week."

I blinked. *"What?"*

He picked up a pen and scribbled on a napkin. "It's not Ty. It's T.Y. Short for thank you."

I blinked again.

"It wasn't what I told the kid to write on the card. He shortened it. You were so confused, it made me smile. All your sleuthing trying to figure it out amused me."

"Why did you send me flowers?"

"At first, because you deserved them. It was only going to be the one time to say thank you. But the way you reacted—as if the flowers were the best gift you had ever received—I had to keep sending them. And the more you meant to me, the bigger the flowers became. You were right from the first run-in, Magnolia. You were, you are, perfect for me. Personally, professionally. In every way. I wanted you to know, yet somehow the mystery made it even better."

"You acted miffed every time they were delivered."

"I was a little pissed this Ty person was getting all the credit."

I laughed. "But he didn't exist. You just let me think he did."

"I had to—I didn't know how to tell you it was me. But I loved seeing your reactions. The way you touched the petals. Took the flowers home." His lips twitched. "Your concerns about poor Ty and his girlfriend never getting the flowers he sent." He chuckled. "I was sure you'd figure it out."

I shook my head. "I wondered at one point, but it was too out of character for you."

"You are too out of character for me. It's another reason I love you so much."

"That is the grandest gesture I've ever heard of. A little twisted when I think about it, too. Over the top."

"I am over the top when it comes to you."

I sniffled. "So, you'll stop sending them?"

"Nope. I want to be your secret admirer. I liked the way you would smile when the bouquets arrived. Excited, yet worried. When they were late, you were disappointed. I loved watching your reactions." He cupped my face. "I love you, Magnolia Myers soon-to-be Bane."

A sob escaped my mouth. "I love you."

He smiled. "Can we start now? Living our life? Come home with me. Let me move your things. Stay."

"Yes."

He bent and kissed me, his lips tender. Everything was in that touch. His love, his devotion, his promise.

"And I'm coming to the doctor."

"I know."

"Add it to the schedule."

"I will."

"And marry me, Maggie darling. Soon."

I sighed, snuggling closer. "Okay."

He huffed a breath. "Finally, some cooperation."

"Don't get used to it."

He smiled, then tickled my chin. "Never. And by the way, when you were listing my attributes a few moments ago, you didn't say I was a good boss. To you."

I bit my lip. "Maybe we should just leave it."

"Magnolia..."

I laughed, and he joined me.

"Good man, good husband, good dad," I murmured.

"And?" he said, lowering his voice.

"Good boss. My favorite boss."

He smiled widely, tucking me close. "I'll take it."

"Good."

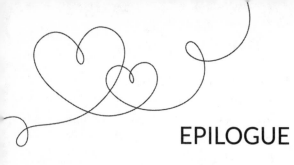

EPILOGUE

Bane

"Myers!" I called, looking at the file on my desk.

She shuffled in, clutching her notebook, her belly swollen. She glared at me as she sat down with a loud huff.

"That's Bane, thank you."

I chuckled. "I can't call you Bane. You call me Bane. We can't both be Bane."

"But we are. Maybe I could hyphenate. Myers-Bane."

"No. I like Magnolia Bane."

"Then call me Maggie."

I shook my head. "That's my name at home for my wife. I'll stick to Magnolia." I sighed. "If I remember."

"What do you need?' she asked, trying to bend to touch her feet. I stood, rounding the desk, tutting when I saw her swollen ankles.

"Magnolia Bane," I scolded. "I told you that you need to stop working. Look at your feet."

I lifted the offending appendages to my lap, pulling off her shoes and massaging the puffy skin. I knew they had to be hurting when she didn't protest, instead shutting her eyes and emitting a contented little sigh.

"Today is your last day."

"What am I going to do at home?"

"Nest."

"The nursery is finished. We have enough clothes washed and ready to dress the entire maternity ward at the hospital. I have nothing left to do."

"Nugget man is due in three weeks. You can be a sloth on the sofa until then."

She opened her mouth to protest, but I hit a particular sore spot, and instead, she groaned, the sound low and sexy. My cock noticed and stood up, and I had to remind myself we were in the office.

As if on cue, Jessica walked in, stopping in the door and staring.

"Why does this feel like déjà vu?" she asked, laughing.

I chuckled. "My wife's feet are swollen. I'm trying to convince her it is time to call it quits."

Jessica pursed her lips and nodded. "As much as I fear for the temp pool, I agree with Bane, Magnolia. The last few weeks are hard enough."

My wife stared at Jessica as if she had just wounded her. No doubt, she had expected Jessica to take her side, joining in the "I am woman and hear me roar" moment Magnolia was attempting to have.

"Fine. Tomorrow is my last day."

I was about to argue, but Jessica lifted an eyebrow, and I shut up. Then I huffed. That used to be my signature move to get people to stop talking. When had she stolen it?

"I'll get the paperwork ready." Jessica handed me a file. "I need your signature on these."

"Sure." I began to get up, but Magnolia gasped and grabbed my arm.

"I'll just be a minute," I assured her.

"No," she gasped. "Bane—my water just broke!"

Jessica met my panicked eyes. "Call your driver," she said calmly.

I picked up the phone. "Darryl—"

"Out front in five," he responded, reading my voice well. "Her bag is in the back."

"Good." We had two bags packed just in case.

Then I bent and scooped up my wife. "I can walk," she protested even as she grasped my bicep. "Bane, he's coming," she panted. "Fast."

I rushed to the elevator, trying not to laugh as she kept talking. "The papers you need to sign!"

"Magnolia?" I asked as Jessica pressed the lobby button. "What?"

"Shut up about the paperwork. You're fired."

She leaned her head on my shoulder. "Okay."

I stared down at my son, his red face, chubby cheeks, and tightly clenched fists the most beautiful things I had ever seen.

Aside from my amazing wife.

I met her sleepy eyes. "He's perfect, Mommy."

She smiled. "He needs a name." He began to fuss, and she sighed. "And his mommy."

I settled him beside her and sat next to her bed. "Do you still like Jensen?"

"I do."

"Jensen Daniel Bane."

"Oh," she whispered, tears gathering in her eyes. "My dad would love that."

"I love it. I love you. I love Nugget Jensen."

She laughed and winced. "Stop it."

I ran my knuckles down her cheek. "You were incredible today, Magnolia Bane. So strong and brave."

"You were so calm it helped me," she muttered sarcastically. "Honestly, Bane."

I laughed. I had been a mess. Twice, the doctor had asked me if I had a medical degree and, if not, to step aside. But he let me cut the cord and take our son to his mother. It was a memory I would hold forever.

"Good thing I have you."

She smiled at me. "You have us."

I kissed her. "Even better."

Bane

Four years later...

"Higher, Daddy!"

"That's high enough, Jensen," I replied. "Mommy said so."

"And Daddy's heart can't take it," I added silently.

He pumped his legs, not really caring. Then he pointed to the slide. "There!"

"Hands on the chains, Jensen!"

He laughed at me.

Laughed.

Then he jumped, landing squarely on his feet in the sand and heading to the slide. I looked over at Magnolia, who was laughing at me, shaking her head. "He's fine, Daddy. Come sit."

I sat beside her, leaning over to kiss her cheek and peek into the pram. Our six-month-old daughter, Ciara, was sleeping, her fist jammed into her rosebud mouth. Her brown hair was a mass of curls on her head, and her dark eyes were like her mommy's.

She had me wrapped around her finger.

And my wife had me by the balls.

I was good with both.

"When did Jens get so...*big*? He always needed me to lift him off the swing, help him up the ladder." I groaned. "Now he's hanging upside down on the monkey bars. By himself."

Magnolia rubbed my back. "He's growing up too fast. I know. He wants to go to school. Be a big boy."

"I'm not ready."

She laughed. "You never will be."

"At least Ciara will grow slower."

"In your dreams." My wife laughed, then sighed. "Maybe the next one."

I sat back, slinging my arm over her shoulder. "It took us three years to get her. Not sure I can face being that old when another one comes."

"Nine months in the future isn't that long."

It took a moment for her words to register. I turned to her, gaping. "Are you—really?"

She smiled. "Yep."

I grabbed her, wrapping her in my arms and kissing her hard. "Maggie darling," I breathed. "That is amazing!"

She laughed, nestling close. I held her, knowing she needed my embrace. The closeness. She always did in emotional moments, and I loved being the one to give it to her. It made me feel ten feet tall that it was me she turned to. I made her feel safe and secure.

"We need a bigger house."

She laughed. "We have a big house."

"Four bedrooms. We need five."

"Or we can turn your office into a bedroom and build you an office downstairs."

"We can afford a bigger place."

"But I love our house. We picked it out together when Jensen was just a little nugget. We made it our home. I love the neighbors and the big trees and the gardens you made."

I laughed, kissing her sweet, sentimental mouth. "Okay, how about the idea we had for a man shed out back? I can work there."

She snorted. "And escape the kids."

"It crossed my mind."

She nudged me. "You'll have to make it up."

"Oh, baby, I will."

Jensen came running over. "Mommy, I'm hungry."

Magnolia dug in her bag, handing me a container. "Sit beside Daddy."

I helped him onto the bench, opening the container. He dug in, munching on the crackers, and I unwrapped a string cheese for him.

"Did you see the paper this morning?" Magnolia asked casually.

I chuckled, brushing the hair off our son's face. "About Terry? Yep. I figured karma would catch up to him. I hope he rots in jail."

"Your, ah, mother must be horrified."

I sat back, swinging my leg. "Don't care."

"What if they came to you..." She trailed off as I turned and met her gaze.

"Never. After how she treated you, scoffed at our marriage,

and walked past us as if we were dirt at that event when you were pregnant with Jens? Absolutely not."

"Okay, just wondering."

"She will never change. Neither will he. I want nothing to do with either of them."

"I just don't want you to regret—"

I took her hand, cutting her off. "I regret nothing. I have a family. Our family. All of you mean more than anything in the world. I want nothing of them to touch us. To touch our kids. Or you. All of you are wonderful, perfect, and mine. They mean nothing because that was all I ever was to them."

"You're everything to us."

I kissed her. Then again. I did it a third time. Each longer. Harder. She was everything to me. The center of my world. The reason I was alive. Really, truly alive.

"I think our kids need a nap."

She hummed and touched my lips. "A long one."

"Or maybe we drop them off with Auntie Rylee and Uncle Sam. I'll order dinner for them. Take my time celebrating another miracle you've brought to my life."

She laughed. "Even better. Take me home, Mr. Bane."

I kissed her again. "Always, Mrs. Bane. Always."

OUTTAKE

Magnolia

I heard the door open and shut, then the sound of Bane's footsteps hurrying down the hall. I waited for him to come to the kitchen, but when he didn't, I went to find him.

I found him in his den, opening a package and talking to Hedgy.

"You are going to love this one. I promise."

"What's going on?"

He grinned at me, his smile huge. It appeared a lot these days. His laughter rang out in the condo.

That had changed too, the barren rooms now filled with my furniture pieces, many of my paintings, and warmer colors.

It felt like home.

"Ta-da!"

I frowned at the bulky item Bane pulled out of the box.

"Um, is that some sort of space suit?" I laid my hand on my rapidly swelling tummy. "A little too soon for the baby."

"It's for Hedgy."

"Hedgy? What does he need a space suit for?"

He shook his head. "It's a backpack carrier for him. He can come on walks with us. Hiking. Maybe even slow jogs."

I bit my lip. "Bane—"

He glared. "Alex. We're married. I'm Alex."

"Except when you're acting like Bane."

"How am I acting?"

I sat down, trying not to laugh. "We've tried four leashes, endless harnesses—even a custom-made carrier on your chest. Hedgy doesn't want to go walking, hiking, or jogging."

"I agree the chest carrier was a mistake. He couldn't see anything, and it upset him." Bane rubbed his chest reflexively, no doubt remembering the pain of Hedgy's claws embedded in his skin. "But this has the bubble, and he can see everything. He'll love it."

"I don't think he wants to be outside," I said. "Maybe it's residual fear from being abandoned as a baby. The only time he likes to be outside is on the balcony with one of us."

Bane frowned, stroking Hedgy's head when he jumped up on the back of the sofa. He smiled as Hedgy climbed his arm, settling on Bane's shoulder—his favorite place to be. I loved teasing Bane that he reminded me of a modern-day pirate and that Hedgy was his parrot. After the first time I teased him, he started calling me a wench and chasing me around the condo wanting to ravish me with his "wooden leg."

"He'll be fine."

He opened the plastic bubble that looked like an astronaut helmet. "It's got a nice thick bottom that's lined, so he'll be comfortable. Lots of air holes for ventilation. We'll go for a walk later and build up to the jogging. I'll let him get used to it." He plucked Hedgy off his shoulder, showing him the contraption. Hedgy sniffed at it suspiciously, not looking impressed. He jumped off the sofa, slinking away, and I was certain I could guess the outcome of this experiment.

I rolled my eyes, knowing I couldn't talk Bane out of trying. He was determined Hedgy wanted to go out with him. I was pretty sure it was more that Bane wanted Hedgy with him.

He leaned over, kissing my stomach. "Your mommy doesn't think I know what I'm doing."

I stroked his hair, letting the silky strands run through my fingers. "I think you're amazing. Just a little odd."

He grinned at me, his blue eyes twinkling. "You taught me everything I know about being odd." Standing, he pressed a kiss to my lips. "Let's have lunch, and we can go for a walk. We'll stop at that coffee shop you like in the park, and I'll get you a decaf latte." He winked. "I'll bring Hedgy a Churu. He loves those."

"Okay."

Bane helped me off the sofa, the action becoming increasingly more difficult as the weeks went by. I hadn't seen my feet in days, and I knew I wouldn't again until after the baby was born. Bane laid his hand over my stomach, caressing the large bump with a tender expression on his face.

"Are you too tired for a walk?"

"Nope. I'm good. Maybe not a jog or a hike, but a walk is doable."

He wrapped his arm around my waist. "Okay. Sandwiches, a walk, a latte, and a nap."

I sighed. "Sounds perfect."

The walk started out all right. Hedgy climbed into the carrier of his own volition—once Bane bribed him with treats that he threw in first. He sat beside the carrier, petting Hedgy's head and talking to him. I smiled watching him—the man who couldn't love, determined to take his cat on walks and trying everything to make it happen.

Hedgy looked unhappy when Bane zipped him inside, and he was downright scandalized when Bane swung the carrier over his shoulders so Hedgy was facing outward. As he adjusted the straps, I slipped my hand into the pocket, stroking Hedgy's head. "It's okay, baby. Be patient with Daddy."

Hedgy gave me the look. The one that said "I am not putting up with this shit for long, human."

"We should go," I advised.

Hedgy started looking rather murderous in the elevator, but Bane assured me once we were outside in the fresh air, he was sure the cat would relax.

Except, outside was loud, filled with pollution, and lots of people.

Hedgy was not a fan.

We headed to the park, me walking behind Bane so Hedgy could see me. At first, he'd looked around in curiosity, then he huddled down, glaring at the world.

"I'm not sure he's enjoying this."

Bane extended his hand behind him, not stopping. "Stop fussing. Walk with me and let him get used to it."

I gave Hedgy an apologetic smile and took Bane's hand. We walked along, not getting far before Bane frowned. "What is he doing? It feels like a bouncy castle on my back."

I stepped behind him, trying not to laugh. "Um, he's on his hind feet trying to find the escape hatch."

"I doubt it. He's just being curious." He tugged my hand. "Let's keep going."

A few moments later, Hedgy started making low yowls of protest and prowling the small enclosure, clawing at the inside, clearly unhappy.

Bane pressed forward until he suddenly stopped. "Why is my back wet?"

I checked, trying to hold in my amusement.

"Hedgy, ah... We need to go home."

Bane looked horrified. "Did he piss on me?"

I nodded.

Bane grabbed my hand. "Let's go."

I hurried to keep up with him, knowing there'd be no latte. And the nap would be postponed as we cleaned up the cat. I was trying not to laugh, but I was finding this all very amusing.

Bane glared at me. "Do not even start, Myers."

"Oh, I'm Myers now."

"Right this second, you are. You and the cat are in cahoots."

I bowed my head, biting my lip. He was the epitome of Bane at the moment. Grumpy, growly, and barking words he didn't mean.

People passed us, and I turned my head, watching. Many of them looked amused. I stopped, checking out Hedgy and gasping. "Stop, Bane."

"What?"

"He's half out!"

"What? How?"

He tugged the backpack off his shoulders and set it on the ground as I tried to push Hedgy back in.

"It's supposed to be escape-proof," he grunted, struggling with the snaps.

"He's supposed to like it too," I pointed out.

"Most cats do," he retorted. "The reviews were great."

"They never met Hedgy."

A second later, our very affronted cat sprang from the carrier, racing away. I gasped, calling his name, and Bane was up on his feet, chasing after him.

Hedgy rushed to the closest tree, clawing his way up, going higher until he settled on a branch. Bane glared at him. "Hedgehog Hedgefund, get down here."

Hedgy turned away, ignoring him, beginning to clean himself. I picked up the damp carrier, wrinkling my nose at the smell and sat on the bench. I couldn't help at the moment.

"If I have to come up there..." Bane threatened, once again using his intimidating voice.

I laughed out loud. "You can't climb that tree. He's too high up."

"What do you suggest?"

"Sit here, and once he's calmed down, he'll come down. We'll go home."

Bane shook his head. "He's coming down now."

He shrugged off his jacket, studying the tree. A couple of other men came over, and they discussed the best way of getting to the cat. One man offered a boost, and Bane nodded decisively. I groaned, taking my phone from my pocket. I was either going to need the paramedics or the fire department. Might as well get ready.

Bane climbed the tree slowly, calling to Hedgy, who continued to ignore him. He reached the branch below Hedgy, reaching up to grab him, but Hedgy hissed at him and moved away, meowing loudly and attempting to crawl down the tree. I went to the base, calling up to him, encouraging him to come to me. Crying the entire time, he dug in his claws, sliding and clutching his way down the bark. One of the men reached over my head, grabbing him and handing him to me. I held him close, cooing in his ear. I looked up, calling to Bane. "I got him. You can come down."

"Right," he replied, but he didn't move.

I thanked the men, and they left. I looked up with a frown. "Bane? Are you coming?"

He sighed, the sound echoing down through the leaves. "No."

"Why?"

"I'm stuck."

I patted Hedgy in the backpack. He didn't look happy, but he was safe. I had thrown out the wet bottom lining and kept my fingers on the broken zipper so he couldn't get out again. Bane climbed down the ladder, the firefighters helping him, kind and encouraging. With as much pride as he could muster, he shook their hands and thanked them, then approached the bench, sitting down heavily.

"Hedgy okay?"

"He's fine."

"I'll carry him home wrapped in my jacket."

"Good idea."

"I don't think I'll be trying cat walks again."

"Probably a good plan." I was quiet for a moment. "I didn't know you were afraid of heights."

"Neither did I."

Hedgy meowed, and Bane reached over, taking the carrier. He released the broken zipper, lifting Hedgy from the bubble contraption and settling him on his shoulder. Hedgy immediately nestled close, content not to try to run. I handed Bane a Churu, and he let Hedgy lick the creamy treat, smiling as he purred.

"Your mommy was right. As usual."

"At least you tried."

"And got pissed on by my cat and rescued by the fire department. Banner day."

I began to laugh, unable to keep it in any longer. After a moment, Bane joined me, then stood, holding Hedgy to his chest, wrapped in his jacket. "Come on, wife. I need to go home and shower with the cat, then crawl into bed and nap with you. I'm done with this day."

"What do you want me to do with this?" I held up the carrier.

Bane took it, pitching it into the garbage. "Someone else can have it. I'm done trying."

We started to walk home, and I glanced at him.

"Have you ever bathed a cat?"

"No. How hard can it be? I'll soap him up, soap me up, we'll rinse off and be done."

I couldn't reply.

I just couldn't.

I was too busy counting the number of bandages we had in the house.

We were gonna need them.

ACKNOWLEDGMENTS

Thank you to my team.

Betas, sensitivity readers, editors, proofers, designers—thank you to each and every one of you. You made this project so enjoyable.

Lisa, your notes made me laugh so hard. I appreciate your observations—and you.

Karen—who knew all those years ago... would you have run? Love you!

George and Atlee—thank you for everything you do—your make Karen's life easier so she isn't as grumpy... sometimes. We can't expect miracles... LOL

Abby—your artwork brings my words to life. I am in awe of your talent.

To my Minions, my Literary Mob, my hype team—thank you for all your efforts and support. I appreciate and love you all.

All the bloggers and book lovers—thank you for sharing your passion.

And as always Matthew—just because of you.

I love you the most.

ABOUT THE AUTHOR

New York Times, Wall Street Journal, and *USA Today* international bestselling author Melanie Moreland lives a happy and content life in a quiet area of Ontario with her beloved husband of thirty-plus years and their rescue cat, Amber. Nothing means more to her than her friends and family, and she cherishes every moment spent with them.

While seriously addicted to coffee and highly challenged with all things computer related and technical, she relishes baking, cooking, and trying new recipes for people to sample. She loves to throw dinner parties and enjoys traveling, here and abroad, but finds coming home is always the best part of any trip.

Melanie loves stories, especially paired with a good wine, and enjoys skydiving (free falling over a fleck of dust), extreme snowboarding (falling down stairs), and piloting her own helicopter (tripping over her own feet). She's learned happily ever afters, even bumpy ones, are all in how you tell the story.

Melanie is represented by Flavia Viotti at Bookcase Literary Agency. For any questions regarding subsidiary or translation rights, please contact her at flavia@bookcaseagency.com

Also by Melanie Moreland

My Favorite Series:
My Favorite Kidnapper
My Favorite Boss

Vested Interest Series:
BAM - The Beginning
Bentley
Aiden
Maddox
Reid
Van
Halton
Sandy

Reynolds Restorations:
Revved to the Maxx
Breaking the Speed Limit
Shifting Gears
Under The Radar
Full Throttle

The Contract Series:
The Contract
The Baby Clause
The Amendment
The Addendum

ABC Corps Series:
My Saving Grace
Finding Ronan's Heart
Loved By Liam
Age of Ava
Sunshine and Sammy

Standalones:
Into the Storm
Beneath the Scars
Over the Fence
The Image of You
Changing Roles
Happily Ever After Collection
Heart Strings